The First Year

97 Stories Distilled from
87 Years of Successful Living

BY

D. BURTON SMITH

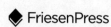 FriesenPress

Suite 300 - 990 Fort St
Victoria, BC, V8V 3K2
Canada

www.friesenpress.com

ISBN
978-1-5255-8329-2 (Hardcover)
978-1-5255-8328-5 (Paperback)
978-1-5255-8330-8 (eBook)

1. FICTION, SHORT STORIES (SINGLE AUTHOR)

Distributed to the trade by The Ingram Book Company

Table of Contents

Dedication

This book is dedicated to my lost love, **Jean Isobel**, and to **Carol Eliza** for reasons that become clear toward the end of the book.

Introduction

I lost my lovely wife, Jean, to cancer after sixty-three wonderful years together. Last year, to help deal with loneliness, I joined a writing group at Centre Wellington Writers, www.thewellies.com. I have written hundreds of reports, cases, articles and teaching notes in my sixty-year career as an accountant, general manager, university teacher and productivity consultant, but for the first time, I was writing from what was in my head.

This book is a collection of stories from my first year of writing for fun. I found story opportunities everywhere in my life experiences. Business flavours many of them, some my university experiences, and I can't seem to escape a teaching/learning bias.

One of our group's exercises was writing fifty-word stories, not 49 words, not 51 words, exactly 50 words. It had to be a complete story, beginning, body and conclusion. Dozens of these microblasts are scattered among the more comprehensive stories.

I hope you enjoy reading my stories as much as I enjoyed writing them.

Section 1
Fiction - Short Stories

THE AUCTION

Driving down a gravel country road, I came across a line of cars parked on the shoulder in front of an old farmhouse. A truck in the driveway had a sign on it, reading, "Dave Jones, Auctioneer." I pulled in about twenty cars past the house and walked back to see what was happening.

The back yard was full of people. The auctioneer was up on the porch. As I arrived, he sold a bundle of garden tools for $15. Next was a lawn mower for $52. A young couple, barely out of their teens, bought an old metal-topped kitchen table and four bentwood chairs for $35. And so it went.

A colourful set of china dishes, Bird of Paradise according to the auctioneer, went for $380 after a spirited competition between two city types.

I saw an old woman sitting on the porch in a magnificent black high-back rocking chair with gold filigree trim. She showed no emotion as she watched the proceedings. A young woman, crisply dressed in what might have been a uniform, sat beside her. They were talking. I sidled over to listen, but there was too much noise for me to hear.

I noticed a heavy wood dining-room table and eight solid wood chairs over to the right, with an old dog lying under the table. The dog was chained to the iron bar of a horseshoe pit. Two hours later, as the auction was winding down, two burly men lifted the table over the dog's head and brought it and the chairs to the front. By now the crowd had thinned, and I could hear the old woman tell her companion, "Harold made that table for me in the barn the first year we were married. He was very good with his hands." The table and chairs sold for $85.

Finally, with the yard nearly empty, the vegetable garden churned into a sea of mud, a flower garden trampled to death, even the lawn demolished, the grizzled old dog was led to the front. It sold for the opening bid of $2 to a tall, spare man in a plaid shirt and a wide-brimmed straw hat.

I heard the old woman say to her companion, "That was Abner. He's a good man, but not much of a farmer. I don't know why he bought Dog, he has one of his own. But I'm glad he did. I thought Dog would have to be put down."

Then the young woman said, "We need to get back now, it's almost dinnertime."

As they stood up the older woman said, "But my chair, Matron said I could keep my chair."

The younger woman replied, "Don't worry, Adelle, Mr. Jones will put it in his truck and drop it off at The Manor on his way through town. It will be in your room before dark."

With that, they stepped through the back doorway into the empty house.

The Challenge *(50 words)*

She grew up with five brothers and a pool table in the basement. When she picked up a cue in the sticky bar the drunk laughed at her, so she challenged him. She won the toss, ran the table, then asked, "Double or nothing?" He paid up and walked away.

Chance Encounter *(50 words)*

He tried online dating with a fake name and doctored photograph to look attractive. She tried online dating, also using a fake name and doctored photograph. They really clicked so they decided to meet. She arrived and said, "Dad, is that you?" Big laugh, but they didn't tell their spouses.

Negotiation *(50 words)*

Dave and I were scheduled for a negotiating meeting with an important customer. Dave is pretty forceful and hard-nosed. At the last minute he told me to get lost. He said he didn't want me in the meeting because I was capable of seeing the customer's point of view.

Warped Sense of Humour *(50 words)*

After a business dinner someone pounded on my hotel room door. I saw a large, rough looking woman through the peephole. I mentioned it the next day. Laughing, our agent said he gave her half of a fifty-dollar bill and told her I had the other half waiting for her.

ANDY

She's a bitch! No other word for it. Last night I was in her bed and this morning she fired me. Bitch! Then she tells me not to slam the door on my way out. Bitch! As if I could. Bitch! Two burly guys in fake-cop uniforms were waiting at the door and frog-marched me out past the other employees to the atrium. Bitch! Not a dignified exit. Bitch!

Her name is Julia Knox, Knockers in the men's washroom. Maybe she thought I underperformed. Not true. Definitely not true.

My name is Randolph James II, Randy for short. I am the only male on the admin team, or at least I was. We like, or liked I guess, to call ourselves executive assistants. I think what might have got Knockers in a twist was me romancing a sweetie named Jennifer Davis.

I'm like most guys my age: when something is offered free with no strings attached, we gratefully accept. But maybe Knockers thought there were strings. Sexual harassment won't fly. It sure was consensual on my part. Besides, I have never heard of that applying to a male employee pursued by a female boss. I can't go the fired-without-cause route anyway. I was only there four months and still on probation. Mom will be pissed. Her connections got me that job.

But I have something on Knockers. I found it while snooping in her apartment last night, when she was showering. There is an employee in her department named Andrew McTaggart. Andrew must be a ghost, because I never came across him and the department isn't that big. I wonder who cashes Andrew's paycheques. I wonder who pays Andrew's income tax. But now I'm out on the street and I don't have any proof. What is my best way to use it?

I'm working my way through college taking night and weekend courses, mostly business subjects. Maybe Knockers cutting me loose is a good thing. My trysts with her were interfering with my studies. But I really need a paycheque. I don't think I'll use her as a reference, though. That would take some finessing.

Andrew McTaggart. That name was niggling in the back of my brain. Then I had it. I knew him. He's the guy in the fancy electric wheelchair with the levers on it in my Accounting 212 class on Saturday mornings.

Now I know how to take Knockers down, but if I do, good old Andy goes down too. Do I want to do that? This situation would be a beaut for my ethics class, better than any case in the course.

It could even be legit, sort of. Knockers might be related to the company's owner. If Andy is connected to him too, Knockers' department would be a good place to finance him from. I'm not sure how Revenue Canada would take it, though. I remember seeing something about income splitting by putting non-working relatives on a payroll. Revenue Canada pays whistle-blowers part of the proceeds of a successful prosecution. I need to find out who good old Andy is connected to.

But back to basic survival. The whistle-blower route would take years to pay off, if ever. Checking out the job postings on the bulletin board, I spotted one that might fit. Payroll clerk. At least it would be indoors. Probably boring, but also not freezing my butt off. Mom won't have any leverage in this, so she should be impressed if I pull it off on my own. She's always telling me to show a little initiative.

Mom could easily support me, but she cut me off. She said she was through financing my useless lifestyle. She did help me get the job that Knockers fired me from though. Mom knows the owner of the company.

I got the payroll clerk's job. I was right, it was boring, but I was able to squeeze in a couple of hours of studying on most days, except near the end of the month.

It turned out I was good with numbers. An interesting thing about payrolls is that even the least educated employee can calculate complicated piecework bonuses and overtime premiums to the last penny. If a paycheque was even two cents short, I was called on it. Funny though, no one ever found an overpayment.

I did get to know Andrew, or Andy, as he liked to be called. He usually sat alone in his electric wheelchair after class, drinking some concoction that smelled like a milkshake, through a straw, waiting for the afternoon lab. I just sidled over and started talking to him. He turned out to be a good guy, upbeat, making the best of each day. He was older than I thought.

I asked and he explained his disease. It goes by the imposing name amyotrophic lateral sclerosis. The abbreviation is ALS. It is sometimes called Lou Gehrig's disease after the great New York Yankee baseball player who suffered from it. It usually doesn't hit until middle age and is fairly rare, but Andy got shortchanged in life's lottery. It started with his hands being tingly when he first woke up in the morning, and not working very well for about ten minutes. He jokingly called it "laughing hands disease." To the best of his knowledge, no one else in his family has ever suffered from such tingling, and it was too trivial to mention.

Then one day when he was playing touch football his legs folded and he couldn't get back up. He underwent a battery of tests and got the evil word: ALS. With the help of a physiotherapist, he regained some use of his legs, but touch football was beyond them. The wheelchair soon followed. Andy did everything he could to keep his body in condition, but it was a failing proposition.

When he became so weak he could no longer work on a computer, he had to give it up. Swallowing was difficult and his diet was mostly liquids. Accounting 212 was the only course he was taking. A wheelchair van brought him to school and took him back home. He could scoot around in that wheelchair faster than I could walk, controlling it with small levers near his hands. He was fearless. People had to jump out of his way or get run over.

Andy's memory was prodigious. He had a calculator on a stalk by his left hand, but he also remembered numbers and could manipulate them in his head faster than I could write them down. He was still planning for a career as an accountant despite all the odds against. I really, really liked him.

Andy was unable to attend several classes during the term. I took notes for him and led him through them at his house. By the end of term, I was teaching him. The saying "if you want to really know a subject, teach it" is true. I aced the exam.

Andy didn't take that exam. He died two days before, with a smile on his face and my hand on his shoulder. It was so fast and unexpected that only his nurse and I were with him.

If anyone asks me to define courage, I will just tell them about Andy.

At Andy's funeral I was asked to say a few words. I was so emotional I flubbed it. After the funeral, Andy's uncle, Joshua, the owner of the company Julia fired me from, came over to talk to me. He thanked me for being Andy's good friend through the last round of his battle with ALS. Joshua had checked me out and knew about my affair with Julia. He also knew I was aware of the payroll scam. Security cameras in Julia's apartment? He thanked me for not using my knowledge.

Originally Andy was a real employee in Julia's department, before ALS sidelined him, Joshua explained. They just left him on the payroll so Andy could feel independent. Joshua also told me to come and see him when I graduated.

I think I passed Life 101 that day.

Oh yes. I got an A in Accounting 212, the first A I have ever received. It feels good. I think I just might buckle down and get some more.

Guest List *(50 words)*

My nieces and nephew were organizing an 80th birthday party for their father, Blake. Two weeks before the planned party Blake was rushed to the hospital's Intensive Care Unit with congestive heart failure. He didn't get out. They used the list to notify all of us of his funeral arrangements.

Burnt Bread *(50 words)*

I was in a huge bread factory when sirens started shrieking. Workers rushed from all over the plant and started throwing pans of bread right and left from the conveyor. Turned out the tunnel oven was on fire and they couldn't turn off the conveyor until the last loaf cleared.

Salvage *(50 words)*

A friend was assigned to manage the company's Brazil operation. Inflation got so high he didn't dare hold cash overnight. Then currency exporting became illegal. He traded the Brazil operation for a freighter on the high seas and flew out that night. The diverted ship was all his company salvaged.

147 CHESS SETS

According to her will, I had inherited Aunt Lisa's large collection of chess sets. They were really Uncle Frank's I suppose, but Aunt Lisa inherited them when he died. About forty of those sets were laid out in fighting formation in glass-covered trays on top of cabinets in the display room. Over a hundred more were in locked drawers below. One hundred and forty-seven in total, according to the letter I received from her lawyer. I had only three months to decide whether to accept.

I wondered if the garden set was included. The pawns are a metre high. The kings and queens are taller than I am. I once played a game with this set. We sat on high, highchairs overlooking the chessboard lawn while Uncle Frank's butler, Walter, walked around moving the pieces for us. Naturally, Uncle Frank thrashed me. After all, he was the university faculty's chess champion for twenty-three years straight.

Where could I put 147 chess sets? Not in my apartment, for sure. It would have been nice if Aunt Lisa had left me some money to look after them. But no, the money all goes to her only child, that weasel, Hans. Hans was lucky. He was the default heir when Uncle Frank died leaving Aunt Lisa between husbands again. The tables had turned on Aunt Lisa, though. Instead of being the trophy wife, she was about to take on a trophy husband.

In the women's locker room at The Club, they call Hans "Hands." It suits him. He grew up touchy and smarmy. He is so fat he waddles. Mothers hid their daughters from him, but now that he is worth upwards of $50 million, I imagine they will present their daughters on a platter. But the mothers better hurry. Aunt Lisa bailed Hands out more than once when his gambling got out of control. I guess every casino on the continent will comp him now.

I suppose Aunt Lisa's leaving the chess sets to me was Uncle Frank's idea, because I spent time with him in the display room talking about them. Hands was never interested. He wouldn't give his stepfather, Uncle Frank, the time of day, and might just throw the chess sets out. Or maybe Aunt Lisa did it as a joke, knowing I couldn't follow through.

There is the Maasai warrior set Uncle Frank got in Kenya. That was the time Hands gut-shot a lion using a guide's rifle. Uncle Frank and the guide had to track the lion for two dangerous days to finish the job. That safari was Aunt Lisa's idea and Uncle Frank only carried a camera. That poor beast's head is still on the family room wall. I think that was Aunt Lisa's idea too.

One time, Hands and I got into the display room and played soldiers with the Civil War set. Hands got angry and stomped Jefferson Davis. Uncle Frank sent the chauffeur, Jerry, all the way to Gettysburg for a replacement. Jerry couldn't just buy a Jefferson, so he had to buy an entire set. I never saw the Civil War displayed after that.

I've always liked the hand-carved ivory chessmen from India. The rook is a fighting elephant and the basket on its back for the rider looks just like the castles in traditional chess sets. An elephant would be just the right symbol for that piece's movement, charging straight ahead. The Disney set is fun, but I don't understand why they made Pluto king.

The Met offered me $50,000 for the set Napoleon used. I offered them the entire collection for that price, but they declined. That was part of my problem. The collection can't be broken up. What was I going to do with 147 chess sets? I hardly ever play chess anymore.

Let me introduce myself. My name is David Dodge. My mother was the cook in Uncle Frank and Aunt Lisa's house, so they were not really my uncle and aunt, at least not officially. Mom and I lived in a small house at the back of the property. Mom never told anyone who my father was. I have my suspicions, though. When Uncle Frank died, Mom retired to a pretty luxurious senior's home someone must have paid for.

Mom is dead now too, so I guess I'm a triple orphan. I got to be a close member of the household because I am about Hands' age and we were playmates. Hands has always been bigger than me and used that whenever he could. I am smarter than him and used that, so it was a fair trade-off. Hands is Aunt Lisa's son from her first marriage.

About the time Hands was six, he took on Aunt Lisa's attitudes about their high status and became impossible. The big estate and raft of servants were Aunt Lisa's doing. I suspect she thought she was living in an F. Scott Fitzgerald novel. Uncle Frank just put up with it, but he also took advantage of it when it suited him.

Uncle Frank got the start on his fortune in his early twenties by developing and selling a computer database program. He was a successful investor the rest of his life. Aunt Lisa bagged him after losing Hands' father to old age. Uncle Frank and Hands had little in common and mostly ignored each other. Uncle Frank and I got along fairly well. I spent a lot of time listening as he recounted his adventures.

Uncle Frank was an adjunct professor at the business school for twenty-three years. Adjunct meant he didn't have the academic credentials but had so much to offer that he was on faculty anyway. That rarely happened, so I guess he was very good.

Uncle Frank managed to get both Hands and me into the business school and paid my way. The deal was that I would look out for Hands on the academic side and he would look out for me on the physical side. Hands wasn't much use to me because he was mostly partying. On the other hand, I coached him on course content and actually wrote some of his term papers.

I refused to take Hands' exams for him, though, so I graduated, and Hands didn't. I moved on to be a teaching assistant in the doctoral program, paying my own way and living in a tiny student apartment. Hence my problem with housing Uncle Frank's chess sets. But if I declined the inheritance, Hands might throw them out. I really wanted to take them and find a home for them. Uncle Frank loved those sets. They were markers of his life's events, and I wanted to do this for him.

Although I was never a member of The Club, I was often an invited guest. I was right about Hands. His status had elevated and several young women, two of them who looked under twenty, paid attention to him. I seemed to attract an older group of women, mostly in their late thirties or early forties. Carole with an "e" was an attractive, youngish widow who listened to my problems and offered good advice. She was intelligent and had enough money to solve whatever was troubling me. Very tempting.

My other obvious path was the university. Uncle Frank had connections there. By then, I was just looking for a place that met the terms of the will. I went to the alumni fundraising offices, where I met Andrea, the receptionist behind the counter. After listening for about a minute to my prepared speech, Andrea walked around the counter, took me by the arm, and marched me out the door. She let me finish my pitch in the cafeteria over coffee. I was focusing on doing it for Uncle Frank. Then she explained the facts of fundraising.

My proposal to finance and display the chess sets was too small to interest the Alumni Association. The university would not sanction or allow competitive fundraising. They were after real money from their graduates and would not allow any graduate to think he or she could meet his or her obligation to the school for a few hundred or even a few thousand dollars. I could not use the university's name on any fundraising efforts I undertook. Andrea also assured me that I did not want to leave any record of having been in her office.

But Andrea was sympathetic too, and she was very familiar with money and fundraising. She was also extraordinarily attractive and intelligent. WOW! We kept talking and moved over to the bistro for lunch. She was full of ideas on how to go about raising money for the chess sets and thought crowdfunding might be a good route. She even knew which crowdfunding groups focused on what kinds of projects.

Andrea! WOW!!!

Over dinner, Andrea outlined the steps we had to take. We. Did you notice that? *We!* Andrea had signed on. First, we needed to find an organization that could and would house and display the collection. Then we needed to work out a budget, since it was clear we would need to entice the target recipient with seed money. How much seed money depended on the deal we could make. The recipient also needed to have enough prestige so their name would help sell potential donors.

It still seems weird to me that we needed to bribe someone to take a gift.

The next day Andrea had a list of potential recipients. She risked her job pulling the names, contacts and thumbnail descriptions from confidential files. We studied the list over dinner at her place that night and rated them from most likely to least likely. We even agreed that I should approach some unlikely ones first, to practice my pitch. That way I wouldn't waste a good prospect while learning. Andrea is really intelligent. I left at midnight after a brief hug.

Obviously, I had to keep Andrea out of sight. Her job and reputation were at stake. My budding academic career was, too. If I approached someone, I needed a story about how I found them. Creative obscuration. Of course, all our target organizations had websites so I could appraise them. Most also had parallel websites commenting on or evaluating them and their products or services. I looked over their published financials. It was usually easy to come up with a good story for each one, based on what the internet told me.

We picked a local one to start on. I got an appointment with the owner. It was a disaster. I was laughed out after less than twenty minutes. But I learned something. My pitch was all about what I needed. He couldn't see why he needed it. I hadn't thought that through very well. I had it backward. It should have been all about his needs.

Andrea and I went back to her list and re-evaluated, based on our targets' needs. I went out three more times with the revised approach and got a better hearing, but no scores. Not even close. I was really discouraged, but Andrea kept pointing out that we were still working through the doubtful prospects, and it only took one score to win this first round of our campaign.

One of our issues was the timeline. I had to make a take or decline decision on the inheritance very soon. That was the crunch for me. Carole is quite attractive and made it pretty clear that she wanted to acquire me. Problem over. On the other hand, Andrea and I were really compatible, and I thought I could probably win her. A sure, easy thing or a maybe amazing thing. When I saw it in these clear terms it was a no brainer.

I rented a big storage unit and notified the lawyer that I was going to take the sets. The rent was ruinous for my budget, but it gave me a year before I had to arrange the display part of the inheritance terms. It was a gamble.

Then I had a win, sort of. A newish internet marketing firm was interested. The problem was, they had no money. They showed me their financials and my analysis said they were verging on bankruptcy. It was pretty clear they were more interested in a way to raise money than in the chess sets.

A recurring problem I met was the need to run our project past a board of directors. Directors are usually focused on profits, so the odds of getting approval were really low. I often thought it was a polite way of saying no.

We had four private firms on Andrea's list. Approaching them was dangerous because I didn't have enough information to concoct a good lead-in story. One had an internet gaming site that was attractive and sophisticated. I went in cold and met Geoff, their president and Chief Operating Officer rolled into one. It was a small start-up populated by techies who talked a strange language. Geoff was a techie too, but he did speak competent English.

I barely started my pitch when Geoff interrupted and challenged me to a game of chess. It was a test model of their next game offering, chess. Bingo! Geoff won. I asked to see their financial statements. All they had was a big, big spreadsheet driving an even bigger database. Geoff asked me if I could pull their financial statements off of it since the auditors were due in a couple of days and he did not understand that side of the business.

I was there past midnight, slicing and dicing their database. Their spreadsheet was incomprehensible, so I built my own. I did it! I produced credible financial statements an auditor could work with. Of course, they were broke, but they had good margins and could be winners with a larger subscriber base. The chess connection was magic. Their lack of commonsense business smarts was terrifying, though.

The next day, Geoff and I talked about the synergy between his firm's future and my chess sets. He was enthusiastic and could see many marketing opportunities, so he wasn't totally a techie. He had an amazing imagination and thought ahead faster than I could follow. Another problem was their crowded space. They needed more area, "elbow room," he called it. We saw that as part of the same problem as housing the chess sets.

With input from Geoff, I worked out a plan and a budget to rent a larger space with a big playroom for reception and the chess set displays. It was not as costly as I had expected. We had a plan. The firm would need a venture capital infusion in about a year, but with the high margins that was a reasonable expectation.

The chess sets arrived in two large trucks. The garden set was included. Andrea and I arranged them in some sort of order in the storage unit but kept out one particular set. These were magnificent Venetian crystal chessmen that were actually small drinking cups. The idea was to put alcoholic drinks in each piece. When a piece was captured, the capturing player had to drink the contents. This could be a great equalizer, because the better chess player would get drunk faster.

That night, we celebrated my big gamble. Andrea's pieces were loaded with clear Cointreau, mine with amber Grand Marnier, both orange flavoured. I started out winning but quickly lost ground and my wits. Then Andrea pulled ahead, and something snapped. Suddenly, spontaneously, we both stopped playing and headed for the bedroom, scattering clothes on our way. By morning we were no longer a two-person team; we were one.

I had to let Carole off as gently as I could. I decided to play it as if she was a substitute mother and I was showing her my future wife. I hinted a warning as Andrea, and I invited her to dinner at a very nice restaurant. Carole understood there was something special coming and took it extremely well. She and Andrea actually liked each other.

Carole was also interested in our venture and the internet start-up. The next day, her accountant dropped in on Geoff and asked for me. I wasn't there, of course, but Geoff showed him around and gave him a copy of the financials I had prepared. They played a game of internet chess. Naturally, Geoff won.

Carole's accountant must have been impressed, because soon after her lawyer came with an offer to invest half a million dollars in exchange for a substantial block of shares. It would make Carole the second-largest shareholder behind Geoff. One of the conditions of Carole's offer was that I had to set my academic career aside and commit to the business full-time for at least three years. I was already so engrossed in its affairs that changing over was an easy decision. I had already vacated my student apartment to move in with Andrea.

Carole's half-million dollars was enough to take us over the top to an Initial Public Offering (IPO). We didn't even need to crowdfund. The IPO was oversubscribed, selling more shares than we expected. Our company was listed on a public stock exchange, where trades between buyers and sellers placed a value on Carole's shares at about $10 million, a pretty good return on her half-million-dollar investment.

We moved our business to larger quarters and guarded our cash jealously. All of us took out minimal funds and were mostly paid with shares in the company. We are on full payrolls now.

Geoff still holds the largest number of shares but sold a small portion of them to pay off his mortgage and become debt-free for the first time in his life. The rest of us are holding onto all of our shares because we think they will be worth much more once the company consolidates its hold on its market. My shares made Andrea and me millionaires on paper. Most of Geoff's team are also millionaires on paper.

I am now the Chief Operating Officer responsible for day-to-day management. I love the work. Geoff is the CEO and focuses most of his time inventing and developing new products with his extraordinary team of techies. Carole is president and chairwoman of our board of directors and has brought in some amazing talent to steer us down good paths.

Our big breakthrough came out of a brainstorming session initiated by Carole's board. We analysed our strengths and weaknesses in depth and concluded that there was nothing special about our web presence except that our games had more depth and detail. We were too small to have much impact on the industry and growing would be tough slogging.

As a result, we changed our business strategy. I went on the road, licencing our games to other internet gaming companies. Our prices were low enough so it would seem foolish for them to develop their own games, but a small amount from a lot of sources still adds up.

We privatized our internet presence to about two thousand diehard gamers to test and perfect our new games. We did not want to compete with our clients. Oddly, being in this inner circle became a point of pride and we now have gamers knocking on our door to get in. We even pay small amounts for useful feedback on new games.

Geoff's team went on a development tear. Once his creations passed the testing phase on our private site, he customized them so the same game would appear different to provide each of our clients with products that had their own unique feel and features.

We call them clients, but the reality is that they are more like franchises. Although each one's offerings looks and feels different, they aren't, and we own the games we licence. Thus, over time we actually come to own their internet personas. We are very careful to downplay this and treat each client with absolute fairness and deference. We are also aware that we might be breaking antitrust laws by pulling all these business into one business envelope, but we hope we are too small to be noticed.

Some of our clients have infiltrated our private website and know what is coming down the pipeline. We are very careful to release new games to all of them simultaneously, so no one has an advantage. We have even started acting as an advertising agent, booking and selling ads for most of them and collecting and distributing the revenues after taking a small cut.

The advertisements don't generate much money, but they allow our clients to operate two-tier sites, where tier two is ad-free. Tier one is usually no charge and they charge varied amounts for the second tier. It seems a gamer doesn't care to have his or her concentration broken in the midst of, say a chess game, by an advertisement.

Our new offices are amazing. The playroom lobby is a huge atrium. We can display thirty chess sets at a time on counters and the rest are in pull-out glass-topped drawers for easy viewing. Ten small tables are set up for people to play chess on and a lawn chess board in the garden hosts the giant chess set. We have open house days for our local gamers. Some of our clients also drop by to see the displays and play when they are in town.

Geoff figured out immediately how I got to him, but he loves games and thought my getting into the university's files was brilliant. Being wealthy hasn't changed him. The university's alumni fund people figured it out too, after Andrea surfaced, but a tacit understanding will keep them quiet as long as the privacy breach does not get out.

Hands is divorced and broke. Easy pickings.

It has occurred to me that Carole has acquired me indirectly. Carole's office is next to mine and we see each other regularly on business matters and occasionally at social events. This arrangement is a win for everyone, especially me. Carole and Andrea are still friends.

Andrea and I are married and have two children with a third on the way. Our oldest child's first name is Frank. We live in a very nice old house in the suburbs. Andrea is as good at being a mother as she is at everything else.

Oh yes, I forgot to mention, there are only 145 chess sets in the atrium, plus the huge garden set outside. Andrea and I held back the Venetian crystal drinking glass set. Every now and then when Andrea isn't pregnant, we challenge each other to a game, but we have never managed to finish one.

RESCUING LOONS

I woke up to pounding on my front door. There was a voice shouting, "LOONS ARE TRAPPED! LOONS ARE TRAPPED!" Johnny!

I was awake quickly because this was an emergency needing my full attention. Some winters a few immature loons delay flying south until it is too late. Often their pinfeathers take too long to develop. Loons need long runways to take off.

I went downstairs and let Johnny in, then put on a pot of coffee. We were going to need it. Johnny saw three loons trapped by ice on Little Lake in his headlights on his way to work. He called the rest of The Crew on his cell phone while I called Agnes Doherty and told her to round up three cat-carrying cases. I also called the mill to let them know we wouldn't be in for work that morning,

We call ourselves The Crew. We are the town's six-person volunteer fire brigade and occasional loon savers. We work at Carson's Mill turning softwood logs into lumber. Everyone, including Mr. Carson, knows that saving loons comes before work or anything else, except fires.

Less than ten minutes later, Agnes delivered three cat cases. Johnny put the coffee into a thermos. Finally dressed, I collected my long-handled fishing net and we strapped my red canoe on top of his 4x4. We dropped by the fire hall to collect Emory, two ropes and a long pole, then headed down the gravel road to the campground on Little Lake.

Sure enough, three loons were swimming in a small open space on the mostly ice-covered lake, diving and resurfacing. We unloaded the canoe and put it on the shore ice. We tied a long rope to its stern and loaded the cat cases. Being the lightest, I got in the canoe. Emory, the strongest, was wearing his ice-fishing cleats and he started pushing me across the ice toward the open water. Emory had the other rope tied around his chest so the rest of The Crew could pull him out if he fell through.

When we got close to the opening in the ice, Emory pushed me the rest of the way with the long pole. The loons dived in panic but had to eventually resurface. It took a few tries, but I was able to net two of them as they came up and I put them in the cases. I had heavy leather work gloves on to protect my hands. I waited and waited, more than half an hour, but the third loon never resurfaced. There was nowhere else for it to go, so it must have drowned.

The Crew pulled the canoe back to shore and we strapped it back on Johnny's 4x4. We took the two loons back to town on Lake Ann and released them. Lake Ann is large and would not freeze over for three more weeks, giving our loons long enough runways and a fair chance to survive. We all got to the mill around 11 am and finished our shift. Mr. Carson didn't even dock our pay for missed time.

I went by Little Lake on my way home that night, hoping, but the lake was completely frozen over. The only thing that had kept that spot open was the coming and going of the loons. I felt sad, but at the same time if we hadn't been quick, we would have lost all three loons.

DON'T ALIENATE NEIGHBOURHOOD CHILDREN

I was delighted when the "For Sale" sign went up on the house next door. Hooray! Mean Dave Shelby was moving. He is a mean one for sure. Last week, our rocket parachuted onto his roof and he told us we couldn't come onto his property to get it back. We have regular fights with him. Last year, he put up a six-foot-tall chain link fence. We didn't like the fence because it broke up our football field, but Mean Dave made Dad pay half for our part anyway.

Mean Dave's got two snarling Doberman dogs. It was fun teasing them through the fence. They ran up against it and bounced back, then they tried to climb the fence and fell back. One of them bit through part of his tongue barking at us. With those dogs in his yard, we didn't dare go in to try and get our rocket back. We waited till Mean Dave and his wife, Phyllis, were away and used Dad's extension ladder to climb up at the front of his house and walk up over the ridge to get it.

Mean Dave accused us of doing that. I think a neighbour ratted us out. We just said the wind blew the rocket off his roof and what could he do? He complained to Dad and Dad chewed us out, but Dad's heart wasn't in it.

Mean Dave didn't like how Dad kept our lawn. There was a strip about ten feet wide between our driveways. Mean Dave weeded and mowed the entire strip, even though half of it was ours. Then he complained to Dad because he had to weed our dandelions. We liked our dandelions. Once Mean Dave moved my bike off the strip of lawn between the driveways and onto our driveway and Dad backed his car over it. Dad shouted back at Mean Dave that time.

Mean Dave's wife, Phyllis, was always coming over to have tea with Mom. Phyllis was crying a couple of times. I heard her say Mean Dave made her vacuum their bed every day before changing the sheets and he hit her if she didn't do it right. One time the police came, and Phyllis left with them. She was gone for two weeks but she came back.

Mean Dave had tires with studs on them that chewed grooves in the road and in his driveway. I heard Dad tell another neighbour that tire studs were illegal, so we reported Mean Dave. The police came and Mean Dave had to get new tires and change them right there in his driveway. We liked watching that.

You know, teasing Mean Dave was kind of fun. Maybe we'll miss him. I wonder why he's moving.

HOMECOMING

Basking on a lounger in the warm sun, I watched ducks bobbing on the pond and white egrets stalking in the reeds. A kingfisher, perched on a high branch, swooped periodically to touch the water with its beak. A regal sandhill crane with red patches over each eye strutted by and stared down at me through the lanai screening, then moved on.

The next day, scrunched in an Air Canada seat designed for a child, I came back to the land of ice and snow. Riding in the Red Car through snow squalls on treacherous roads, the only saving grace was that I had exclusive use of the coach. I was the only passenger whose flight made it.

The weather was much nicer in Tampa.

LIES, DAMNED LIES & POLITICIANS

There are lies, damned lies, and politicians. I never said that / Next year we'll balance the budget / We will meet our carbon target / The war to end all wars / There'll be peace in our time.

There are kid's lies and grown-up kid's lies. Santa Claus / The Easter Bunny / The Tooth Fairy / The Wishing Star / The Great Pumpkin / In God We Trust. I don't see Americans sitting on their hands waiting for divine intervention.

There are feel-good lies and not-so-good lies. You'll be better soon / You look good / I'm glad to see you / That was great / Come again / Drop in anytime.

There are self-serving lies and self-deceiving lies. I didn't do it / It wasn't my fault / I'm sorry / I did it for you / I didn't mean to hurt you / This might hurt a little / The dog ate my homework.

There are terrible lies and hopeful lies. Those people really *are* different / I'm not prejudiced, *but...* / Work will set you free / Global warming is a hoax / *You* will burn in hell.

Speaking of Hell, I've been to hell and back. It was a 1960s-era iron foundry in Hamilton, Ontario. There were big, sweaty, half-naked men lit up by a bright orange glow, reaching long-handled pokers through holes in the sides of blast furnaces to stir up the coals and intensify the deafening roar of the fire. There were enormous cherry-red ceramic crucibles travelling across the ceiling on a gantry. The stink of sulphur was almost overpowering. The air was so thick that bright sunbeams shining through high-up windows did not make it to the floor. I am *certain* that Hamilton iron foundry was the model for Dante's Hell.

Perhaps the most hopeful lie of all time was:

There'll be love and laughter   *Vera Lynn, born March 20, 1917*
And peace ever after   *Died June 18, 2020, at age 103*
Tomorrow when the world is free

The world revolves around lies. The issue is knowing when to tell a lie and when not to.

There are times when it is OK to tell a lie; the truth can be so bleak and so inevitable.

A GOOD LIE

James descended on us last week. We love him, but not his sleeping day and night on our living room couch. I needed to move him on without insulting him. I dialled the telephone number that makes my phone ring and faked a conversation ending with a loud "O-mi-god!" I turned to James and said, "My bridge partner just found out there was a case of coronavirus on her Vancouver flight and she might be quarantined. That could be our fate too, since I played bridge with her last week."

James rallied quickly and was soon gone, saying, "Maybe Jack can take me in." He didn't even say goodbye.

Phone Bill *(50 words)*

The memo was in his handwriting, and it drew a blank. It said, "phone bill." He could not remember why he wrote it or which Bill he should call. Two weeks later he got a delinquent payment notice in the mail from the telephone company for his unpaid phone bill.

Reported Stolen *(50 words)*

He woke up and discovered his car was missing, so he reported it stolen. An hour later the police called back to let him know his car was parked at a minimart two blocks from his house. Turned out he drove to the minimart the night before but walked home.

Negotiating *(50 words)*

The hobby farmer backed over her dog. The vet quoted $2,400 to treat a crushed leg. Dad, a senior manager, said, "I am a farmer you know," and started walking out. His small daughter started crying. The vet dropped the price. Outside Dad said, "Don't worry, we were just negotiating."

THE OPPORTUNIST

Evan Sloan was driving far too fast on the gravel road when he turned into his driveway. Elaine, his daughter, heard the crash while gardening and ran down the driveway to find him. She was the first person on the scene. His convertible was leaning on its side against a large maple tree, totalled. He was cradled in a juniper bush at least five metres beyond, dead.

Elaine could not process the scene. She was standing there screaming when her neighbour arrived, out of breath from running. The neighbour called 911 on his cellphone, then gathered Elaine in an embrace and helped her back to her house. He sat her down in a wicker chair on the patio and went inside to get her a full tumbler of single-malt scotch.

In the following investigation, some information was fact and some was speculation. One fact was that Evan was driving too fast. The smashed speedometer was locked at a reading of just over a hundred kilometres an hour. Another fact was that Evan had a blood alcohol reading of almost twice the legal limit. At Evan's funeral, a friend was overheard saying, "Double the limit wouldn't impair Evan because he was adapted to that level." There was speculation that the "accident" was suicide, either intended or unintended.

The funeral was a grand affair. The pallbearers were Evan's business associates. Evan's wife, Marguerite, was dressed in flamboyant black that accentuated her trim figure and generous breasts. A gossiping guest joked that Marguerite was already trolling for a replacement. Elaine, who was Marguerite and Evan's only child, was in a state of shock and could hardly process what was happening.

Marguerite discovered that her Mercedes was leased when it was repossessed out of her driveway the morning before the funeral. A frantic phone call revealed that Evan was three months behind on the lease payments for both cars. Fortunately, the funeral home was supplying the transportation that day, but Marguerite and Elaine were reduced to driving to the lawyer's office in Elaine's Miata the next day.

At the lawyer's office, it was Marguerite who went into shock. Although she was the sole beneficiary of Evan's will, there was precious little to bequeath. Incomprehensibly, her property had first, second and third mortgages registered against it, totalling more than its market value. The family business, MacDougal Enterprises, owed lenders, notably Merchant Bank, over $2 million and was losing money.

Marguerite could not understand what was happening. Her father, Francis MacDougal, built his manufacturing business from nothing to a powerhouse over thirty years. When he died, leaving everything to Marguerite, the business was valued at $5.5 million. How could Evan run that business into the ground in less than five years? But then, she didn't know anything about the business or ever wanted to.

The country estate was valued at just over $2 million. Marguerite could not understand how Evan could take out three mortgages on her property, since he was not in any way an owner. Her family's lawyer, John Barry, agreed to investigate, but wanted a retainer since Evan had not paid his legal bills in over a year. John assured Marguerite that he was not involved in the mortgages and was fully aware that Marguerite was the legitimate owner. However, he said, the registered deed shows that Evan was the sole owner.

John advised Marguerite to contact the Merchant Bank as soon as possible to deal with the mortgage and the business debt. He thought the mortgage was probably enforceable since it was very likely that the bank's lawyers were diligent.

Marguerite took John's advice and called Merchant Bank later that day, setting up a meeting with Harold Maynard, the account manager.

Elaine knew even less about the business. Her sheltered upbringing and private girls' school education did not prepare her for things like that. To her, the most important part of the disaster was that her tuition for the upcoming semester at Darien College was not paid. Her place in her final year was forfeit, so she would not graduate with her classmates. The fact that she could apply for readmission the following year was of little comfort.

The next day in the meeting at the bank, Harold told Marguerite that the bank was going to insert an overseer into the business to evaluate the bank's business loan. He also told her that the bank, as first mortgage holder on the estate, would have to foreclose if the monthly payments were not caught up within thirty days. If that happened, he said, the bank would almost certainly put it up for sale.

Harold pointed out that Merchant Bank would get the first $1,400,000 to retire their mortgage, plus an administration fee that could amount to another $140,000. The potential real estate commission of 5% could take out another $100,000. As a result, the second mortgage holder would lose most of his money and the third mortgage holder would almost certainly lose all of his money.

Harold suggested that Marguerite investigate the possibility of one of the other mortgage holders paying out the Merchant Bank's loan to protect their position.

From Marguerite's socially conscious point of view, that was the worst part of the entire disaster. Marguerite's cousin, Edgar, held the third mortgage. Evan had borrowed half a million dollars from her cousin, pledging almost worthless collateral. Evan had not only squandered Marguerite's wealth, undermining her position in society, but it seemed he was taking down her entire family.

The next day Peter Anderson, the bank's appointed CPA, arrived at the business, took over Evan's office, and started sifting through mountains of information. He wrote the following report four days later.

Memo – Confidential – Property of Merchant Bank

Re: MacDougal Enterprises – Preliminary Report

The company is operating at a loss of about $200,000 a year. The owner/manager, Evan Sloan, was paid an average of $250,000 a year, so without his salary the business might have been marginally profitable. He has also personally borrowed $487,000 from the company, which invalidates the loan covenant and has caused the cash shortfall.

The profit margins on the company's products have been shrinking for the past five years but are still in an acceptable range. Product development has not kept up with their competitors and many product lines are trending toward obsolescence. The company has not increased its prices in four years as its costs rose with inflation, causing the eroding margins. Despite holding the line on prices, the company's sales volumes are declining.

If sales volumes were returned to levels of even two years ago, the company's profitability would be adequate for it to meet its present obligations, including dealing with Merchant Bank's loan. However, new product initiatives are an absolute necessity for longer-term success.

Accounts receivable aging shows that 40% of the company's customers are behind in their payments by at least thirty days, 10% by over ninety days, yet sales and shipments to all customers are continuing. With an increased collection effort, it should be possible to reduce receivables by up to $200,000. It could take three to four months to do this. At present there are no employees dedicated to collection activities.

Factoring the receivables that are current could raise another $500,000.

The layout of the manufacturing plant is a disaster. There are no aisles marked out for moving product through. There is overcrowding of equipment with excess inventories scattered around every workstation. Rationalizing inventories with a partial just-in-time system could free up as much as $500,000. This could take eight months to a year to complete.

A discussion with the plant manager suggests that 10% to 15% of the company's inventory is obsolete and worth only scrap value. Getting rid of it would help clear floor space. Identifying obsolete inventory could take up to two months. Any cash recovery would be negligible.

The machinery is old and outdated, but functional and well maintained. Many of the operations could be automated if computer-controlled equipment was available.

Bringing in such equipment would significantly improve productivity and margins.

Payables are badly in arrears and suppliers are starting to withhold materials, parts and components. In order to bring payables down to industry norms, the firm needs to commit $400,000 very quickly.

The controller does a good job of tracking financial transactions but prepares no budgets and produces no future-oriented analysis. "Controller" is not an appropriate title for her activities. With better operating information and analysis, productivity could be improved, and accurate pricing could take better advantage of market opportunities.

The marketing manager, Larry James, spends most of his time making sales calls and is rarely in the office. The company has lost many of its sales representatives, adding to his workload. Evan Sloan often involved himself in this area of the business, undermining Larry's authority. Larry might be successful if left to do his job.

The plant manager has relied heavily on decisions made by Evan, who as an engineer, should have been competent in this area of the business. This manager has been with the firm for almost forty years, starting as Francis MacDougal's first press operator. He does not have the presence or energy to fulfill this function and says he wants to retire. I have suggested he stay on long enough to help a replacement learn the ropes.

Overall, Evan appears to have spent most of his time micromanaging in every area of the business and does not seem to have delegated real authority to any of his managers.

Both bringing the receivables into line with industry norms and rationalizing the inventory will take time, but it can be done. Of immediate concern is the need for a cash infusion to bring key suppliers back on board and meet the next payroll. The obvious source is factoring the accounts receivable that are current. For that to happen, Merchant Bank would need to waive these receivables from the blanket assignment it now holds on all of the company's assets.

Most of the 217 employees have been with the company for years. If the company was liquidated the severance costs would take up most of its value. At least two members of the management team need to be replaced. In the short run, it might be best to keep them on the payroll in some capacity to postpone their severance costs.

Summing up my major conclusions, MacDougal Enterprises is still a viable business provided a competent general manager assumes control. A cash infusion of $200,000 is needed immediately to keep it afloat, but this $200,000 can be recouped as the inventories and receivables are brought down. There is room to take out an additional term loan on their committed facility.

My interviews with senior managers did not identify anyone currently employed who could be considered capable of managing the company out of its current situation.

I see three options for Merchant Bank.

Call the loan by accelerating the installment payments since the covenant is in default.

1a) This could lead to the company being liquidated by selling the assets, collecting the receivables and using the proceeds to meet the company's financial obligations, or

1b) Having the company put up for sale as a going concern.

2) Continue to support the company financially and appoint a competent manager to bring it back to profitability.

Recommendation:

I recommend **Option 2**.

With **Option 1a**, there will not be much left over for Merchant Bank after the company's legal obligations are met. The inventories would be almost worthless.

With **Option 1b**, the company in its present condition does not have sufficient value to cover the money owed to Merchant Bank.

My analysis indicates that **Option 2** gives Merchant Bank the best path to recovering all of its loan, provided a competent general manager can be installed.

Option 2 has additional advantages. It retains a potentially good future client. It provides a social good by helping more than 200 older workers remain gainfully employed. Laying off 200 older workers with Option 1a could lead to negative publicity for Merchant Bank.

Option 1b would not guarantee job retention for the employees. A buyer would most likely value the product sales but move production to a more efficient facility. Merchant Bank might still have negative publicity as employees are laid off.

I am preparing a detailed analysis, which will follow in about seven days.

P. Anderson, MBA, CPA
C. Burns & Associates

Harold Maynard was also in favour of Option 2. The bank considered any loan that had to be called a failed loan, even if all the bank's money was recovered. Either of options 1a or 1b would record a black mark against his performance record. He already had two of those this year. A third would be very bad for his career. Option 2 gave him a chance to avoid that, with the consultant's report providing cover.

It did not occur to Harold that Peter Anderson already knew that and took it into account in writing his report. For reasons of his own, Peter also strongly preferred Option 2.

Charles Burns started the search for general manager prospects immediately. One of his associated firms was in the Executive Placement Business, commonly known as headhunting. No one other than Peter had any level of authority in the firm, so Marguerite accepted Harold's recommendation and assigned Peter to do the vetting.

No candidates with appropriate experience or credentials met Peter's approval. This was not surprising, since the challenges facing the company were large and the company was small, and Peter had other plans.

Meanwhile, Peter began the process of resurrecting the company. He found a tough-minded junior employee in the accounting department who was willing to tackle the overdue receivables and gave her the new title, Credit Manager. He gave her the authority to cut off shipments if she thought that was an appropriate tactic. He gave her guidelines for making extended repayment deals. He bypassed the plant manager and instructed the shipper to take his direction from the new Credit Manager. She was the first person in the company that Peter felt comfortable delegating authority to.

Peter started a search for a new plant manager through Burns & Associates. The existing manager was almost seventy years old and never had much authority because of Evan's management style. After several interviews, Peter did not consider any of the department foremen capable of assuming the plant manager role.

Product development was another area where Peter was acting fast. One of the company's product lines included gas fireplaces that were controlled by a battery-powered handheld wand with a thermostat built in.

This wand could turn the fireplace on and off automatically to maintain a steady temperature at the wand's location.

Peter signed a development contract with an engineering company to incorporate these existing components into a design for a small portable propane gas heater that could be located on an external wall of an enclosed space such as an ice-fishing hut, hunting camp, cottage, or even a tent with vertical walls.

His detailed list of specifications included:

An external airflow system to feed the flame and exhale the exhaust.

An internal airflow system to put heat into the enclosed space.

Heat sensors on the exhaust stack and internal components to modulate the flame and limit temperatures. (This was essential because the convection airflow would take a minute or two to develop as the system started up.)

Reliance on convection for the air flows for both systems, so no electricity source is required.

An automatic shutoff feature if it is tilted more than a few degrees.

An on/off function triggered by the handheld wand and its thermostat.

Next, Peter tackled the sales manager, Larry James, telling him to cut back on his sales calls and start finding space at cottage and recreation shows in Ontario, Manitoba, Minnesota, northern Michigan, and the New England states. The purpose of the shows, Peter said, was to find new commission sales agents in these areas, as well as to sell the company's products through these new agents. He did not tell the sales manager about the new product.

Peter had no authority to make any of these decisions, but nuances like that had never stopped him. He carried such an air of authority that everyone in the company just assumed he had it. Operating out of Evan's office helped.

Peter was working sixteen-hour days. The company needed a cash infusion to help meet a payroll five days after Peter started. He took that problem to Harold Maynard, pointing out that Harold either needed to waive the bank's assignment on the receivables or increase the company's credit limit. Harold opted for the credit limit increase because changing the basic terms of the loan would involve the bank's legal department. which could bring this mess to head office's attention.

As sole owner, Marguerite had to sign off on the new loan arrangement. Out of deference to her new widowhood, Harold took the forms to the estate for her to sign. He brought Peter along to explain what was happening at the company and why the larger loan was important. Harold also wanted to look at the estate he had taken as security for such a large mortgage loan.

This was Peter's chance to meet Marguerite. He wanted to make a good first impression, because he hoped to run and eventually own the company. He outlined some of the things he was doing and explained how they would bring the company back. He described the new product line that still existed only in his imagination and outlined the market he wanted to take it into.

Elaine was present at the meeting. She was not much impressed, thinking Peter was brash and overconfident. He did not pay much attention to her, and Elaine was not accustomed to holding second place for any man's attention. It did not occur to her that this was a business meeting.

Peter was definitely aware of Elaine, although that was secondary to his need to impress Marguerite and Harold. He was conducting an unscheduled job interview. It worked! Harold Maynard realized the company already had the competent general manager it needed. When he was back in his office, he called Marguerite and advised her to offer Peter the general manager's position. She had already made that decision on her own.

In the negotiation with Marguerite and her family's lawyer that followed, Peter "agreed" to take a reduced salary to help the company "over the hump." Instead, he proposed taking the difference in newly issued shares of the company at the end of two years, with the amounts based on how successful he was. He pointed out that this arrangement aligned his incentives with the bank's needs and with Marguerite's objectives.

It turned out to be a lot of shares.

Elaine visited the plant the following Monday morning. When she arrived, Peter was in a telephone conversation with a Boston-based Canadian Trade Commissioner. They were discussing how "his company" could benefit by exhibiting at a New England Outdoor Show. Peter was after the $75,000 support available from the Trade Commission Service as well as their assistance in booking the show and finding good sales representatives.

Peter's secretary, Kendra, knew who Elaine was and settled her in the anteroom with a coffee and reading material. Peter was astonished to find Elaine there when he came out. He told Kendra to postpone the morning's meetings and invited Elaine into his office as he poured coffee for himself. Elaine started in on him before he even sat down.

"Who do you think you are, taking over Dad's office? And where are Dad's trophies?" She wanted to fire Kendra because Kendra had been her dad's mistress on sales trips. Elaine based her mistress judgment on the fact that Kendra and her dad went to exhibitions together. She made several other demands.

Peter told her to stop being silly, that he was employed by the company not by her, and that his contract gave him complete authority. He told Elaine that Kendra was good at her job and he relied on her experience and knowledge. He also told her he had not picked up any suggestion of a personal relationship between Kendra and Evan in his factfinding around the company and anyway, he didn't care if there was one. Had it occurred to Elaine that their travelling together might be about business?

Elaine was not accustomed to being called silly, but she was not about to be chased off either, so she agreed to let Peter show her around and explain what he was up to. She might have been looking for an angle to get even.

From a shelf in the anteroom, Peter provided headphones with a microphone attached, a white hardhat and safety goggles for her to wear. He took down another set for himself, and they put them on. He explained that no one went into the plant without wearing them and the headphones and mics were tuned to the same band so they could talk to each other. Then they went onto the production floor.

Even with the sound muffled by the headphones the noise hit her like a wall. Giant machines were pounding. Smaller equipment was grinding. Forklifts were humming. To her it looked and sounded like chaos. They were met at the door by an older man who also wore a hardhat, goggles and headphones. Peter introduced him by name and said he was the plant manager.

They stopped near a tall stamping press that rose and fell in a steady rhythm and the older man explained its function. It was stamping panels for one of their gas fireplaces from an enormous coil of shiny steel fed into it by an operator. They went on to look at a conveyor carrying large shiny parts from one sunken, liquid-filled tank to another similar tank in a steady flow. Peter explained that it was a chrome-plating machine. He said the tanks held strong acids and having them below floor level was a safety precaution in case of leaks.

Then Peter paused, toggled a switch on his mike and said something to the manager that Elaine could not hear. The manager left them to go over and talk to a man wearing another white hardhat sitting at a desk. The two of them went over to a big horizontal machine and talked to the operator. Elaine noticed that the operator was wearing a blue hardhat. Then she noticed that most of the people in the building were wearing blue hardhats.

As they moved on, Peter switched back to her frequency and explained, "That man was not wearing wrist cuffs. That is really dangerous. The cuffs are designed to pull his hands out of harm's way if he hasn't already pulled them back, when the cutting blade comes down."

Elaine asked, "Why are there two different colours of hardhats?"

Peter explained, "Managers wear white hardhats and workers wear blue hardhats. Sometimes being able to identify a manager quickly can be important. The man at the desk is the foreman of the stamping department."

Elaine asked, "Why did you go through the plant manager and the foreman to get a problem fixed, instead of just fixing it yourself?"

Peter's answer startled her. "Your dad would have done just what you suggested. By doing that he was undermining the authority of his management team. It's called micromanaging. I'm trying to rebuild their authority and self-confidence. To run a business this size, you need to delegate and rely on a lot of other people succeeding for you to succeed."

Elaine realized that Peter had just criticized her father without even knowing it, but it sounded like the criticism might be justified. She was starting to see Peter in a new light.

As they left the plant, Peter explained how the layout was inefficient and how the workflow could be improved with reorganization. He pointed out that there were no defined aisles or corridors for moving product between workstations. He told her the mounds of inventory beside the machines were obsolete and were headed for a scrap dealer. He talked about the labour-intensive equipment she had just seen and how computer-controlled adaptations could displace quite a few operators and reduce payroll costs.

Then he took her into the general office where she knew several employees. He explained how cracking down on delinquent customers could bring desperately needed cash back into the business.

He took her through the materials warehouse and explained how just-in-time purchasing could bring down the investment in the inventory to also help with cash issues. He took her to the shipping department where products were packaged and loaded on large trucks backed into spaces in the wall that were equipped with overhead doors.

Wherever they went, he addressed people by their names to introduce her. She was amazed, since he had been there less than a week.

Two women in the shipping area were making backdrops for the company's exhibition booths. That caught Elaine's interest. She had designed and built props for plays at her college. She pointed out a couple of ways the women could improve the backdrops. Then, at Peter's suggestion, she put on a smock and started painting. Peter left her working happily and went back to his office for a scheduled meeting, saying, "I'll come back to get you in time for lunch."

Over lunch he talked about exhibitions and how the backdrops fit in. He talked about sales representatives and why the company needed to expand sales into the United States. He told her how the Canadian Government was going to help him do that. He explained why the exhibition booths needed to be staffed by the company because the reps each carried several company's lines and took their customers from booth to booth. That was why they could not be relied on to commit their time to any one company's booth.

It was like a foreign language to Elaine, but she was interested, intelligent and learning. Peter asked her, "If I was running a sales booth and needed help staffing it, do you think I could find a better support person than Kendra? She is attractive and pleasant, she knows our products and our production schedules, and she knows our sales reps. By helping our reps with product presentations, she is actually educating them about our products. They could represent as many as eight or ten companies, so getting them to focus on and know about our products is important."

Peter continued, "We have two classes of competitors. One is companies that make and sell products like ours. The second is the other companies our reps sell for. We need to keep our reps focused on our company, giving our products a higher priority than products from other companies they represent."

Elaine got it. It dawned on her that Peter was very different from the young men she was familiar with. It was unsettling.

She told Peter about the problems on her home front. "Dad has taken out mortgages on mother's house and the Merchant Bank is threatening to foreclose."

Peter thought about it for a minute, then said, "Harold Maynard doesn't want to foreclose. That would be bad for him. All you need to do is catch up on the mortgage payments and keep them up and the problem is solved."

Elaine asked, "How can mother do that with Evan leaving her broke?"

Peter suggested they could downsize by moving somewhere else and leasing the estate out. He even told her how to do it. "There are any number of temporary assignments in senior management or diplomatic postings where an estate like yours is mandatory. They will want it furnished. Merchant Bank has a high-end real estate partner, so get Harold on it. He has a big incentive to make that work. While he is doing that, you can probably skate for another couple of months on the payments."

Skate?

Over dinner that evening, Elaine told her mother about her day, her impressions, and Peter's suggested solution to their debt problem. Marguerite understood and said, "We could move to the compound. It is only a couple of hours away and we could come back to visit if anything interesting is happening. That would even keep Cook and Gerald employed. I wouldn't need to dismiss them. I'm beginning to like your young man."

"My young man?" Elaine was startled but almost liked the sound of it, although Peter was at least ten years older than she was.

Marguerite and Elaine moved to the family compound. Some cottage! Almost anyone would be happy to have it as their primary residence. The bank backed off on the foreclosure, as Peter suggested they would. Less than a week later, Marguerite received a cheque for $10,000 for the first and last month's rent on the estate, paid by the Peruvian embassy.

She deposited the cheque and told Harold to take two months of arrears payments on the first mortgage. She kept the rest for living expenses.

Elaine telephoned Peter to tell him his plan worked. Peter told her Marguerite didn't need to catch up on the second and third mortgages because those holders couldn't do anything unless they bought out the first mortgage holder.

Then he said he could use Elaine's help staffing the company's display at the Outdoor Show if she was interested, although he couldn't pay her. One of the terms of the company's extended loan was that he couldn't add anyone to the payroll. He said her dad usually hired models from an agency for the show, but she looked as good as any model he ever saw, and she would do a better job because she had skin in the game.

Skin in the game? It was another new term to her. As good as any model? Maybe a compliment? She was confused. It seemed that everything about Peter caught her off guard.

She asked, "Will Kendra be there?"

"Absolutely," Peter said. "Kendra is going to introduce me to our reps. I want her to introduce you to them, too, to show ownership continuity. There are rumours around that the company is on the rocks and your dad committed suicide. We need to stop that cold. It could be really bad for business."

"Oh yes," he continued, "Kendra also wants to talk to you about your dad. She liked him and she was crushed when your mother called to tell her to stay away from the funeral. I think you'll find that you and your mother gave her a bad rap."

Rap? Peter sometimes talked a foreign language.

Elaine asked where she would stay if she came back to the city. Peter asked, "Don't you have any friends? During the show you will be staying at the Castle Royal Hotel, down the street from the show. We have a large suite booked with two bedrooms off it, but you could have a separate room if you wanted."

He continued, "The suite will be our off-hours operating base. It will be stocked with beer, booze and eats. The idea is to entertain our sales reps and some of our important customers who are staying in the hotel. This show will be a twenty-four-hour-a-day operation. We will try to snatch shuteye between laps."

Laps?

Elaine agreed to help and would arrange to stay with a friend for a few days. Isolated at the compound with Marguerite in the off season was boring. What Peter offered sounded interesting.

When she came to the plant the following Thursday, Peter took her down to the shipping department and got her working on the still-unfinished backdrop. He collected her at the end of the workday and took her out for dinner. Kendra was waiting for them in the restaurant. Peter introduced them to each other, although they had previously crossed paths in the anteroom.

Peter had caught Elaine off guard again. She was angry, but a high-class restaurant is not a good place to act out, so she was determinedly polite. Kendra was embarrassed, too, and mimicked an old TV show, saying, "Peter made me do it." Peter ordered a good bottle of Cabernet Sauvignon and waited for the waiter to fill their glasses. Then Peter asked Kendra to tell Elaine about her relationship with Elaine's father. That shocked both women and almost made them allies against him. The nerve!

Kendra started talking. She said she did travel to exhibitions with Evan and they did share a suite, but not a bedroom. In any case, they were so busy feeding and entertaining sales reps and customers that they were almost never alone. The work was exhausting, she said, and she looked forward to sharing it with Elaine. Maybe she would get some sleep for a change.

Magic happened. Elaine believed her and apologized for her mother's suspicions and behaviour. Actually apologized! Right in front of Peter!

Kendra told Elaine that Evan once took her to a casino after an exhibition closed. She saw Evan play at one blackjack table for at least three hours. He was terrible at it, drawing cards too often and going over twenty-one, so the dealer didn't even need to compete. Kendra guessed Evan lost about $50,000 before she could drag him away. She never went to a casino with him again, but she could always tell when he lost big because he had a bad temper for days afterward.

She continued, "When he was in one of those funks, he was accident-prone. One day he fired Randy for no good reason. The company paid $125,000 to settle a wrongful dismissal suit over that."

By the time dinner was over, Elaine and Kendra were on pretty good terms and Peter felt relieved. It had occurred to him that he needed both of these women in his life.

Showtime. The three of them plus the sales manager, Larry James, went into the exhibition building the evening before to set up. The furnishings for the booth were quaint and rustic, in keeping with the spirit of the show and of their products on display. Back in the suite Peter and Larry took a twin bedroom on one side of the suite. Kendra and Elaine took the twin bedroom on the other side. Larry explained that the firm usually booked several more rooms, but this year they were conserving cash.

They were back on duty at the exhibition by eight the following morning. The first four hours, nine to one, were all business. Reps came through one after another, bringing customers with them. Elaine studied Kendra and started learning what to do. Sometimes two or three reps with customers arrived at the same time and Elaine found herself completely involved. The reps were happy to meet her and flirted gently. One said she was a lot easier to talk to than her father.

Then the floodgates opened as the public surged in, the crowds of people overwhelming.

All four of them were selling, selling, selling. They demonstrated the company's products and helped each visitor identify the closest participating dealers by entering the visitor's postal or zip code into a computer database. Each visitor got a prenumbered coupon with these dealers' names and addresses printed on it. This coupon gave the visitor a 20% discount off the retail price if they bought one of MacDougal's products from one of these dealers within a month. Peter said the dealers could redeem the coupons with MacDougal Enterprises for half of the discount amount and that was a good deal for everyone.

Later Elaine asked Peter whose idea the coupons had been. Peter said Larry put it together. Peter also said Larry made a deal with the show's management to trade their database of visitors' postal and zip codes for a double spot at the end of two aisles, where they had exposure on three sides. He said their database gave the show's management a profile of who attended the show.

The crowds thinned about seven, so Peter and Larry went back to the suite to schmooze with their reps and customers. Peter said there would be pizza waiting for the women when they got there. The show shut down for the day at nine. Both Kendra and Elaine were exhausted after their thirteen-hour day as they trudged back to the hotel.

But the day wasn't over. The pizzas were waiting and so were several people munching on them—reps and customers. There was a fully stocked bar and Kendra took over as bartender immediately. Elaine offered to help but Kendra declined, saying, "Only after you get a bartender's licence."

Bartender's licence?

There were breads and crackers, pâtés and dips, and an enormous wheel of Oka cheese about fourteen inches across and three inches high. People came and went for hours. Finally, the four of them were alone and Peter closed and locked the door to the hall. They dragged themselves off to bed about two AM.

Back up at seven, they chugged down coffee and orange juice and crammed in scrambled eggs and bacon as Kendra and Elaine tidied the room, ready for the next onslaught. The women were a good team and Kendra complimented Elaine, saying, "Thank you. The rent-a-models never helped me clean up."

Back in the booth, their second day was a repeat of the first, except that Elaine knew most of the reps by name and started giving them back as good as she got. It was actually fun. Then another five hours of turmoil in the suite.

By the end of the week they were all exhausted, but Peter was also elated. The show went exceptionally well. It closed at noon on Sunday. Two men from the plant came to pack up and cart away the booth. Kendra and Larry begged off to go home and collapse. Peter asked Elaine to stay awhile and have an early dinner with him. He had a surprise and he hoped she would like it.

Over a glass of chardonnay, he told her she had done exceptionally well. He apologized for not being able to pay her. He told her the reps and customers were sizing him up and that having her involved showed an important continuity for the company – that having Evan's daughter there made a difference. He also complimented her on the way she got involved in the business and contributed to the show's success.

Elaine was pleased as they toasted her with raised glasses.

Then the surprise. "Ed Moore, owner of Moore Modelling Agency, checked you out and was impressed. He wants you to sign an exclusive modelling contract with his agency. If you do, his agency will invoice MacDougal Enterprises for your time at this exhibition at $500 a day. Ed will skim 20% off the top and pay you $3,200 for the eight days. I can't add you to our payroll but it's what I would have paid for a model if you hadn't signed on."

Elaine was stunned. $3,200 was a lot of money to her!

Peter went on, "Ed won't use you for runway work, you aren't skinny enough, but he often places models in marketing assignments like this exhibition. He thinks you'll be in demand once people find out about you. He shot a short video of you from the booth across the aisle and plans to use it to promote you. I saw it yesterday before you got back to the hotel and you looked great. Very professional. You better sign up with him because I already booked you with him for the April Home and Garden Show."

Elaine almost laughed when Peter said, "The $500 is for eight-hour days. I couldn't get you more because having you work sixteen-hour days is illegal."

They paused to order dinner and make small talk. Elaine finally found her voice and thanked him enthusiastically.

After dessert and an aperitif, Peter started talking business again. "When I have the business built up and we are selling big time in the US, I want to steal you back from Ed, so don't get too comfortable there. Larry is impressed with you and thinks you would be a great assistant in his marketing department."

Peter went on, "One other thing, your mother owns all the shares of MacDougal Enterprises. The agreement she signed with Merchant Bank doesn't address dividends. Harold slipped up there. I think MacDougal Enterprises could pony up, say, two thousand dollars a month in dividends. Dividends are a pretty good deal. The tax credit on CCPCs actually makes them tax-free. With her living at the cottage and what she gets from the estate rent, your mother might even be able to start paying back some principal on that third mortgage she seemed frazzled about."

When Peter dropped Elaine off at her friend's house she was exhausted, but also floating on a cloud. This amazing man cared about her family. He cared about her. He had invited her to join him for dinner and a concert Tuesday evening.

She had no idea what a CCPC was though. So much to learn.

Revelstoke (50 words)

Flying out of Revelstoke was an adventure. A tractor pulled the plane back against a cliff face. The pilot revved the engines full RPMs with the brakes on. Released, the plane lurched forward until it ran off the edge, sinking as it gained speed. There were mountains on every side.

Sputnik (50 words)

Jim's mother interrupted our bridge game to tell us Russia had put a satellite up in the sky with a live dog in it who wouldn't come back. We went out to see the Sputnik drifting across the evening sky. That was a terrible thing to do to a dog.

Inclusion (50 words)

As the last of the Valentines cards were distributed to students in our grade two class it was clear that the new student, Carlos, had received none. Then Andrea, by far the most popular girl in the class, marched over to his desk and, smiling, gave him one of hers.

Section 2
Nurena, A Novella

Chapter 1

My name is Anthony Carter. My friends call me Ant. I live on Corona, a tired, used-up, old planet, in a small country called Nurena. The country's capital city is also called Nurena. I am a Fractional Alien. My mother was an alien migrant who came from another planet on a starsled, along with 127 other migrants, by accident. This was not their intended destination. Perhaps they slipped into an adjacent vector of Humanity's Grand Migration. This journal is my attempt to leave behind a record of our existence.

Aliens, any aliens, were not welcome in Nurena, which was already vastly overpopulated, as was the rest of Corona. Fractionals, a result of a liaison between a Nurena citizen and an alien, were barely tolerated and had few civil rights. Living conditions were deteriorating everywhere, with industrial pollution darkening the air and smothering every creature's lungs, including human lungs. Even then, carbon dioxide levels were reaching dangerous levels and life-giving oxygen levels were diminishing.

This planet started out with a carbon dioxide atmosphere. Over millions of years, one-celled life forms and plant life absorbed most of the carbon, storing it as oil, natural gas and coal, in that order. Industrialization managed to undo much of this in just a few generations after humans arrived, with the atmosphere reverting toward its original mix.

The planet was warming rapidly. Traditional rainfall was diminishing and glaciers, whose annual melt provided water for much of Nurena's food production, were vanishing. Ocean levels were rising, threatening to drown entire countries, including Nurena's neighbour, Caprico. Caprico's river deltas—their most productive farmland—were drowning. Their coastal cities were struggling to hold back floods. The average altitude of Caprico's territory was less than a metre above the rising sea level.

Hordes of people—both economic and climate migrants—were trying to move to safe and productive ground. The inhabitants of still-productive areas were resisting. Both sides used conventional weapons, with nuclear weapons and biological weapons as an ongoing threat. The planet was entering a death cycle. Despite its problems, Nurena held some of the more productive areas.

My mother's group were escaping from a planet experiencing a similar fate. In fact, hers was the last starsled out. There would be no time to build more and critical material resources were exhausted anyway.

My mother described the scene as they boarded that last interstellar transporter. Soldiers were holding back a mob clamouring to be included. The dead were piling up along the perimeter barriers. She saw her youngest brother fall as guards held back the mob to give her group its chance.

This is my life story. I chose to tell parts of it in the words of the amazing people who were involved, to help bring them to life. I had to bridge gaps with my own words. Jeremy is an example. He was a wild man, living life to the fullest. He was intelligent, resourceful and self-promoting. He had a photographic memory, which made him a perfect spy. He was quick to size up a difficult situation and ingenious at finding a path through it. Yet people saw him as simple. I have detoured off my main story in places to include some of his experiences, to help you see the truth about this amazing man.

My father was a social misfit who lived in a large cave, a cavern really, with several other social misfits. They made a marginal living digging minerals out of the wasteland, transporting them to the city in an old hovercraft, and selling them on the black market. They used the money to buy food, booze and other necessities of life.

Nurena was ruled by an extended family headed by their patriarch, Angus Robertson. Angus was old and tired and often befuddled. The head of the police and Nurena's military was his son, James Robertson. James was the real power in Nurena, and he was held up by the army. He also had cadres of unofficial militia that enforced some of his extrajudicial activities.

The Justice Department was run by James Robertson's cousin, Andrew Robertson.

My mother told me about her arrival on this planet, a story I never got tired of hearing. Their starsled touched down in Nurena on rocky, barren badlands. Hurricane-strength winds pelted the refugees with sand, gravel and stones as they set up a temporary site. There were 128 of them and they all survived the trip, exhausted but unhurt.

Early the next morning my mother's group was attacked by a ragtag militia. She and her people were not armed. The militia leader segregated the men from the women and killed all the men. Anton, my father, says the soldiers would have had a grand party with the women then killed them as well, to hide the crime of killing the men. By law they should have turned all these unarmed migrants over to the authorities for trial and, presumably, deportation if they had come from somewhere else on Corona.

The soldiers might have seen their actions as just taking a shortcut. No doubt they were also anticipating their party.

Just after all their men were murdered, a rock exploded behind Mom. Then another rock exploded. They all looked up to see a large scruffy man standing at the entrance to a cave about three metres above the desert floor. Several other man-shapes were in the shadows of the cave entrance behind him.

The large man shouted something, and the attack stopped. The militia leader shouted something back. They argued. There was a buzzing sound and two more rocks exploded near the militia leader. The man in the cave mouth obviously won the argument, because the soldiers fell into a sloppy formation and slouched away.

The large man, my father-to-be, waved to tell my mother's group to come into his cave. They didn't have much choice. They needed to get to shelter and safety, and this man did save them. The women, still dazed, straggled over to the cave and shuffled past Dad and about a dozen other scruffy young men. One of Dad's group started cooking something that smelled noxious and gave the women stale water that was badly needed.

The cooking food might have smelled nasty, but Mom said it tasted like heaven. Probably after that ordeal, anything would have.

Mom thought about the situation. They had no male survivors and were over a hundred young women. Now she was their leader, third down in the original line of command. She started trying to communicate with the large man, Dad, obviously the men's leader. It was difficult. She said his language used guttural sounds she did not even know how to make. Finally, he started pointing at things and naming them to give her nouns. Then he started motioning actions to give her verbs. And so it went. She was impressed by his intelligent approach to communicating.

At the end of about an hour, they were in a crude conversation. She was able to get across that they were migrants from another world. Dad got across that migrants, any migrants, were not welcome in Nurena, but he didn't mind personally. He also got across the notion that he and his small group were pleased to have a group of young women under their care.

Mom soon realized that these generous men had given up most of their food and all of their water. She also realized that her group had much they could trade, because the men had so little. It occurred to her that, with all their men dead, her group would need the cooperation of these cave dwellers to fulfill their mission of establishing a colony. These were not men they would have chosen if they had a choice, but Mom was a practical person.

Mom organized work parties and the women got going. She assigned one group to find water. They located some in a small aquifer under the cave floor about three hundred metres down and brought it in with a laser probe the next day. Soon the cave had cool clear water. Dad, Anton, the cavemen's leader, was astonished.

Dad's group had a store of coal to burn on cold nights. Another group of women activated a conversion kit and started modifying coal into digestible food. That was just in time. A third group went out to bury the dead. Two of the cavemen helped, using a digging contraption like nothing Mom had ever seen. Another group went out to carry in the rest of their gear, with Mom leading. Dad joined them and carried in about as much as the rest of them combined.

Here is a description of these events as told by Dad in an interview on the occasion of his fiftieth birthday.

Chapter 2

RECOLLECTIONS OF ANTON CARTER
(MY FATHER)

I quit school soon as I could. They was tryin' to cram stuff into my head that was useless. Mom wanted me to go in the army. The last thing I wanted was someone tellin' me what to do, so I buggered off to the boonies and found this cave. If I'd signed up the army, they woulda likely put me here anyway, but this way I don't owe nobody nothin'. The army sends losers to the boonies, mostly to hide them from city folk.

This cave is big, so I don't mind sharin' it with a few other free guys that come along time to time. We had a good gig diggin' phosphate and totin' it to the city in a clapped-out hovercraft, to sell. That way we could buy groceries, booze and other good stuff. We had to tote water in too 'cause there weren't none here.

We was gettin' along nice when I woke one morning to the sound of weapons firin' and women screamin', just outside. I looked out and saw Kenny roundin' up a bunch of people who wasn't there before the storm. Kenny's bunch was sortin' them and killin' the men. Guess they was plannin' on a big party with them women, but not much fun for the women I s'pose. Once Kenny started killin', he had to kill them all or he'd of been in a shitload a trouble.

Kenny was the commander of a ratty troop of them Guards set up by the Supreme Council. He was even more a loser than Guards mostly are. His troops were losers too. If I'd gone in the army I coulda been one of them.

Anyhow, I told Kenny to bugger off. He shoulda known better than to try that right in front of my cave. If I'd killed Kenny or one of his men I'da been really skunked 'cause the Council takes a dim view of their men gettin' killed. Kenny shoulda rounded up them people and turned them in for deportin'. Killin' them woulda killed his career in the army if he'd got caught 'cause they wasn't armed.

Mexican standoff. Kenny pulled his men out. I knew there won't be no reports 'cause Kenny was really outta line. I waved the strangers into our cave to get them outta danger, just in case. My buddy Jim told me later there was 112 of them, all women. Kenny musta got a clean sweep of the men. But what he was doin' just ain't right.

I never did get along with women. They was always thinkin' forever and I was thinkin' tomorra is another day. I sure had that right. These women took over my cave. They conned us to carryin' in their stuff and while we did, they buried their dead. Then they went to work. Next day we had water right in the cave, pulled up from what they call an aquafer that was a few hundred metres under the floor. That was good. Real good. No more totin' water.

With all them new people the cave was kinda full. They started makin' it bigger by buildin' new walls outside on the desert. They called it printin', but that was nuts. I know printin' and that ain't it. We dug up coal for fires to keep us warm at night. These women knew how to turn coal into food. Tasted like crap but we needed it, what with us bein' 'bout five times as many. It kept us alive 'cause our supplies went in a snap. Havin' food at the cave were good too. We was still totin' groceries what with so many of us, but about the same as before, not ten times more. Less booze though.

Their lingo was full of squeaks and hand wavin' but in a coupla days they could talk our lingo some and in a couple of months they talked it better than me. A couple of our guys who stayed in school taught them.

These women was hell-bent to fit in with us, build a colony and have kids. Me and my pals were 'bout the only way they could do it. Why they cared I never got, what with the planet overcrowded an' all, but they did. They picked choices among me and my buddies and I ended up with Margaret and three other sweeties. I ain't complainin'. Never coulda got this on my own and I liked it. I really liked it. We set up in a side cavern that was kinda private. Forever's not so bad after all.

Soon there was babies, lotta babies. If you wanna really bugger up a good thing, babies will do it every time.

As the first babies got older I noticed a little girl who was real perky, kinda pretty, and into every mischief goin'. Her mom called her Maria. Later I noticed my kid, Ant, 'cause he was bigger than the rest, a loner, and kinda took after me. Might end up bigger'n me. Ant followed Maria around like she had a ring in his nose.

About the time Ant and Maria was in school a couple of years I noticed they was outta sight a lot at the same time. One day I saw Ant goin' in a tunnel one side of the cave and Maria goin' in a tunnel the other side. I know this cave backward and forward and I know those two tunnels meet in a nice little room higher up, with a chimney ventin' through to outside so sunlight comes in. I didn't tell their mas. I just wished I had a Maria when I was growin' up. I mighta turned out better. You're a lucky bastard, Ant.

Chapter 3

ANTHONY CARTER (ANT)
(BACK TO MY STORY)

As Dad said that, he saluted me, raising a jar of our potent beer in his enormous hand.

The preponderance of women soon brought social order to the cave. The cave dwellers each settled in with a few young women to form loose families. Genetic records were kept, and relationships were strictly maintained.

My dad, Anton Carter, settled into a relationship with four of the women. My mother, Margaret, was one of them. They got some privacy by taking over a small chamber off the main cave. Anton's and my mother's union led to my conception, the oldest of four full siblings and twelve half-siblings. They named me Anthony, a derivative of the name Anton. I learned all of this from history lessons as the women organized formal schooling.

Other children were also conceived and born in the cave. Growing up, my favourite playmate was Maria, a few months older than I was. Maria was a vibrant, dark-haired little vixen. Our cave had a labyrinth of branches, tunnels and hidden rooms that let Maria and me rendezvous without our parents' knowledge, although I always thought Anton knew. In our early years, Maria and I played a well-known children's game called doctor and nurse as we explored each other's bodies.

We were also allowed to play outside in the desert. A concern was random Council flyovers looking for migrants. One of the inventions the women developed was a light blanket that formed into a rigid dome shape that looked like a rock when it was plugged into an energy pack. They called the combination a rockit. Everyone carried a rockit when they were outside. We practised setting them up and slipping under them to get faster at it, because seconds after we heard an aircraft it could be above us.

Maria and I found these portable hiding places also good locations for our mutual exploration, literally under a rock.

About the time we were eleven years old, one of our classes dealt with the topic of sex. Boys and girls were taught separately. Maria and I could hardly wait to share the course content and check it out. She wanted to experience everything.

We were not concerned about the main negative aspect the courses mentioned, because a recent test showed that Maria was sterile. I think that, thanks to Maria's guidance and feedback, I got to be quite good at the course material.

Nurena was ruled by the Supreme Council, a hereditary group made up of members of several prominent families. This Council required every citizen to be surgically implanted with an electronic identification tag immediately after birth, so she or he could be tracked. The Council established listening posts around the country to monitor their citizens. One of the listening posts is on top of a tower just four klicks from our cave.

An early priority for our community was getting around this surveillance. We could not use electronics because the signals would reveal our presence. We developed masking, a negative force-field that absorbed all wavelengths. We used it to surround the area of the cave so we could use electronic devices inside without detection. We hardwired listening stations on the perimeter outside to monitor our surroundings.

Dad mentioned this system to one of our Nurena trading partners when making a delivery and pickup. The trader commented on how useful a portable model would be to him and his cohorts. One of our engineers followed up by developing a portable model she called a Tag Blocker. It cloaked electronic tags, so the wearer was invisible to the Supreme Council's surveillance system.

A few Nurena citizens joined our colony, escaping the suffocating rule of their hereditary rulers. Many were scientists, who had a wider range of freedoms than ordinary citizens. They usually found our colony through our underground market contacts. Tag Blockers made their escape possible.

Tag Blockers were soon the most successful trading item we had. As an added bonus, Tag Blockers allowed criminals and dissidents to operate undetected, undermining the hated central authority.

The efforts of the Supreme Council to track our people down were focused on a wide area around our base. Our underground contacts told us there were rumours of our existence and suggestions that we were the source of Tag Blockers. We needed up-to-date information about the Council's plans.

Our leaders decided to place spies close to some of Nurena's most influential citizens. They asked for volunteers from our sterile second-generation women. We had too few fertile young women to risk any of them on such a dangerous assignment. Maria was the first to volunteer, always up for a new experience.

The plan was for these young women to involve themselves with influential male Nurena citizens in extramarital relationships. As Maria explained it to me, "Men are simple. They have two brains, one in their head and one in their penis, but the one in their penis is dominant. We can't miss."

We created counterfeit IDs and Tag Blockers for our young women, using the identities of dead citizens who would have been about their age. We delivered them to the edge of the badlands at night by hovercraft and our underground trading contacts helped them integrate into Nurena's society. We paid for this service in a way that rewarded the contacts substantially for successful integration, so they would not go after the smaller rewards the Council offered for turning migrants or Fractionals, children of a citizen and a migrant, in to the authorities.

Maria hooked up with Karl, a high-ranking officer in the militia. The fact that he was over seventy years old didn't seem to arouse suspicion. This was a prime posting for learning about planned military action.

Other young women hooked up with members of the Supreme Council and one, Judeth, the first to be inserted, became secretary to the chief justice, Andrew Robertson. She was our earliest insertion into Nurena's society, and actually completed her education at Nurena University.

Unable to use electronics for communication, we established information channels through our commercial contacts. Our couriers, usually sterile young men, brought the information to our leaders. This information helped us avoid some confrontations with the military and our young female agents often redirected or moderated the plans against us by manipulating their patrons.

Then a freak setback happened with Karl, Maria's honeytrap victim. Karl's wife of forty years reported that he was harbouring a migrant. She had no idea this was true, but she was upset by Karl's shacking up with an attractive young mistress and wanted to cause him trouble. She reported him while he was visiting Maria. In the investigation that followed, Maria was exposed. We learned this from another agent, Cathy, who had established herself as mistress to the prison warden. Prison rumours can be excellent information sources, especially when a regime is oppressive. Good people often find themselves in residence there.

Maria should have killed herself rather than be taken, but she didn't. We never found out why. Perhaps she failed her last assignment. Perhaps she was prevented from carrying it out. Perhaps she thought she could bluff her way out of her predicament.

The investigators thought she was acting alone, just making her way in life. Her forged documents said she was a full citizen. Genetic tests showed she was a Fractional. We had to give her a citizen's identity because Fractionals would not have been accepted.

The record of her tag in Nurena's databases said she was dead. Her interrogators didn't realize she was part of a conspiracy, but they were starting to ask dangerous questions. There were drugs that could make her tell everything, which would be the end for our colony. We had to either get her out or terminate her very quickly.

As an added goal, we wanted to introduce evidence proving that Karl knew Maria was a Fractional, so he would lose his position in society and his traitorous wife would lose her status in the community. We wanted to deliver an object lesson so other wives would not play fast and loose with accusations.

We have professional forgers. One of them practised until she could write and express herself as if she was Maria. Another learned how to duplicate the seal, signature, handwriting and style of Karl. Together they concocted a narrative that had Karl using his knowledge that Maria was a Fractional to blackmail her into performing obscene sexual acts, a nice touch. Our secondary plan was ready.

Getting to Maria was going to be difficult, if not impossible. Our planners could not even imagine a way to get her out. She was held in maximum security on an island in the middle of a dry valley that was once a large lake. We had no flying capability. Our rockits would look out of place on the dried mud, so sneaking up wasn't feasible. Our portable weapons were no match for the prison's fixed defences anyway.

Our one advantage was Cathy. She managed to persuade her sugar daddy to take her on a tour of the prison. She found Maria, slipped a small gas bomb through the feeding hole in the ultraglass cage to suffocate her and bit down on the cyanide-filled glass ampoule she carried under her tongue, severing any connection to us.

My poor Maria, so vibrant, so fond of life, failed her final assignment, putting our colony in jeopardy and costing Cathy her life. Cathy's act is the bravest I have ever known. She went in there knowing that if she succeeded, she would die, and she did succeed, and she did die.

Judeth, secretary to the chief justice, was able to slip our doctored evidence into Karl's criminal file and he was convicted of harbouring a known Fractional. He was sentenced to life in prison. His wife, shamed, ended up living alone in subsidized housing.

The authorities saw a pattern in the similarities between Maria and Cathy, as we expected they would, but they acted much faster than we thought possible. We recalled our young agents acting as mistresses immediately but lost two more before they got out. These two young women used their cyanide ampoules to carry out their final order and were never questioned.

Chapter 4

JUDETH'S STORY
(ONE OF OUR SPIES AND CONTROLLER OF OUR SPY NETWORK)

We needed to set up a reliable network of our own people to keep track of what was happening. All through school I was at the top of my class. I also seemed to attract more than my share of attention from boys. When I was sixteen and ready for university, our Strategy Committee decided to send me to the city for my higher education. They forged academic credentials and gave me the identity of a citizen who died before she was a year old. If she had lived, she would have been about my age now.

My new name is Judeth and my documents say I am a citizen. The reality is that I am a Fractional migrant. The penalty for a Fractional or a migrant masquerading as a citizen is deportation. But to where? Outer space? Equivalent to death? Just one more thing to worry about in this screwed-up world. The Strategy Committee set me up in this private living space and gave me a generous allowance so I could buy my way into important social groups and schmooze – sorry, "network."

I did well, making the Dean's List every year. Majoring in secretarial science, I completed minors in law and computer science. When I graduated, I entered a contest for an entry-level job with The Office of Public Prosecutions. I was one of ten selected out of over seven hundred applicants.

Another of the ten was Bradley Clark, a nephew of James Robertson. Brad wasn't very intelligent, so the family must have pulled strings. I met him my first day on the job. I was not impressed with Brad, but apparently he was very impressed with me. I am accustomed to that. I accept that I am physically attractive but there must be something more going on, because men swarm toward me when I enter a room. I don't understand it, but I use it.

Brad started crowding me from day one. He was there beside me in the cafeteria at lunch time. He would plop down at my table when I dropped into the bistro pub. He ran into me in the halls while I was delivering messages. I don't know when he worked.

Then one evening he pounded on my door at home. When I answered, he barged past me, gloating, and told me I couldn't ignore him anymore. He said when he was finished with me, he would rent me out by the hour on J Street. He had collected some of my DNA in the cafeteria, had it analysed, and knew I was a Fractional.

He attacked me, popping buttons as he tore my shirt open, before I could I take him down. Of course, I could have killed him easily. He had no idea how to control a victim and I am at master's level in quedoh. But killing him would be bad strategy, hard to explain, and he was a Robertson, so I just restrained him and put him to sleep.

The next morning when Jeremy showed up, I put the Brad problem in his hands. Jer is a courier of ours who was picking up our reports. He was sweet on me. He actually brought me here, so we were simpatico. I stressed the danger of Brad's knowing I was a Fractional migrant. Jer focused instead on Brad attacking me. I was afraid he was going to kill Brad right there.

Instead, Jer left and came back an hour later with a laundry truck and a helper. They put Brad in a big hamper, rolled him out, and the helper took him away. Jer was more interested in staying to console and cuddle me. I liked that about him. Good priorities.

Brad died in a tragic accident that afternoon when a scaffold fell on him. It must have been badly assembled because a key brace fell off. Ironically, it happened on J Street. The Supreme Council aren't the only ones who know how to play rough. Jer was halfway back to our base when the accident happened, so we must have agents I don't know about. No one in the office seemed unhappy about losing Brad.

That was the start of a much closer relationship with Jer that led to our making a formal commitment to each other. He changed his work pattern and stayed with me whenever he was in the city.

I went on to complete my apprenticeship and earned a position as one of Chief Justice Andrew Robertson's clerks. I was proud of myself. This was the best placement we could have ever hoped for. Everything passed through that office and I had free rein to look at it. It helped that Andrew liked looking at me and having me around, but he never overstepped proper boundaries.

Soon, Jer was bringing other agents through our home, nine in total. They all managed to get close to important people in the country's administration and seduced their way into useful roles as mistresses. I ended up in charge of our agents, convenient since Jer was responsible for delivering their reports. Jer has a photographic memory and doesn't need to carry documents.

When we lost Maria and Cathy, then two more of my agents, I was devastated. Those women were my friends. Jer gave me needed comfort as he got the other five agents back to our base. It was dangerous work and a miraculous outcome that demonstrated his great talent for outwitting Council operatives.

He and I continued in our roles for many years without ever any suggestion of being found out. I collected mountains of information for our colony and Jer carried it to our base while seeming to be just another common workman driving a supply hovercraft to one of the outcast settlements in the badlands. He was very good at being a spy.

JEREMY'S STORY (JER)
(ONE OF OUR COURIERS OPERATING IN THE BADLANDS)

Oh shit. This should not be happening. I was being flagged down by a bunch of Council Guards at the city's entrance. We pay a potful of denues to keep that from happening. We practically own this entrance, we pay so much. All I was carrying in the hovercraft was a load of phosphate with five hundred Tag Blockers tucked in sealed packages underneath.

This is a really secure way to smuggle Tag Blockers. Only an idiot wants to turn over half a ton of phosphate, digging it out with a shovel. But the captain must be an idiot, because he ordered his men to do it. Dad's generation have been trading phosphate forever, so it was just same old, same old, until now.

Shit! **Shit!** **SHIT!**

If they find the Tag Blockers, I'm done for. They'll arrest me and after that they'll find out I'm a Fractional, and my documents say I'm a citizen. Double whammy. At least ten years in the can. More likely get deported. Shit, **shit**, **SHIT!** I'd get a trial but it would be a setup. The Council owns the juries because Council stooges pick them.

I considered giving the captain my emergency stash, but he was so prissy I thought that might make a bad situation worse.

Just then our broker arrived and started a conversation with the captain. Colin, the broker, is high up in the city's pecking order, so the captain was distracted. While they were talking, I slipped the stash to the sergeant, who was digging in the phosphate with his men, and said, "Don't find the Tag Blockers." They didn't.

I'm part of a group of about four hundred citizens, aliens and Fractionals living in an expanded cave that looks like a mountain, out in the boonies. We are mostly self-sufficient, but we need to trade for medicines, food items and some technical stuff. Officially we sell phosphate to earn the denues to buy what we need. Actually, phosphate earns bupkis but we have other things, illegal things, that bring in big bucks. Tag Blockers are our hottest product.

We sell through brokers and we buy through brokers. That cuts the paper trail.

A few minutes later, Colin came over to me and said, "Jer, blow this thing out of here before that son-of-a-bitch gets a chance to think things over. Meet you at the barn in an hour." The barn is an old, falling-down structure on a dusty farm that was abandoned when the rains quit. We own it through a local citizen and do our business with our brokers there, nicely out of sight.

Once Colin and I were finished dealing in the barn, I went to Judeth's place. Judeth is one of ours and we made a commitment to each other. She is a secretary for Andrew Robertson, the chief justice of the legal system here. She has a nice little place in the upper crust Rono Sector that sometimes doubles as a safe house. I won't make the return journey with our supplies until tomorrow. We want to look legit and moving around at night doesn't.

There were five young women hiding out at Judeth's. The mood was bad. Real bad. Judeth recalled seven agents and only five showed up. I was not supposed to know their names and they didn't know mine. We didn't need to know.

Yesterday, an agent of ours named Cathy took out another agent of ours named Maria at the prison, then took herself out. Both were mistresses to important people, and the authorities saw a pattern. Judeth read the official reports and recalled all of our agents who were mistresses, because they were suddenly in danger of discovery. My job was to get them safely back to base.

Judeth and I didn't get any private time that night, and I left early the next morning for the barn to finish dealing and loading. I was stopped and the hovercraft was searched leaving the city, something that had never happened before. They were looking for women being smuggled out. I was back in the base with the information later that day. Back at Judeth's the following evening, I learned that the missing agents were dead. Again, Judeth read the reports.

Both agents had self-terminated rather than be taken. We were a sad and sombre lot. Four out of Judeth's nine mistress-agents were dead. I knew all of them even if I didn't know their names, so it hit me hard. I had brought them in to take up their assignments. To Judeth they were personal friends and she was destroyed.

We worked out a plan for the remaining five agents. I would start coming in with helpers, young guys who looked kind of girlish. On the following days I would go back to base with one of the agents dressed up as my helper. That would leave five guys stranded at Judeth's over a couple of weeks as we got the women out. I would start by taking back the guy I brought in the day before, to get the soldiers used to the routine.

Later I would travel in alone and travel back with one of the guys I left behind, as my helper. By then the Council soldiers would be used to seeing me with helpers. If they really wanted to check in detail, these were guys and they were looking for women. It was dangerous but it worked.

Caleb, a slight, girlish-looking homosexual was picked as my first helper. He is naturally shy and doesn't make anything of his sexual bias, but he also turned out to be one hell of an actor. We started with Caleb going both ways, into the city and back out, to establish the routine. The first trip outbound, the Guard captain ordered Caleb to drop his pants. Caleb cooed, giggled and said, "I will if you will. I bet your penis is really big. I want to hold it in my hand. Please?"

The captain recoiled, blushed, then turned back and yanked Caleb's pants down angrily. Caleb flapped his surprisingly large penis at the captain with his left hand and giggled again, saying, "Now it's your turn, bet I have you beat."

The second trip out, Caleb went even further, saying he wanted to suck the captain's cock. On the third and fourth trips out, we were waved through without inspection. We were ready to start Operation Bailout.

Getting the first two women out, dressed and made up to look like Caleb, went smoothly. By then we had three Caleb lookalikes in Judeth's safe house. On the third trip out with Candice, we were stopped by a different captain. He told Candy to drop her pants. Shit. If Candy drops her pants, we are all toast. But Caleb had trained and rehearsed all the women on how to act. Candy cooed at the captain and said, "You first, I can hardly wait to see what you have to offer." She giggled.

A voice from the troop said, "Told you so." The captain, embarrassed, waved us on, saying, "Get the hell out of here, you disgusting faggot." If only he had known. Candy is an extremely attractive young woman.

I got the last two women out with no trouble. I got Caleb and the other young men out over the next two weeks. No one noticed there were no helpers coming in but helpers going out, because we timed it so the early in and late out trips took place during different Guards' shifts.

Chapter 5

JEREMY AGAIN

Occasionally I took out citizens who wanted to escape the Council's rule and had skills we needed. These escapees usually found us through our brokers. I used the same strategy for younger ones to smuggle them out. We sometimes put older ones into suspended animation and took them out in coffins. Those "corpses" really spooked the soldiers when we mocked them up to look like fever victims.

I had other interesting experiences running contraband in and supplies out in the hovercraft. One time running back with supplies I was almost hit by another hovercraft, a sleek six-passenger roadster. Settling in behind me, it tried to catch up. Our machine is souped up so that should have been impossible, but the roadster was gaining.

They were also shooting but bouncing over the rough landscape made it unlikely that our machine would be hit. I was glad they weren't carrying a mounted cannon. With its gyroscopic control, it would have taken me out with the first round at that distance.

I know the terrain better than anyone alive and headed for a narrow dead-end side canyon with them less than ten metres behind. As we entered the canyon, I dumped three small land mines out the back. They saw them but couldn't stop. Hovercrafts moving at that speed will drift on their momentum for at least twenty metres after the power is switched to full reverse.

They swerved into a steep side of the canyon wall and tipped over. Two mines exploded, sending shrapnel into the riders, killing three and injuring the other three. I cut my power, drifted to a stop and went back to finish the job. One of them begged for his life right up until I pulled the trigger. What could I do with a wounded prisoner? The other two were resigned. We never found out who they were. We are a peaceable lot, but anyone who attacks us does it at their own risk.

I put the bodies beside their machine and took the camouflage blanket from my craft to cover them and their vehicle, so they wouldn't be spotted from the air. No one was going to go into that canyon on the ground to find it. I picked up the unexploded land mine and reset the safety, eased my hovercraft past their overturned one, and carried on to our base.

The next day I was back with a crew of mechanics and a pneumatic lift. We buried the dead so carrion wouldn't attract attention, righted the hovercraft, repaired and repainted it, and brought it in. It looked quite different.

The bottom line was we had a fast, nifty, six-seat hovercraft roadster to add to our fleet at the cost of two mines and a scare.

* * *

On another occasion, again while I was running back to the base with supplies, a rock kicked up under the skirt of my hovercraft, punched through the screen and took out a fan blade. I managed to drift to a stop without going ass over teakettle and looked over the damage. I was in for a long hike to get help. It takes a lift to get under a freight hovercraft and I didn't have a spare blade anyway.

Then I noticed another hovercraft coming over the horizon. Just in case, I sneaked twenty metres away on the opposite side, keeping low so they wouldn't see me. I activated my rockit and crawled under it. The men from the other hovercraft arrived and started looking for the driver of my hovercraft. I could hear them talking. They were members of the Supreme Council Guards, gone rogue.

They emptied my hovercraft's load onto the ground and sorted through it. They found nothing worthwhile except the booze, so they started drinking it and got very antsy.

They hung around overnight, partying, while I hunkered under my rock. One of them even came over and pissed on it. That close he should have seen it was fake but he didn't, so he must have been drunk as a skunk. I was worried that the piss would short out a circuit, but it didn't. Good job, engineers! Bet you didn't test for that, though.

The next morning, they torched my hovercraft and left, leaving our remaining supplies scattered on the ground. I had to walk two days to our base. Three of us went back in another freight hovercraft and salvaged most of the supplies. The hovercraft was a write-off.

Driving a hovercraft on a dry lakebed is cinchy. I'd imagine driving it on water was even easier, back when the lakes had water. Driving one in the city is downright dangerous because, basically, they have no brakes. You just put the fans in reverse and drift to a stop. Dodging from side to side to pass is clunky because of the momentum. Wheels are better in the city.

Driving in the boonies is another thing altogether. There are obstacles everywhere. You need to plan your route a long way out to sneak past them. Driving a hovercraft at night is downright suicidal, because the lights don't go out far enough and the shadows screw you up. Except for me, that is. I know every boulder and cranny out there by heart. I know every landmark that tells me what to expect next. Judeth says I have a photographic memory.

I also know how to jump a hovercraft over a boulder instead of veering around it. The manual says you can jump it one metre by goosing it and aiming the fans straight down, but you need to have enough momentum to drift over the obstacle. I can jump my hovercraft over two metres by throwing it into fast reverse as I goose it, but I need a lot more momentum to carry me past because of the reverse thrust, so I drive real fast. It's sort of like pole vaulting, only the pole is a column of air. That was handy once when a gunship was after me. I jumped Guilder's Ridge and they didn't. I heard the explosion.

* * *

Last week I was out at night just for fun and hit an obstacle that wasn't there before, a parked hovercraft with a couple making out in it. There are a million square klicks out there and I had to use theirs. Too late to veer, lucky I didn't try to jump them. I might have taken off their heads or some other important body parts. I went through my windshield and landed in their laps. We all went ass over teakettle and landed in a prickle bush. The bush saved us from serious damage, but boy those prickles stung. The couple was mighty pissed off too. I guess I caught them at a critical time or something.

At least I had some clothes on for protection.

When we got dusted off, I realized the guy was Ed, our other hovertruck driver. I didn't recognize the sweetie he was with, but it wasn't Noreen. He made a commitment to Noreen just last month. Now this was going to be hard to finesse. We had to all go to the infirmary to get the prickles pulled and get dosed with a lotion to stop the infections. Everyone says the infirmary is like Grand Central, whatever that means.

Our machines were banged up and we didn't dare start them up without a mechanic's clearance this close to base. What's more, their clothes were scattered all over hell's half acre and we couldn't find most of them in the dark. I gave the sweetie my long coat to cover her up. Actually, I didn't want to cover her up, she looked great buck naked. Don't tell Judeth I said that. Ed was left dangling on his own and it served him right.

We walked the half klick back to base. I went in first to check out the landscape. Shit. The commander was the duty officer and Noreen was running the infirmary. On the upside, the commander was sleeping on the job, he's the only one who could get away with that, and the clinic is back past the entrance far enough so we could sneak in without Noreen seeing us.

The sweetie disappeared, saying she would check into the clinic the next day when someone else was on duty. Man, she was going to have a shitty night. I doubt she'd do that for Ed. Bet she was cheating too. Ed went to his place to get clothes and we concocted a story about practising night driving, and we got away with it. Noreen didn't ask why some of the prickles were under Ed's clothes, but I bet she wondered. I never found out who the sweetie was, and I didn't get my long coat back either. Damn. So much for chivalry.

* * *

My worst run was the time the Council Guards came after me in an aerocar. An aerocar is a lot easier to fly than a hovercraft because it is well clear of ground obstacles. We daren't own any because the Guards have a monopoly and enforce it. This aerocar followed me all the way back from the city, just hanging up there out of range. I wouldn't dare bring it down anyway.

I had to head for a fake base about five klicks from our real one so I wouldn't give our location away. There were Guards waiting there for someone just like me. I didn't know any of them. They realized it was a fake base and laid a trap. Looks good from the air, not so good from the ground. They arrested me on the spot. I guess we detoured there once too often. I thought if I get out of this, me and Ed need to coordinate better, 'cause I hadn't been there for weeks.

Anyway, bribing wouldn't work, too many of them. I'd never be able to kill all of them – again, too many. I was carrying in a load of supplies and some electronics, which was kind of ordinary stuff.

I decided to be an idiot and try to indicate that the driver was out there somewhere. The role came naturally since I was halfway there already, having let them flush me here in the first place. Nobody worries about an idiot. I drooled and mumbled and couldn't understand the captain at all. I flapped my hands and made howling noises.

In the middle of the night, I just walked out and parked myself in the middle of a prickle bush in an arroyo. No one searches a prickle bush. They looked just about everywhere else for me, but city dudes don't see you unless you move. I sneaked back in twice in the middle of the night to get water and munchies. I had to wait five days for those damn Guards to leave, then I had to walk a full day to our real base. The infections nearly killed me.

Ed and I now use different fake destinations.

Chapter 6

ANTHONY CARTER
(BACK TO MY STORY)

Those were some of his favourite stories. He was an original and later he played an important part in my story.

Eight years after we lost her, I still miss my first love, Maria. I grew up without doing anything significant. Perhaps I edged into the highest quartile on intelligence. I graduated with an environmental engineering degree at the appropriate age, earning it through a self-learning program my mother's generation brought with them. Then I entered military service. I never had a dangerous assignment because I was one of only three fertile second-generation males, too important to our colony's future to be risked.

I rose through the ranks at a normal pace and eventually commanded a platoon of ten—five women and five men—when I was twenty-eight years old.

One day, our detectors picked up a brief signal about seven klicks west of our base. My unit was on standby and we went out on foot to scout the area. We found a small group of sport-hunters forming a ring around a large man who was perched on a smaller person, his knees bent in a kneeling position on each side. The man was clearly torturing the small person underneath him. We found them by following the sound of loud voices carried on the wind.

The group was so intent on watching this obscenity that they did not notice us. They didn't even set out perimeter guards. My fury almost overwhelmed me, but I managed to stay calm enough to form my platoon in an arc so we wouldn't hit each other as we fired. On my signal we opened up, killing seven of them immediately. We could not fire at the main perpetrator for fear of killing the victim.

Racing at him as fast as I could, I seized him under his chin and the back of his neck. Twisting as I lifted him clear of the ground, I broke his neck. I heard the snap. I am not that strong, so it must have been a combination of rage and adrenaline.

I fell back with him still twitching on top of me and shrugged him off. Standing, I looked down at a small, delicate young woman with bruises over all of her body, a broken arm, a dislocated jaw, her left eye closed beneath what looked like a smashed bone above the eye socket, and blood seeping from every orifice.

I grabbed the greatcoat belonging to my late adversary and wrapped her in it as gently as I could, folding her injured arm below her bruised breasts. I picked her up and cradled her in my arms as I ran through the setting sun of evening, ran through the twilight of descending dark, ran through the black of night, seeing my way by a light strapped to my forehead. All the way I talked to her, telling her she was safe, telling her she would soon be in a medical infirmary, telling her she would heal, hoping my voice would keep her in this world.

I stumbled into our base in just under two hours, exhausted, and handed her over to our medics. She still had a faint heartbeat.

I mustered a second unit and a hovercraft. The slaughter of those animals needed to be covered up. If we picked up that electronic signal, the authorities did too. They would be investigating. The secret to our survival is invisibility, never letting the authorities know we exist.

In the hovercraft, we covered the seven klicks quickly. My original unit was cleaning up the mess. There were eight corpses and three disgusting female prisoners. I guess all of us only aimed at the male spectators. Our surprise attack was so fast these animals never fired a weapon. We loaded the corpses on the hovercraft with the help of the prisoners, spent two more hours covering up evidence and were back at our base by dawn. I executed the three female prisoners before we went in. Releasing them was out of the question and holding them would be a serious drain on our resources.

The report from the infirmary was discouraging. In intensive care, her chances were slight. She was in a deep coma and might never surface. I went to see her and talked to her again. A nurse said my time with her was her quietest since she arrived. Apparently she was restive even in the coma and was making whimpering sounds until I started talking to her.

I made it a habit to visit and talk to her every day I was on the base, telling her who I was, our colony's story, and about what was happening on the base and in the cities. I kept this up for almost a year. Although her body healed, she did not surface from her coma.

We still maintain spies, but no longer as mistresses of important citizens. Women are better than men at clandestine work, better at keeping up their roles. Jeremy, one of our couriers, brought back information one of them picked up about a missing scientist who was the focus of an unusual level of concern and activity. Her resume was amazing.

An announcement on the communicator network said, *"We ask your help in the search for scientist Juanita Rodrigues. She graduated from our challenging Engineering Physics PhD program at the age of seventeen. Her dissertation was so advanced only a handful of her professors understood it, but it has led to several innovations in astrophysics.*

"Juanita is assigned to the illustrious Robertson family as James Robertson's mistress. She is seventeen years old, 157 centimetres tall, weighs 50 kilos, has light brown hair and light brown skin. When last seen she was wearing a blue sundress and was shopping at the Exford Retail Centre.

"We assume Juanita acquired an electronic Tag Blocker. She vanished from our surveillance system two days ago. James' father, Angus, one of the rotating presidents of the Supreme Council, has authorized a reward of 400,000 denues for her safe return. Contact your local representative if you have any information about this missing person.

A follow-up news report added more information. *"Two days after Juanita's disappeared, our monitoring system picked up a signal from her tag in Sector A4GF, a barren wilderness area known to be extremely dangerous. This signal was so brief we were only able to get a rough triangulation. We organized flyovers and search parties and scoured the entire area. The only evidence that Juanita had been there was traces of blood in some sand. One sample was a perfect match.*

We had a name for our patient: Juanita Rodrigues.

Months later, with things going smoothly, someone noticed that external electronic signals were seeping in through our masking barrier. Panic stations! That meant our internal signals were also seeping out. We immediately shut down all but the most essential activities and all of our electronics. We collected all real and counterfeit tags, often cutting them out painfully, and placed them in a sealed steel and lead-lined box prepared for this possibility.

We could no longer go into the city. We could not carry tags with us, and we could not survive in the city without them. Trading was suspended. Information was cut off. We were effectively isolated. Fortunately, we had stockpiled critical supplies and medicines because of the deteriorating situation as the Supreme Council was losing its grip on the country. Wealthy citizens were also hoarding and goods on legal markets were scarce.

Council engineers must have worked out a way to bypass our Tag Blockers. Our best engineers worked frantically to develop countermeasures, without success. We were hampered by not having a copy of the Council's new device to reverse engineer it, and we had no way of getting one.

As panic descended into despair, Juanita rolled into the room, pushed in a wheelchair by our head nurse. Weak and thin, she had surfaced from her coma and told the nurse, "Take me to Anthony. He's in trouble and needs my help." The nurse was confused for a minute because everyone calls me Ant. I'm big like my father, so it's sort of a joke. Then the nurse figured out who Anthony was. Juanita must have learned about our extreme peril through my one-sided conversations with her. It must have registered through her coma.

Juanita sat down at a computer and went to work immediately, studying our designs and making notes. She reviewed our algorithms at an astonishing pace, line by line, screen by screen. Once she changed a plus sign to minus, murmuring, "That was a mistake." She wrote line after line of new code. She studied our drawings and proposed changes. Finally, she said, "That should do it." and the nurse rolled her out. We followed her revised plans, loaded her revised program, and we had a functioning tag blocking system again.

Juanita was in a state of near collapse, but she didn't retreat back into a coma. She gradually gained strength and her body filled out as she joined in our base's affairs. Her new Tag Blockers were an enormous commercial success as the large and growing market needed to be entirely replenished. We developed direct trading relationships on the black market for what we needed, meeting our distributors at the edge of the wilderness to barter. The value of the Council's currency was collapsing through inflation.

Juanita suffered terrors that caused her to cry out in her sleep and jerk awake several times every night. Her recovery was being held back. Then one night, I woke to find her slipping into bed beside me. She asked me to hold her and just talk to her as I did when I was carrying her to safety. She remembered. She slept soundly. That was the start of her real recovery.

I tried to stroke and soothe her but any time my hands moved over her she seized up in panic. Soon I was just holding her in the crook of my arm and talking her through the night. There was no sexuality involved. It was as if I was a substitute father helping a child through the night terrors.

Lack of sex with Juanita was not a problem for me. We had too few children on the base to provide for natural replacement of our population. There were only three men among our second generation who could consistently help create viable children with women from the migration, so we were in great demand. Our highest priority was servicing women where there was a good chance of producing fertile children.

The assignment officially started on my sixteenth birthday with women from my mother's generation. We had a high success rate in the early years. After all, I was genetically half migrant. Thanks largely to my involvement, there were a lot of fertile children in this second wave.

Later, the few fertile young women nearer my age were added. Sterile women sought my services in the hope of proving their diagnosis wrong, and very occasionally it worked out for them. As the one with most successes, I was the one in most demand.

I found these assignments pleasurable and considered myself lucky. I did my best to satisfy my temporary partners and some indicated that I succeeded. Also, they kept looking for repeats. They should thank my lost mentor Maria, not me.

I kept these liaisons relatively short so I could get back to my own bed to hold Juanita. Protecting her from night terrors gave me my greatest satisfaction. I think I loved her even then, this very special small person.

One night a couple of months later, I woke to find Juanita naked, climbing on top of me. In the nightlight her smooth skin was the colour of nutmeg. This was the first time I had seen her unclothed since that terrible day. Her bruises were a lost memory. Suddenly, our relationship did not feel like father/daughter anymore.

Before I was fully awake, she had enveloped me. She placed my hands on her breasts, her wonderful soft breasts, so different from the last time I had seen them. Leaning against my hands, she started a slow massage. I tried to join in but as soon as I did, she stopped, placed her hands on my chest to still me, and shook her head.

She resumed her slow massage as I held still, rigid, enduring the most exquisite sensations of my life. Holding out as long as I could, I finally exploded and relaxed. Juanita immediately rolled off me and snuggled back into the crook of my arm, placed her head on my shoulder and fell into a deep sleep. I slept too. During this amazing liaison she did not experience climax.

I talked it over with Juanita's therapist the next morning. The therapist concluded that Juanita had overcome her terror to honour me with the greatest gift she could give: herself. She told me Juanita had undergone extensive reconstructive surgery and would never experience climax.

Two weeks later, Juanita scored positive on a pregnancy test. We were with child. I still held her each night and stroking was always out of bounds. In the later stages of her pregnancy, I could feel our child kicking in Juanita's full, round abdomen.

Confused by this new depth of a relationship, I went back to talk to the therapist. She summed it up nicely, saying "The other women are an assignment. Juanita is a commitment, a commitment you made when you saved her."

I resigned my military commission and was assigned to the experimental physics lab. I kept up my responsibilities to other women on the base and fathered more children, but I did not have any important connection with them or their mothers, only with Juanita. She did not object to me fulfilling my duties.

Our communication improved as we talked about our child, about concerns on the base and about the disintegration of order on the rest of the planet.

Juanita told me why she was so close to our base when the sport-hunters took her. From various publicly available records, she had figured out that our colony existed and had identified the approximate area. She decided to try and join us rather than be the property of James Robertson. For someone that intelligent, she didn't think out her strategy very well.

As the sport-hunters approached, Juanita ran away from her companions and threw her Tag Blocker as far as she could before they seized her, revealing her electronic ID briefly in a desperate cry for help. She was taken to the small amphitheatre-shaped valley where we found her.

Our beautiful daughter, also named Juanita, was born nine months after our liaison.

Chapter 7

MORE FROM ME,
ANTHONY CARTER

Later I got the real story on the loss of Juanita Rodrigues. The information came from a criminal complaint filed by one of James Robertson's employees. Chief Justice Andrew Robertson, James' cousin, welcomed a chance to take James down. Some family members were concerned about James' mental condition and wanted to protect the family's position.

Here is Juanita's story.

James was keynote speaker at the graduation ceremony and presented Juanita with the gold medal for academic excellence. Obviously, he was impressed with Juanita, but with her body, not her mind. Juanita was a beautiful, graceful, slight young woman with soft brown skin and large lustrous eyes, in addition to having the best mind to come along in anyone's memory.

He invited all the medallist to his home for the following weekend. To Juanita's surprise, she was the only one who turned up. James was a congenial host and poured her a glass of juice when she declined an alcoholic beverage.

Juanita woke up alone in a large bed in the bedroom of a self-contained suite. While she was exploring it a housekeeper, Denise, came in with clean towels and was surprised to find her there. Juanita asked, confused, where she was and what was happening. Denise was horrified when she realized what was going on and why there was a guard outside the door.

Clever gossips call the building Juanita was in The Robertson Bordello. It houses a collection of attractive young women who were all well paid to be there and found this safer than soliciting on J Street.

Denise left and soon came back to give Juanita some pills designed to cause vomiting, a normal item in a first aid kit. They are used to make a person eject noxious substances in place of a stomach pump. Denise told Juanita to take one whenever James came into the suite and act as if she was in terrible pain.

Shortly after, James did come in and told Juanita he was now her patron, and this was her new home. Juanita swallowed a pill and deliberately vomited on him. James left in disgust to get cleaned up. When he returned later in the day, she did it again.

The next morning, Denise was back in Juanita's suite with breakfast and they talked out the problem. Juanita told Denise about a sanctuary in the badlands, referring to our base. Denise agreed to get her out of the bordello and take her there.

The bordello is an opulent house on the Robertson estate. No man other than James ever gets into it and his Supreme Council Guards there are all women. Putting it bluntly, Juanita was to be James' personal sex slave. That arrogant narcissist devil wanted to deprive a young woman of her freedom and the community the benefit of her intellect, just to satisfy his disgusting lust. He was old enough to be her father.

Juanita didn't stay in The Robertson Bordello very long. Denise rented a hovercraft and a driver who agreed to go into the badlands. Denise spiked the guard's coffee to put her to sleep, dragged her into Juanita's suite, left with Juanita and got into a flexicab to go to the hovercraft. They both wore Tag Blockers so their movements could not be traced.

Contrary to published reports, Juanita did not disappear from the Wexford Shopping Centre. The investigators found the hovercraft rental firm and the documentation connected to Denise, but they could not find the owner/driver.

A criminal docket was prepared but the investigator found no evidence. The complainant, Denise McMillan, had disappeared. The Guard had returned to her unit and the investigator was denied access to her. The other employees at the bordello could add some detail, but it was all second-hand hearsay.

Juanita and I occasionally repeated our union at what seemed to me were random times, always initiated by her. In this way, we conceived a total of five beautiful, intelligent, viable children. Her therapist noted that these episodes came in her cycle when Juanita was most likely to conceive. At some primal level, Juanita's body must have been meeting an ancient need. These liaisons were so spontaneous there was never a chance to take precautions.

We worked together in the physics lab. Juanita told me I was her foil and that in explaining her concepts to me, she refined them in her own mind. She said she knew she had it right when I understood. Later I won a position on our Directors' Council and I ended up as Council President. I teamed up with my Juanita in that role to help steer us to our greatest triumph.

We were both responsible parents. We knew we were the nucleus of our growing family and that our children were satellites who would someday spin off, find mates, and form nuclei of their own. Nita, our oldest, told us she did not realize we were two separate beings until she was about five years old, we were so closely aligned.

My domain was the bedroom, where I helped Juanita fend off her demons.

Although the outside scientists could not predict the movement of celestial bodies in our galaxy, Juanita could. She pointed out modestly that their best scientists had already been jailed or deported, as she would have been once James Robertson got tired of her.

She knew that our galaxy was colliding with another galaxy and that they were pulling each other apart. By deep datamining of information collected over decades, she was able to calibrate the effects and produce accurate predictions for the combination. The situation was an evolving disaster condemning all life in our entire galaxy, not just us.

By the time our youngest was ten, Juanita proposed sending all of our colony's children to a stable galaxy far beyond this calamity. It was a huge gamble into the unknown. Unknown to everyone but Juanita, that is. We debated long into many nights, but Juanita had always been right. In the end we agreed to trust her. She convinced us that our current situation was a hopeless dead end.

That was the start of our grand plan.

Chapter 8

COLIN GUERRA
(GANGSTER AND BLACK-MARKET DISTRIBUTOR)

My name is Colin Guerra. Occasionally someone calls me Col, once. It never happens twice. It's all about respect. In my business, if you don't have respect, you're soon out of business. I own the West Side of Nurena. What I can't take, I buy. Every officer of the Council Guard in my area is in my pocket and I have the evidence on them to enforce it. My official job is brokering for people who don't want to leave a transaction trail. My unofficial job is running the West Side.

My best suppliers are Jer and Ed, two hovertruck drivers working for a bunch of people living out in the boonies. Jer is a wild bastard that scares even me a little. Ed is more civilized and a lot smarter. They bring me Tag Blockers, a thingy that shuts out signals from electronic tags so people can operate outside of Council tracking. In exchange I get them the food and other shit they put on their order sheets, plus a lot of denues because those Tag Blockers are pricey. My deal with them is exclusive. I wholesale to the other countries on the planet but there is not much demand outside of Nurena.

My best distributor was Jimmy Robertson, grandson of Angus Robertson. Angus is the head honcho around here, so hanging with Jimmy was like magic. That name, Robertson, is a password to drug heaven, or whatever else I need him to peddle. He had the Tag Blocker franchise in one of my territories and I make sure there's no competition.

One time, Jer was held up at the entrance to Nurena by a prick of a Guard captain who wanted to find out what was under a load of phosphate. I kept the captain talking to give Jer a chance to bribe the sergeant.

Jer caught on and came through, so maybe he's smarter than I think. The captain died two days later on the practice range when his weapon misfired, driving a piece of breechblock into his brain. Boy am I good! I can't stand people who can't be bought. That can seriously screw up business.

Another time Jer hired me to remove a guy from his sweetie's place and arrange for a fatal accident. I got Adam to take care of it. Fatal accidents are one of my specialties and they're very lucrative. Jer was really growing on me.

The shit really hit the fan the day those Tag Blockers stopped working. Twenty-seven of Jimmy's customers were arrested for antisocial behaviour in less than twenty-four hours. Antisocial behaviour is anything the Senior Robertson doesn't like. Jimmy had hundreds of complaints and I had three hundred useless Tag Blockers in inventory. I hate that. I could hardly wait to brace Ed or Jer next time they showed up, but they didn't show up for a few days.

Then, hallelujah, they did show up, both of them, each with a full load of new and improved Tag Blockers that worked. They took back all my inventory on an even trade. We agreed to price the new Tag Blockers at double the price of the old ones and give a discount if a customer traded in an old and useless one. Jimmy went to work. Ed took the trade-ins away with the groceries and dumped them somewhere, I guess. I don't really give a shit. Boy did we clean up on that deal.

Then Jimmy went bad. He started using H and got unreliable. He wasn't meeting his money obligations and he was full of crappy excuses. Then he disappeared with five thousand denues of my product. I had no choice. If I let that slide, next thing there would be pressure from someone in my organization to take over because I'd gone soft. So, I put out a contract on Jimmy.

The top North Side dude sent me Jimmy's head the next day, to give me confirmation of the kill. I sent back the contract fee plus a nice bag of blow as a thank-you bonus for the fast action and it all smoothed over for a bit. Turned out, though, that grandpops Angus was really fond of Jimmy. His private army tracked the hit back to me by getting the info out of the North Side dude before feeding him into a crematorium feet first, alive.

They circulated the video as a warning. All of a sudden the Guardsmen I used to own were my worst enemies because they knew me on sight.

I told Jer about my troubles as I was shutting down my networks. Instead of complaining about losing his distribution, Jer hustled me into a flexicab and took me straight to his place, no stopping to pick up any of my shit, just straight there. I met his sweetie Judeth. What a babe! WOW! Jer went way up in my book right then.

Jer offered to take me to his place in the boonies in a coffin, by putting me in suspended animation and decorating my corpse like I died of the fever. Now I'm not a trusting type, but what could I lose? I was already toast just waiting to be burned—damn, bad choice of words. Anyway, I agreed. I thought that was the end of the line, but I was wrong.

I woke up in a mountain, no shit, really, a mountain. It was hollowed out inside and a bunch of people lived in it. One of them, a sort of project manager named Ant, found me later that day. Ant is huge, not fat, just fit, but a giant. Ant explained that they needed me to set them up with new brokers they could trust. Trust is not a big thing in my profession, but I gave them a few potentials to check out. I also gave them my mark, so Jer or Ed could get passed up the chain and talk to them.

Ant also wanted to bring in a lot of electronic stuff that I knew how to source, so they got double duty out of me. Turned out Jer made an executive decision to bail me on the spot because he figured I could be useful to them. Why did I ever think Jer wasn't swift? Silly me. Jer even filled out a death certificate for me, and Judeth filed it so my family wouldn't suffer reprisals or wonder about me.

These people didn't totally trust me though. They cut out my ID chip and deep-sixed it somewhere, so I no longer existed. They gave me the lowest-level pass, so most of their mountain was out of bounds. But they treated me right. They even set me up with some top-notch women so I could be brought into their gene pool. I treated those women like queens, and they appreciated it. This is one strange place. For such straight arrows, they sure do weird sex stuff.

Ant also found I have pretty good organizing talent. I guess so! I organized the West Side from the ground up when I was just twenty-two years old. Dad sort of let it fall apart and I put it back together. Four years later, when Jake iced Dad to take over, I inherited and Jake started feeding daisies.

Ant put me in charge of organizing the day-to-day stuff for his projects so he could concentrate on the engineering. I didn't need no strong-arming—Ant's reputation was enough. I offered them my other specialty, fatal accidents, but I guess there was no call for that in the mountain. Now I have a second family of two boys and two girls and they are all fertile. That seems to matter. Those women are thrilled with me, and there is a line-up forming. This is the good life for sure.

Chapter 9

PROFESSOR GRANT AMES, CPA, MBA, PHD
(FACULTY MEMBER, NURENA UNIVERSITY)

Those bastards have done it again. I am referring to the Supreme Council, known in private as The Robertson Cabal. They have legislated another head tax across the board, without any consideration for the desperate poverty of our country's unemployed citizens. For many of us, this tax will be is a nuisance. For some, it will be the difference between starving now or holding on for another few weeks. That bastard family lives in luxury as people starve, and now they want to sweat more denues out of us, denues many don't have. The penalty for non-payment is severe.

I am a Professor of Financial Management and Financial Literacy at Nurena University, the most prestigious university on the planet, if I do say so myself. The Robertson Cabal has no effective political opposition, so our faculty banded together to be the country's unofficial opposition. This does not sit well with the Robertsons, so they cut off financial support to our institution. We now depend on wealthy citizens and other generous donors. Tuition alone can't cover it.

My wife, Norah, is Assistant Professor of Human Resources and Employment at Robertson College. I almost dread going home tonight. She will be going through the ceiling in fury. She can't express her disdain for the Robertsons at work. Her job depends on them and they don't take kindly to criticism. The Supreme Council still funds Robertson College, which is not affiliated with Nurena University.

Norah and I live in a very nice suite at The Cascades. We don't have children, a conscious decision mutually reached. We both think this planet is doomed within our lifetimes. This childless state gives us freedom to undertake anti-government activities aimed at taking down the Robertsons. We are heavily dependent on Norah's income. Nurena University had to cut faculty salaries twice this year. It seems the Robertsons are winning by attrition.

I limit my activities to research and publications, trying to undermine Council authority through persuasion. Norah is the risk-taker out on the front lines, a firebrand. If she ever gets caught, the least of our problems will be deep financial doodoo. That's a technical term, in case you didn't notice. There is a distinct chance she won't survive. The Council Guard are not exactly gentle, and recent court cases show they are immune from our laws. The Council owns the juries.

It was worse than I expected. Norah wasn't home, but a visitor was there. Norah was involved in a confrontation in front of the municipal courthouse and was in The Brig. The Brig is a holding facility for people scheduled to go before the court. The student protest was triggered by the court sentencing one of my fellow faculty members, Professor Robert Dorian, to deportation. That amounts to a death sentence, given where he came from.

Professor Dorian's crime was being an alien occupying an illegal position of authority. He assumed the identity of a deceased citizen about his age and was brilliant at what he did. His students rated him in the Top Ten of faculty. Norah's crime was telling our student council president about the secret proceedings so he could mobilize Professor Dorian's students.

On the plus side, the students managed to liberate Professor Dorian and he disappeared into the crowd. A complication for me was that my visitor was Professor Dorian. Bob, that is. We have an informal relationship outside the university, and he is Bob in our house. The authorities were canvassing every possible location to recapture him, and with Norah's involvement, our place had to be on the list.

Bob is an intelligent, inoffensive man, pleasant to talk to, with enlightened views on our society. He loves his work and brings his students along with a combination of incisive lectures, interesting assignments and positive, instructive feedback. Norah and I really like him. Fortunately, he has no family that can be held hostage.

I have an odd relationship with a freight driver named Jeremy. Jeremy runs phosphate in from a secret colony located somewhere in the badlands and he runs supplies back out. He thinks laws are designed for other people, to keep them in place so he can dodge between them. I suspect he is good at violence when it's called for and I know he gets things done.

I contacted Jeremy on my communicator and asked for a meeting, using a code we had. We set it up for half an hour later in front of the Kabella building. Jeremy told me to dress Bob as a woman and bring "her" with me. Fortunately, Norah's clothes were a reasonable, if tight, fit. Jeremy took Bob off my hands and assured me he would ride out in the hovercraft the next morning as Jeremy's wife.

When I got back, two Council Guards were standing by our kicked-in front door. Lucky I hung Bob's clothes up with mine. Lucky the Guards didn't spot them, because they are not my size.

I met Jeremy through Judeth, a slight, attractive, sexy executive assistant at the Supreme Court. Judeth was one of my students a few years ago. An extraordinary talent, she is committed to Jeremy, so I imagine she agreed to this subterfuge. Jeremy doesn't do much without her OK. Judeth is the brains of their relationship, Jeremy is the muscle. It's a good combination.

Now that my problem was simplified, I just needed to get Norah out of the Brig without her being charged with anything that would end her employment. She wasn't spotted at the confrontation in front of the courthouse, fortunately, because she was there. The issue was her telling our student council president about Bob's trial. The student president was picked up and would be questioned. He would tell all under the influence of drugs. All this from Bob.

When I got to the courthouse, I learned the charge against Norah was "Inciting a Riot." I talked it over with a criminal lawyer I know, who was duty counsel that day. He pointed out that Norah must have known telling the student council president about Bob's trial would result in a riot. There was no point claiming she hadn't told the president. With the juries owned by the Supreme Council, I had to finesse the judge fast.

Luckily, Jeremy told me how to do it. He even gave me his "influence stash" as he called it, four thousand denues. Success. Judge Raymond took the stash and dropped the charges on the grounds that Norah could not haven known that her mentioning the trial would trigger the riot. I just love that Jeremy. He really knows his way around.

I was absolutely drained as I brought Norah home. She was exhilarated. She and I are really made of different stuff. I begged her to stop taking chances. She absolutely *knew* she was inciting that riot. She just laughed me off. I still hold my breath waiting for a next time, and there will be a next time as sure as the star rises over the horizon every morning.

But the next time, it was about me. I published a critique on the new head tax in the name of our informal opposition, pointing out that the tax was anti-progressive in that it could be an entire month's income for a day labourer but only a nuisance charge for a Council member or other high-income earner. I was detained without charges the next day and taken to The Fortress, a high-security prison located on an island in the middle of a dry lakebed. Now it was Norah's turn to get me out, if she could.

By our constitution I could only be held for thirty-six hours without a charge being laid. Norah called Judeth. Judeth filed the necessary complaint in Norah's name to start the clock. Nice to have friends in high places.

The Chief Justice is also a Robertson, but he is not sympathetic to the family branch running the Supreme Council. He recalled me from The Fortress, expedited a hearing, and had me released the minute the thirty-six hours ran out. Judeth told me later that he also tossed a charge of fraudulent reporting on the basis that my report was accurate.

Interesting. The judicial and executive branches of government are at odds. The legislative branch has no power. There should be a wedge there somewhere for us to exploit.

I solved my Wild Norah problem by playing dirty. I pricked holes in our protection and Norah got pregnant. She wanted to sue the manufacturer, but I talked her out of that. She absolutely adores our daughter, Virginia, and takes good care of herself now because of her new motherly responsibility.

Chapter 10

DR. MARTHA JACKSON, BA, MA, PHD.
(PRESIDENT, NURENA UNIVERSITY)

The money problems were almost killing me. When I took this job, I thought I would be managing first-rate programs and a progressive faculty. Turns out I am a desperate fundraiser, begging wherever I can find deep pockets full of anti-Council denues. Money was so short I gave up my driver and even my university limo and just used my old rattletrap to get around.

We laid off about 80% of our support staff. That was terrible for me. Some of them had been with Nurena University for more than thirty years. We couldn't even give them severance. We are officially bankrupt, and the overseer said no. Our faculty clean their own offices now and input their own research papers and grades. The Robertson Cabal is winning on all fronts.

The only thing keeping us alive is the constitution. Nurena University is enshrined in it. Unfortunately, government funding is not enshrined. There are two main branches of the Robertson clan and they are at odds. The James Robertson branch runs the Supreme Council, the military and the Council Guards. The Andrew Robertson branch runs the courts and the Office of Public Prosecution. The Council branch wants to change the constitution to close our university down. The legal branch is blocking that. We are the kickball in the middle.

The Council has cut off all our government funding and we are not allowed to run a deficit while in bankruptcy. I'm not sure I should even hang on here now. I grew up in the same enclave as Andy Robertson and our friendship has helped keep him on our side on the constitution issue. Without him blocking the change, Nurena U would be long gone.

I have an appointment in a few minutes with Professor Grant Ames. He heads up our Financial Management and Financial Literacy Department. I don't know him very well, on purpose. He fronts for a faculty group that call themselves the Council's Unofficial Opposition. They are most of the reason the Council wants to shut us down, and they really make my efforts to keep us open harder. Universities have no business in politics. We are supposed to be above partisan rivalries.

Later I met with Professor Ames, and he asked me to do something odd. He wanted me to go with him to a secret place in the badlands and meet some people he doesn't even know. He gave me a letter from Bob Dorian asking me to do that. I knew the letter was real because of Bob's directions so we could find the person we are to meet: Bob said to meet this person at the place where the daiquiri nearly poisoned me. Only Bob could know about that. So embarrassing!

Speaking about Bob Dorian, I was amazed he is an alien. He just seemed like everyone else and he was really good at what he did. I was really glad to hear from Bob and know he got out safely. Out to where, I hadn't a clue. Second, Bob's letter said he had a plan to finance the university. That was a hook I couldn't ignore. Here we come, Bob!

We met a rough character named Ed at Bob's meeting place. Just Ed, no last name mentioned. I doubt Ed was his real name anyway, but who cares. It's just convenient to have a name to address. He was dusty and sweaty and obviously didn't care what anyone thought of him. That must be liberating. Professor Ames wife, Norah, was with him. She was very pregnant. Congrats, Dr. Ames.

Ed had a flexicab waiting and took us to an abandoned farm on the edge of the badlands. He had a nice six-seat hovercraft parked there in a rundown barn. We got in and it bounced over rocks and gullies for half an hour to get to a camp tucked deep in a dead-end canyon surrounded by high cliffs. Ed ran the hovercraft under a fabric shelter, and we all got out. That trip can't have been good for Norah in her condition.

There was a main shelter close by. As we walked over, a very large man stood up and came out to welcome us. He shook my hand and then Grant's and Norah's. He introduced himself as Anthony Carter and told us to call him Ant. Ed just drifted off and disappeared.

Bob Dorian, sorry, Professor Dorian, was there as well and looked fit. The third person was the real surprise: Juanita Rodrigues. She was pale and a lot thinner than I remembered, but hallelujah, she was alive. People who can take in Bob and Juanita and put them at this obvious level of authority have to be truly impressive. Ant was their spokesperson and leader. Their proposal was astonishing, and I soon understood why Professor Ames was included. Bringing along his wife, Norah, also made sense.

The basic idea was that they were planning to take over Nurena U and use its facilities as a development base for their projects. They were primarily interested in our engineering, math and deep data faculties and their labs, but were also interested in some people in our Financial Management faculty. They were clearly anti-Council. The university would continue in its proper role of cutting-edge research and higher education teaching but would also address their needs.

Ant had a list of seventeen faculty members and four staff members they thought had to go. Juanita hacked their social media accounts and Ant thought these people would be "uncomfortable" working against their legal government. I was to employ Norah in the human resources department where she could access employee files and make decisions.

They knew about Norah's bias against the Council and would leave the final decisions to her. If Norah spotted any additional problem employees, she was free to act. Ant did admonish her to keep it honest. No grudges or personal biases. Everything had to be based on objective data. Juanita could get her into any social media files she needed to see.

Norah would also be the hatchet so my reputation as a moderate president would not suffer. Norah was looking forward to "weeding out reactionaries." She was strong-willed. I wouldn't want to cross her.

Once this was accomplished, the financing would begin. Bob assured me the financing was feasible, but the university had to stay broke for now to justify Norah's "weeding."

I agreed to their initial step. Bob trusted them. Juanita trusted them. I trusted Bob and Juanita. Oddly, I also trusted Ant. Such is the power of a straightforward personality. I realized they held most of their plan back from us, but they were trusting me, Grant, and Norah too. It seems they are a group of aliens and Fractionals surviving somewhere in the badlands. A year ago, I would have told them to stuff it, but now I was thinking maybe aliens and Fractionals are people too. Maybe even good people.

Back at the university, I had no trouble hiring Norah. We were down to two employees in the Personnel Department and the workload was impossible, as one after another good faculty member couldn't afford to work for us anymore. Happily, five of Norah's seventeen faculty "reactionaries" and two of Norah's staff "reactionaries" were already outward bound by their choice.

Over the next month, Norah wielded the hatchet vigorously in the name of austerity. She added two more names to the "reactionary" list and subtracted none. The rumour surfaced that we were getting rid of people who supported the Council and our legal government. Very observant. Sometimes rumours are true. Most of the departing people were glad to have the decision taken out of their hands, even with no severance.

Ed took us back out into the badlands six weeks later for a second meeting. This time we took along a deep data professor and a communications professor. Ant and Bob were there but no Juanita. Ant explained that Juanita was deadly afraid to leave their base and go into the badlands and couldn't bring herself to do it again. She did it that one time because she thought having another woman in the meeting would give me comfort. Apparently, she had suffered overwhelming harm out there sometime in her past.

Their proposal for the next step was astounding. They planned to launch their own currency—an electronic one they called a crypto. They were the only successful manufacturer of Tag Blockers on the planet and they were exporting their updated version into our society at a high rate. They stopped taking denues six months earlier because their value was crashing with hyperinflation. Instead they resorted to barter. Now they had a large surplus of odds and ends of goods, far more than they could possibly need, and not always a useful mix.

Their analysis of the denue's hyperinflation concluded that it was caused by two situations that compounded on each other. First, the reduction of the country's productive capacity was reducing outputs. Second, the

Supreme Council was increasing the pay for their employees by increasing the supply of denues, particularly to pay their Council Guards, to keep the Guards buying power stable and keep them onside. In effect the Council was taking up a larger and larger share of a shrinking pie.

Ant's group planned to set up an electronic market to sell their surpluses that would accept only cryptos in exchange. Their crypto was going to be pegged to the price of Tag Blockers at one hundred cryptos per Tag Blocker. Since Tag Blockers were an illegal product distributed in underground markets, Ant thought they could control that price. They would limit the initial issue of cryptos to the equivalent value of upgraded Tag Blockers already in circulation and increase the quantity of cryptos proportional to their new production of Tag Blockers. They would be the only ones able to introduce new cryptos into the system.

An interesting wrinkle was that they were going to inflate cryptos at the rate of 2% a year by gradually increasing the number of cryptos it would take to buy a Tag Blocker. For example, next year a new Tag Blocker would sell for one hundred and two cryptos. Their purpose was to persuade people to use their cryptos instead of saving them. They wanted maximum crypto circulation. They would increase the crypto supply by 2% a year to maintain balance. Two percent was almost nothing compared to the 30 to 40% denues had inflated each of the past two years.

Anyone who owned a pocket communicator could register as a crypto trader by downloading the crypto application, but only one registration could be loaded onto each communicator. This communicator approach could include almost every adult on the planet and many children. Cryptos would become an international currency. Communicators are basically small, powerful computers, so each registrant would be part of their crypto computer network.

When I asked if cryptos could be counterfeited like denues, my own expert, Grant Ames, jumped in with the answer. He called it "blockchain." Grant was excited and animated for the first time since we started down this path. He was in his element.

He said it would be impossible to change a transaction in a read only application. If anyone managed to change a transaction, the majority of members' communicators would undo the change in the reconciliation stage anyway. To change one transaction successfully after the fact, it would be necessary to change every subsequent record, even as new transactions rolled in to extend the chain.

Grant asked if there would be a master computer running the system. Ant said there would be two, one at the university and one at their base. They would mirror each other so if one went down the other could carry on, then update the down one when it came back online. Ant thought they could process about a million transactions an hour, based on the speed of current computer processors. Juanita had a team working on upping that by a factor of 128.

Grant asked if the private network would be secure. Ant answered, "As secure as anything can be. Juanita hacked into the ring of satellites running the planet's communicator network and Nurena's identity tag system and took control. She left the current applications in place and put her applications one level higher, so they can't be seen by Council engineers. Juanita left the Council's applications untouched but controls them so they can only be changed as she allows. She also took over the on/off switch on each satellite. It should look like a programming glitch to satellite engineers if they ever try it."

I asked why Juanita didn't disable Nurena's hated identity tag system. Ant pointed out that would tip off the engineers about the interference. Also, he said, smiling, it would undermine their market for Tag Blockers. On the upside, he pointed out, his group could now track every Nurena resident better than the Council could, because his group could see through Tag Blockers.

Then we got into my main issue: financing Nurena U. Their plan was to run a separate payroll system out of their base's computer as a supplement to our official system, adding to our system's pay with cryptos. As they had explained earlier, they planned to open an online market dealing only in cryptos to move their surpluses. This would bring the cryptos full circle.

They expected others to enter the crypto marketplace as well, to sell excess products of whatever they had managed to hoard, and thus diversify what they held. Ant thought a marketplace based on stable cryptos would unblock the flow of commerce around the planet.

Student scholarships and bursaries would also be paid in cryptos. With denues falling in value through hyperinflation, this should increase the attractiveness of Nurena University to top students. Finally, Nurena U would receive substantial amounts of cryptos to run their business. One of the objectives was to attract and concentrate the absolutely brightest people on the planet at Nurena U. Another objective was to get a lot of cryptos into circulation fast, to catch up with the number of Tag Blockers already out there.

Again, I agreed to their proposal—enthusiastically as a matter of fact. Salvation for Nurena U was at hand. Their plans were the most audacious thing I have ever heard of, and I have been around the track more than a few times. Basically, a group of four to five hundred disenfranchised non-people was planning to take over an entire country's commercial system, starting with the capital city of Nurena, and it would probably work.

Chapter 11

ADAM JONES
(GANGSTER AND COLIN GUERRA'S FORMER SECOND-IN-COMMAND)

I got a message from my old boss, Colin, tucked into a Tag Blocker ship-ment. Surprise! I thought he went to boot hill long ago. I knew the message was from him because he used a codeword only known to our inner circle. He asked me to keep everything confidential to protect his wife and family from Robertson reprisals.

Colin was a rough one, but that was what it took back then. Now my business is so sophisticated, it takes someone with an economics degree to understand it. For all practical purposes I and my fellow Capos running the other territories are Nurena's real economic system. The official one is dying or dead.

Colin wanted me to go with Jeremy, the Tag Blocker smuggler, to meet him and a couple of other people somewhere in the badlands. Colin's message said I could trust Jeremy, and I would anyway. He's a rough one but a straight shooter, and he needs me to move his Tag Blockers.

Jeremy took me to a small dead-end canyon in a remote corner of the badlands in a sweet hovercraft. He parked it under a temporary cover, and we walked to another shelter close by. A large man and a smaller one met us, along with Colin. Nice to see Colin still alive and looking good. He always treated me right while bringing me up through the organization. Truly forward-thinking for such a rough character.

Colin and I shook hands and he introduced his large companion as Anthony Carter. The smaller man was a university professor I once took a course from named Robert Dorian. Anthony told me to call him Ant, Professor Dorian told me to call him Bob, and we were on friendly terms right away. I was finally meeting the principal stakeholders in my very profitable Tag Blocker business and they impressed me.

They had an interesting proposal for me to think about. They were going to launch a new currency to supplement the failing denues and eventually to take over management of the commercial transactions of Nurena. They had barns full of products they had taken in barter, both with me and with other Capos. They wanted a way to move their products and pick up others that they needed in exchange. Barter wasn't cutting it for them.

They wanted me to get together with the other Capos and join in their electronic market, which would deal only in their new currency. They wanted us to take physical control of their surplus goods and arrange delivery to buyers. They wanted us to collect what they bought through the market and deliver it to destinations for them to pick up. They would continue to supply Tag Blockers but wanted the purchase price to be paid only in their new currency. They called the units of their currency cryptos.

In payment for this activity, we could charge a 20% commission in cryptos on all completed exchanges.

It made sense. The collapsing value of denues was gumming up commerce. Hoarders were holding big quantities of goods off the markets that they had no way to use. The proposal would tie the value of cryptos to the value of Tag Blockers and hyperinflation would be contained by limiting the quantity of cryptos in circulation, proportional to the number of Tag Blockers in circulation. Part of the deal would be fixing the price for new Tag Blockers at one hundred cryptos each, something we could easily control.

Ant had a great presentation ready and suggested I use it when I talked to the other Capos at our semi-annual gathering the following week. Colin must have been keeping track. I couldn't see how we could lose. These people were taking all the risks.

They were also going to score bigtime if it worked, and I got the impression they knew how to make it work. We would buy Tag Blockers from them at a 20% discount with cryptos. Then they would introduce new cryptos into the float at the value of the additional Tag Blockers in circulation, kind of double dipping. Everyone won, but I wanted more than a 20% discount. That negotiation was for a later time when I had the other Capos lined up. More leverage. Right then I was just listening. They didn't explain the double dipping. I just figured it out.

They also didn't go into how they were going to get the initial infusion of cryptos into our hands to prime the pump. Something else to negotiate. My guess was that they already had about two million new Tag Blockers out there. At one hundred cryptos per Tag Blocker, they were planning to get about two hundred million cryptos into circulation fast to float their system. Interesting times.

After the presentation, Jer drove me back into the city and let me off where my vehicle was parked. My driver was waiting. My mind was churning as I turned over their concept and examined all the pros and cons I could think of. The current denue system wasn't working. Barter really screwed up the economics of my business. Too clumsy. Conclusion, if they could make it work, I wanted a piece of it. Those clever bastards had turned me into their star salesman.

When I got back to the office, the first thing I did was put a new item on the agenda for next week's get-together. One word: cryptos. That should get some of the other Capos curious. Meantime, I would go on a tour of my territory and get all my people ready, also so the other Capos couldn't find me. That way I wouldn't need to lie to them. They needed to see this in the proper perspective at the right time where I could field all the questions and put it to bed. I didn't want any ignorant half-assed understandings to circulate.

The meeting day arrived. We were at a top hotel in South River with Rick Knowles as host. Couldn't be better. Rick is also a university economics graduate and runs a tight ship. Everyone pestered me with questions. Well, not Rick, but everyone else. Rick just made sure cryptos was the first item on the agenda. I think he already thought some of it out.

I went through Ant's presentation, asking the other Capos to hold questions until I was finished. Even at the end, some of them just looked puzzled. The entire concept was over their heads. Rick jumped in with some baby questions that let me downmarket parts of the plan without seeming condescending and I got a few more nods. Rick was totally with me, already sold, visions of cryptos dancing in his head.

The clincher was my explaining that from then on, they could only buy Tag Blockers with cryptos. No cryptos, no Tag Blockers. Rick announced his support and everyone else was on board. It was unanimous. Rick and I were voted to negotiate on behalf of all the Capos. Perfect. Rick and I were simpatico on many levels.

I contacted Jer and I was back talking to Ant less than a week later, with Rick in tow. We bounced ideas back and forth with Ant and Bob and started doing some horse-trading. Ant wouldn't move on the 20% handling and delivery charge, pointing out that our customers would be paying it and too high a charge could hamper business. He said that his group was not taking any cut on the transactions. He did agree to increase the Tag Blocker price discount to 25%.

On the float, we got everything we wanted and more. Ant agreed to give us 150% of the equivalent Tag Blocker value in cryptos in the first round of Tag Blocker deliveries immediately after we signed, right there in the badlands. Up front for us, and the same for each of the other Capos as soon as Ant had their electronic signatures of agreement. Colin knew who they were. Of course, it was a one-time shot, so it didn't affect their big picture much.

And that's how it went. Cryptos were launched. I heard Nurena U got a big initial float as well, spread among their faculty and staff. I had trouble organizing the delivery part at first, but there were a lot of unemployed grunts out there, some nearly starving, and I could get it done on a piece-work basis if I paid in cryptos. Everyone wanted cryptos. No employees, and it only cost me after I had the cryptos in my wallet. Great cash flow. I had a special crypto business wallet with no size limit.

The crypto app was in the communicator app store free of charge and could be downloaded onto any communicator on the planet. The word was getting around fast and we were becoming legitimate businessmen, except for the Tag Blockers, of course.

Chapter 12

DR. MARTHA JACKSON, BA, MA, PHD.
(PRESIDENT, NURENA UNIVERSITY)

Ed got back to me. I went back into the badlands with Grant and Norah to meet Ant and Bob Dorian. Ant and Bob had worked out a crypto pay scale for every one of our employees and would put it in an oversized university wallet as soon as I signed on. Ant added an extra million cryptos for general purposes to let us purchase much-needed supplies and to set up scholarships and bursaries in cryptos. Their support in cryptos would be ongoing at 30% of their wholesale Tag Blocker sales.

Their electronic market was up and running, so there was a place to spend cryptos and good things were beginning to show up on it.

Bob had searched the literature in several disciplines and had a list of doctoral candidates and junior faculty they wanted me to approach as soon as cryptos were a known commodity in academic circles. The emphasis was on engineering and the sciences. I actually recognized four of the names, and if they were representative of the whole list, Bob had done his homework. Norah would stay on after the baby was born and help with the recruiting.

I took the deal. I loved the deal. Nurena U was saved. I still didn't know why they were doing this, not exactly, anyway. In my experience, there is always a reason. The only clue I had was one phrase I heard Ant use when talking to Bob: "Exodus is on track."

The faculty and staff were also enthusiastic once I explained it. They all downloaded the crypto app onto their communicators and found they already had a crypto balance in their wallets. They also found the electronic market, which was already filling with items they had been unable to afford or even find for months. They discovered an unofficial market had already started to sell cryptos for denues and the exchange rate was an astonishing forty thousand denues to buy one crypto.

Several faculty members and some staff members bought enough denues at that inflated rate to pay off their mortgages and retire a lifetime of debt in a few keystrokes. I was able to rehire several of our laid-off staff members, offering only cryptos as pay. More than one of them was crying with relief before my call to them ended. That made me feel really good.

Norah started on the list of junior faculty and doctoral students Ant wanted, again offering only cryptos as pay. Word spreads fast in academia and she was very successful. I got a lot of calls from more senior and established faculty and had to say no to almost all of them. Only three extremely desirable ones passed Ant's screening. He had explained to me that his group wanted to build a strong, creative faculty of near geniuses to pursue a development that could take up to ten years to bring in and he wanted a team that could stay intact for that long.

I was also getting more insights into what he was up to. The strongest research focus was intergalactic travel. I know about interstellar travel within our own galaxy, although Nurena hasn't launched any expeditions in at least two decades. It is well established that travel between galaxies is impossible. There is no way to pick a destination or to send advance preparation proxies. The nearest galaxy external to ours is 2.2 million lightyears away.

Norah hired twenty-two doctoral students from Ant's group in the badlands, seventeen young women and five young men. They were trained by Juanita and no one had ever heard of them before they arrived. I asked Norah about them and she said they were part of the deal. OK by me. I really liked the deal and it wasn't my money. If they couldn't cut it, we would soon find out. Meanwhile we were bringing in almost everyone on Ant's list plus seven more I wanted, to beef up the humanities. Obviously I still had some authority.

It soon became clear that Juanita's students were exceptional, and they were channelling Juanita into our university by proxy. Several became leaders among younger members of the faculty, and all were well liked by the staff, not always the case with really bright people. Juanita's students actually organized research programs and kept track of progress against targets only they seemed to know. Juanita again, I suppose. A most remarkable person. There wasn't a man or woman alive who could come anywhere near her for raw talent. Truth be told, she was running Nurena U from a distance and doing a damn fine job.

On the outside, trouble was brewing as the old order financed by denues was being displaced by our new order financed by cryptos. The most dislocated were in the military and members of the Supreme Council Guards, once top dogs but now just impoverished gunmen. Norah needed to hire some of their senior officers, using cryptos, to protect Nurena U and our employees. We started developing housing and other infrastructure inside the campus and moving our employees and their families inside our boundaries. We also started reinforcing the university boundaries, using technology provided by Ant and his Fractional second-generation aliens.

Trouble was brewing in Nurena and we were preparing for it. Ant had predicted all this and was getting us ready to deal with it. This small band of aliens was truly amazing.

I sent word that I needed to talk to Ant again through one of his faculty nominees. I got a message back telling me where to meet Ed with the usual coded reference to something that happened on my last visit with him. This time Ed whisked me all the way to their lair, a hollow mountain out in the middle of a vast nothing.

Juanita took time off to show me around. We visited a class of four-year-olds learning about a planet they might never see. The teacher was effective. Her approach could be described as discovery learning. We visited a class of eleven-year-olds and they were discussing relativity intelligently. Our students don't go there until secondary school. We visited a university-level graduate school where content was taught by computers and the professor provided individual challenges and feedback.

Their computer-based library had more titles in it than Nurena U's did. We ate in a communal dining room to fine background music and intelligent adult conversation all around me. Everyone made an effort to include me. We visited a small hospital equipped with the best our planet could offer plus some equipment that I had never seen before. We visited two private residences, which were small but comfortable and well appointed.

We ended the evening in a large amphitheatre at the apex of their artificial mountain, listening to great music I had never heard before played by a combo that worked in their computer lab during the day. These migrants and their Fractional children were an impressive, civilized people. Maybe better than my people, certainly better than some of my people.

My overnight accommodation was as good as a five-star hotel.

The next morning, I met with Ant and presented my case. We needed to bring Andrew Robertson and the Justice group into the safety of Nurena U's campus. The university depended on their support where the constitution was concerned, and they ran a double risk if civil unrest resurfaced. First, they would be a convenient target for mobs and upheaval. Second, James Robertson might use a civil disturbance to sic his Council Guards on his cousin Andrew and the court system Andrew represented. I pointed out that I grew up with Andrew and he was one of the good ones.

Ant was with me in a second. Slapping his hand on his forehead, he said, "Stupid, stupid, stupid." I pointed out that he couldn't think of everything. His answer was, "I have to think of everything." We started making a plan right there on the spot. I was to be Ant's access to Andrew. Ant wanted to go the badlands meeting route again and I could see no reason not to. It worked for me. In the end we decided going to Andrew would be easier to work out.

We talked about where the Justice Department could go on the campus. It had to have a separate and secure location. Obviously there was no time to build one. I suggested sacrificing the gymnasiums and the field buildings they were in. It wasn't ideal but we could bring in temporary space dividers to allow some privacy. Andrew could use the recreation director's offices. We had a plan. Now I had to get Andrew to agree to a meeting.

Chapter 13

CHIEF JUSTICE, THE HON. ANDREW F. ROBERTSON, BA, LLB

Martha Jackson, Marty, dropped into my office unexpectedly and asked me out to lunch. I told her I had an appointment, and she told me to cancel it because what she had to say was more important. I told her to tell me right there. She held a hand up to her ear and waved at the door. Did she think someone was eavesdropping? My office was swept just that morning and nothing was found.

Anyway, I told Judeth to cancel and went out with Marty. She took me to a noisy dive off the main streets, really just a greasy spoon. If she wanted secrecy, no one would look for us there. The shaggy host at the door was expecting us and led us to a separate room at the back. A giant waited for us there. Marty introduced him as Anthony Carter. Shaking hands firmly, the giant told me to call him Ant. A finance professor I knew slightly, Grant Ames, was also there.

Marty explained that Ant was a representative of a business group responsible for the new cryptos that were replacing the collapsing denues in our monetary system. I was amazed. I thought James – Jimmy – had just started a new money scam. It never occurred to me that an independent third party was messing in his sacred territory.

Grant explained the crypto system to me. I got enough of it to realize no one was running the crypto system, or rather everyone was. It was based in the entire citizenry using a distributed network operating on their communicators with no government involvement. That must be driving Jimmy crazy. Of course he's already crazy, so even more crazy. He likes to control everything, especially everything involving money.

Marty explained that Ant represented the group that put the system together and they had a foolproof way to prevent the inflation that was destroying Jimmy's denues. I asked what could do that. Marty asked me to hold that and other questions until the end of the presentation. Sure. It was her meeting.

Marty told me how Ant's group was actually profiting from it and how they were using that profit to save Nurena U by financing it with cryptos. Of course, I already knew about their difficulties with Jimmy and his Supreme Council, and I was glad they were back on a good financial footing, but what did it have to do with me?

Ant stepped in and described how the collapsing denues were devastating the criminal justice system. He knew how many people I had laid off. He knew how much debt our courts had taken on. Hell, he even knew I couldn't keep up the mortgage payments on the family estate. How in hell did he know all that? So, I asked.

Ant told me they had taken in Juanita Rodrigues and that every database on the planet was an open book to her. Juanita? Great! Stupendous! I thought Jimmy killed her. Marty confirmed that Ant was telling the truth, saying she had met Juanita twice in the past six months and Juanita was just fine.

Then the real shocks started. Marty told me I and my fellow judges were in mortal danger. Civil unrest was going to morph into rioting, burning and killing, and Robertsons were going to be major targets. With Jimmy's ass covered by the Council Guards, I and my group were the soft targets. I already figured some of this out, but what could I do about it? Jimmy had already refused to send any Guards my way. Marty pointed out that Jimmy might even use civil unrest to take us out himself.

Marty's proposal was to move our entire justice system onto the university campus. She was ready to turn over the athletic buildings to us, including letting us change the locks and keep all the codes to ourselves. Complete independence.

I couldn't see why that made us safer. The university has no soldiers and for sure Jimmy wouldn't protect them anyway. They wouldn't be much of a target as things stood, but taking us in could run up their danger level.

Ant stepped into the discussion to describe a protective dome his group was deploying as we spoke, to cover the university's entire core campus. His group was already using it successfully in a different application. Again, Marty confirmed it was true and told me she had been inside one. Ant offered to demonstrate it later if we could reach agreement. Ant went on to say his group was funding Nurena U out of the profits they made trading in cryptos and he was prepared to offer some crypto financing for my justice system. What was the downside? Obviously there must be one.

Then the ton of bricks fell on my head. Ant's group manufactured and distributed Tag Blockers. They were criminal gangsters. My courts have been prosecuting and jailing Tag Blocker traders for years. Marty's proposal would have our justice system protected and financed by criminals and criminal activity. I almost walked out, but Ant stopped me by saying it was even worse. What could be worse?

It was worse. Much worse. Ant's group started as migrants from another star system who accidentally landed here. Ant's generation were almost all Fractionals. By masquerading as citizens, they were proscribed. Every one of them should be jailed or deported. I sat back down, astonished. Marty must be out of her head. And I thought Jimmy was crazy.

But Marty wasn't finished. She quoted the old saying, "The enemy of my enemy is my friend." Ant and I were natural allies. She told me if I walked out now, she would deny the meeting ever took place and she was certainly going to continue running the university on cryptos. That was really working for them and nothing could stop cryptos anyway. Then she pointed out that I was not going to stop Ant or his group either, so my real choice was to have the justice system form a temporary alliance with them or go bankrupt, maybe die, with me probably dying first.

Ant suggested we take a time-out and get back together the following day. He offered to take Marty and me to their main base for the meeting if I could withhold judgment until after that meeting. Astonishing! Marty said she had already visited their base and I would be impressed too if I went ahead with Ant's proposal. Marty also said Ant had already agreed to proceed if I decided to. He had signalled that to her and I hadn't noticed. Ant had decided to trust me. Marty continued the sales pitch, saying

Ant's group were a commendable, civilized people we should admire, not hunt down.

As the shock subsided, I could see some merit in Ant's proposal. Marty has always been level-headed and pursued the main chance. Maybe there was something wrong with me that I couldn't see it. Marty pointed out that our meeting place was a closed restaurant up for sale and Ant's people had stage-managed it for today. It was already an empty property again. She said Jimmy's Guards were likely to check it out, since they could track me.

And the capstone of the day, Marty offered me a Tag Blocker to wear if I decided to go forward. Heaven help me, I took it and joined a criminal conspiracy. Possession is a crime and I have convicted and jailed people for it. No more tracking of my activities for Jimmy if I went in on this venture.

I didn't sleep much the early part of the night. There was no one I could talk to. It was all up to me. I held the future of the criminal justice system in my hands. Then I came to the almost forgone conclusion. I was in. After that I slept like a baby. I have never regretted this decision. I suppose I really made it when I took the Tag Blocker. It just took me a while to get my head around it.

The following morning, I dropped by Marty's office, a fairly normal thing to do, to say I was in. She was ho-hum as she smiled and nodded. She turned on her wave interference system to give us privacy and we both activated our Tag Blockers. I was surprised at how much that made me feel free. I don't think I've experienced that feeling since childhood. I was on the move and no one knew where I was or where I was going. Except Marty, of course.

We went out to the quadrangle where a guide named Jeremy was waiting. Jeremy had a flexicab on hold and took us to an abandoned factory on the outskirts, where he had a hovercraft parked. Jeremy drove like a wild man, swinging around boulders with a hairbreadth to spare, jumping up ridges of impossible heights, leaping over gullies that should have swallowed us. I was too terrified to keep track of where we were.

He slowed to a near stop as we ran up against a mountain. Then he proceeded at a sedate pace as we entered a gap opening up ahead of us and we were inside the mountain. This was no ordinary mountain. It was hollowed out and contained a small city. The effect was awesome. A people who could do this must be very impressive. Now that I thought of it, Ant was very impressive, and Jeremy was an impressive driver. At least he had made an impression on me. Maybe Marty was used to it.

As we got out of the hovercraft, Ant came up to greet us. He pointed to the surrounding walls and said an electronic dome as powerful as this could shield the university's central campus on a minute's notice, just by throwing a switch. He introduced his companion as Juanita Rodrigues, the famous Juanita Rodrigues. She is a happy, smiling, small, trim woman with light brown skin and lovely eyes. I could see how she would have captivated Jimmy, although that was no excuse for what he did. I got the impression that Ant and Juanita were more than just a welcoming committee.

Juanita took me on a tour while Ant settled in with Marty to work out something. Juanita and I dropped in on a couple of primary classes run by competent teachers. We dropped in on a learning centre where senior students were pursuing individually tailored programs with tutors giving assistance and direction. We also visited a law reading room that could have been the one in my building back in the city. I tested the librarian by asking for five relatively obscure titles and she retrieved every one of them from her system.

Next we went to lunch, where we joined up with Marty and Ant again. White linen and gleaming cutlery, very pleasant and very tasty. Then down to business.

I asked how my files were going to move to the university.

Juanita said, "We have already set up a computer system at the university that is compatible with yours. All we needed to do is shut down your backup computers for maintenance, dismount the memory wafers, and physically carry them to our machines to create a new backup. We can then update our new backup from your main computers with only a few minutes of data transfer. Finally, we can copy this continuing backup to create a new primary record on the new computers safely at the university. In a few hours the move can be complete."

I asked, "Why can't we use electronic data transfers between the locations?"

She answered, "That would take three days, while moving the wafers could be done in three hours. A three-day process might be too vulnerable. It is unlikely anyone can act fast enough to stop a surprise three-hour blitz."

Then (why should I keep on being surprised?) she gave me a list of seven people I could trust to carry out the mission. She knew my staff better than I did!

Ant came back into the conversation. He told me his group was prepared to dedicate 25% of all Tag Blocker sales at the wholesale price to financing my justice system, no questions asked. He told me how much that was at their current level of activity. They were doing a lot better than I imagined. It was enough to offset the bind that the devalued denues had me in.

Before I could accept, Ant pointed out that it was a trap. "Every time your people intercept a shipment of Tag Blockers or imprison a distributor, you would be undermining your revenues as well as the university's revenues."

Apparently, Martha had a similar deal. Talk about a conflict of interest. What could I do about it? Nothing. I agreed and we were finished. Ant said I would have an account with a million cryptos in it by the time I was back in the city.

I asked, "What did you want in return, a repeal of our migrant laws?"

Ant answered, "No, we just want the same things you do: a peaceful, orderly country. In fact, the migrant laws help us by keeping us together. Getting around them keeps us sharp. Without them, your people would just absorb ours."

As we shook hands to seal the deal, Ant said something that had never occurred to me. "You know, we have always been natural allies. My people arrived here by accident. You want us out of Nurena. We want to get off your planet. The only difference is we want to do it on our terms, not on yours. We want to survive the experience. Help us do that."

Chapter 14

JUDETH
(ONE OF OUR SPIES AND CONTROLLER OF OUR SPY NETWORK)

Chief Justice Andrew Robertson, my boss, told me that we would be shutting down the backup computers for maintenance. This didn't surprise me, since I was involved in planning it. Andrew said we would be starting the backup on new computers at Nurena University. I had to pretend ignorance once again. Same old, same old.

I called in the six people that I had chosen and that Andrew told me to use, and I explained that we would be pulling the memory wafers and reinstalling them on new computers at the university. Joseph asked an intelligent question about the operating system and I assured him the new computers were already set up with it from a download completed the previous day.

That was a small risk, since Andrew didn't tell me that so I shouldn't have known. Ant and I agreed to do this switchover the week before, when we developed the plan. Like so many other times, knowing both sides of a story when I was supposed to only know Andrew's side was dicey, but no one noticed. I suppose knowing too much is always a risk for spies.

Shutting down the backup computers was a complicated process, but we closed everything out in a couple of hours. Pulling the wafers took maybe two more hours. Jer was managing the transfer of the wafers with Ed's help, using two Nurena U transport vehicles. This was the dangerous part where we were exposed, but the Nurena U logos gave us some protection. Two Council Guards even helped us push though the crowds. That might have increased the risk since many citizens don't like Guards.

My small group got to the U safely and set out installing the wafers and booting up the computers to start running the programs. I restarted the backup download of the day's data using conventional channels, but something was wrong, and the transfer wasn't happening. Four of us headed back to the Supreme Court to track down the problem. By then it was dusk, and the crowds were getting ugly. It was scary being on the streets.

We made it safely to the Justice Building and started test protocols. We finally got the data flowing just as a flaming bottle that smelled like rocket fuel crashed through the atrium roof. An intense fire started in the entrance area. We slammed the fire doors shut and retreated into the main area when another flaming bottle started a new fire near the computer rooms. This time there was a lot of smoke as furniture started burning. We could hear crowds shouting and cheering through the hole in the glass.

My companions decided to retreat into the fireproof vault. I tried to stop them, but they were panicked and wouldn't listen to me. By then the fire was intense where we were, as well. The last thing I saw of them was Stacy pulling the vault door closed.

I ran up the stairs, darted through a fire door just as it was closing and found temporary safety in the executive lounge. Soon the fire door was radiating heat, then glowing red hot in its centre. It should have held out, but I guess rocket fuel burns hotter than fire doors were meant to resist. As the doors started melting, I retreated onto the balcony one storey above a mob screaming and cheering as the building erupted into an inferno.

They saw me against the orange backdrop and started chanting "BURN! BABY! BURN!" I was terrified. My knees turned to jelly, and I nearly fell off, into their waiting rage. I thought maybe Stacy had made the better choice.

Just as my life was over, a large hovertruck popped up over the edge of the mob and rode right over it to just below where I was teetering. I heard Jer yell, "JUMP!" and I toppled into the bed of the truck. It hurt. I hurt all over as the truck bounced me around its almost empty bed. Objects banged against me and I blacked out.

I woke up in the infirmary at our base. Jer was sitting beside my bed.

A nurse told me later that I was out for five hours after being admitted. I had a concussion, a broken wrist and collarbone, and I was bruised all over, but I was alive. Jer had seen me on that balcony on his communicator.

Seems I called him a few minutes earlier, although I couldn't remember doing that. He was still in the area after delivering the wafers and was going to pick up a load in the hovertruck. He sped over fast and blew the hovertruck over the top of a mob of several thousand people to rescue me.

We watched the news reports of that night's rioting. The media were far more informed than usual, with no sign of the usual censoring. Someone videoed Jer's hovertruck rising over the outer edge of the mob. Other shots showed it smashing people to the ground under the thrust of its powerful fans. One embarrassing shot showed me falling into the truck, not jumping, just falling. What a wimp. And then the fast retreat into the dark over more people. In all the shots you could hear the chant, "BURN! BABY! BURN!"

A government report said Jer killed eighty-seven people and seriously injured an estimated 200 to 250 more. Apparently, the Council Guards didn't kill or injure anyone that night, although they were actively engaged in several places. I think Jer was getting all the blame, rather than having the Council stoke the anger people already felt toward the Guards. Government agents later arrested every injured person in the hospitals whether they were at the riot or not. They were all charged with insurrection, a capital crime.

Jer, hidden in the hovertruck cab, was not identified and the report said the hovertruck could not be traced. I was identified and a wanted circular on me was issued. It was going to be a frosty Friday before anyone could find me at the base, but my spy career was probably over. The riot collapsed after Jer ran over it, with the mob just fading away.

Another communicator broadcast featured a new face and a name, Dargon. Dargon praised the brave people murdered by a government agent using a hovertruck and urged them to keep resisting. He shouted and waved his arms and made a big noise. The performance was almost mesmerizing. Juanita analysed his image later and told us it was a holograph of a computer-generated composite and not a real person. She speculated that it might be a destabilizing attack sponsored by Caprico, a neighbouring country in even more social and economic difficulty than Nurena was. Their people were already surging against our borders.

Dargon attracted quite a following. His performance was repeated over and over on all the news channels with lots of analysis, much of it favourable. Some news anchors claimed he was the new saviour. Small shrines popped up on street corners and people started bowing down. To a fake-human holograph? I thought maybe a new religion was being born with all the fuss. Dargon said the mob was justified in killing government agents like me and the murderous act to save me was an atrocity that called for revenge.

The Robertsons, all the Robertsons, were under siege. The Robertson Bordello was torched. Several of the young women in it were burned alive rather than trying to escape into the mob. Two women did try to escape and were literally torn to pieces. An amateur photographer captured some of that grisly scene on his communicator. The authorities were able to identify two of the participants in this monstrous act and they were captured and executed without benefit of legal process.

Martial law was declared. Groups of more than three people became illegal gatherings. Council Guards enforced the new law violently. Flyovers used live ammunition to kill larger groups and sometimes even legal-sized ones. Thousands died. Thousands more were taken captive. The vicious attacks and reprisals were unprecedented, but in the end the Guards restored some semblance of order.

Then Angus Robertson died and James took over the chairmanship of the Supreme Council. In normal circumstances, there would have been a state funeral with all the trimmings, but these were not normal times. Instead the crowds of protesters grew larger and property damage increased. Autos were overturned and burned. Two members of the Council were caught in one confrontation, trapped in their auto and burned alive.

The tactics of the Guards changed too. No more prisoners. Their orders were shoot to kill. Drone overflights were even happening at night, the remote pilots seeing the way with infrared receptors. Explosives and nerve agents were dropped on any groups found in the streets.

Dargon became more active. People were projecting his image onto walls with their communicators and all communicators in range were hijacked to broadcast his voice. In a crowd, the effect was overwhelming. It was total war: the Council against the people.

As a result of their brutal tactics the Council won again. Gradually, order was restored, and life carried on with some semblance of normalcy.

The funeral business thrived. The day Angus was interred, there were over a hundred other funerals happening and his was barely noticed. Hundreds of unidentified bodies were dumped into a pit and incinerated.

Later, I heard on the news that my three co-workers died inside the safe. The feature that made it fireproof was an airtight door. They must have suffocated in less than an hour. The interior of the safe obviously reached a high temperature, but lack of oxygen prevented fire inside. The first responders reported that it smelled like roast pork when they opened the safe door the morning after the Justice Building burned to the ground.

I found out later that we lost a full day's transactions but recovered most of them by having outlying regions recycle their submissions. We pulled off that transfer barely in time and Andrew Robertson let everyone believe the files we resettled at Nurena U were lost in the fire so no one would try to destroy them again.

JEREMY
(AGAIN)

I was just switching from the wheeled truck to the hovertruck when Judeth called me on her communicator. She must have pocket-dialled because all I could hear was the roar of a thousand voices chanting "Burn, baby, burn." It showed a large mob below her. Then she must have dropped her communicator because all of a sudden it showed her on a balcony with a fire raging in the building behind her and flames licking out to claim her.

The Justice Building! The north balcony! Got it!

I raced through the streets faster than was possible, knocking a couple of cars aside as I practically flew. I jumped the hovertruck over a larger vehicle, taking half of its roof off. When I got to the back of the crowd, I just jumped up over the outer group and kept the fans on full blast all the way to that balcony. Those bastards wanted to kill Judeth. I didn't care how many I schmucked. I just needed to get to her.

As I swept under the edge of the balcony, Judeth fell into my truck's bed—didn't jump, just fell. One split second later and she would have been in the hands of the mob reaching for her. The hell with them. I just gunned back out over all of them and dropped onto J street. Cars were after me. I bounced from building to building, side to side, so they couldn't get past me. Then I jumped a crowd barrier and smashed down on some Guards.

Once free of the city, I headed straight for our base. A couple of drones checked me out but didn't attack. By the time I got there with no fancy misdirection, I was finally able to check Judeth out. She was a mess. One mucked up arm and unconscious. The medics rushed her into the infirmary and started treating her. I told them if they let Judeth die, I would take them out with her. Ant finally came in and tamed me down. Ant is very big.

Chapter 15

ME AGAIN,
ANTHONY CARTER

Cryptos were in trouble, a victim of their success. It seemed everyone wanted to convert from denues at the same time and there were simply not enough cryptos in circulation. Cryptos were also becoming an international currency. Instead of inflation, we were experiencing deflation. Grant Ames said we needed to abandon the Tag Blocker standard, create millions more cryptos and use them to buy real assets wherever we could buy them, from as wide range of people as possible, to get more cryptos into circulation.

I asked Professor Ames to recruit the best of his graduate program's finance students to participate in a massive purchase of shares of successful companies. With his help, his students set up their own securities trading firm. Two of the students already had their trading licences so the rest were organized into research groups. They were to identify companies that still held their management talent and had a record of profitability before the troubles.

There were nine companies we wanted them to buy into regardless of their circumstances, because their products and services would be critical to our plan.

The research groups started by going through past financial reports of hundreds of firms in the public archives. Once they spotted one that met the threshold criteria, they started interviewing the managers on their communicators. If they could talk to someone senior enough, they would arrange a visit for a personal interview. They played it as if they were completing a course assignment. If they thought the firm could be a worthwhile investment, they brought it back to a group assessment session.

The registered traders started buying shares of firms that passed these group session evaluations, buying on the various securities markets and registering them in the students' names. The students signed blank sale and purchase agreements to protect us from fraudulent activities they might think of. As Fractionals we were not allowed to own these kinds of assets directly, but in this way we could control them.

We paid normal commissions in cryptos to the new securities firm and duplicated that for the students who first brought the investment to the committee's attention. Professor Ames had some very happy students and they were earning a course credit as a bonus. We were also buying massive amounts of denues with cryptos on the open markets to finance the purchases.

Nurena U had an active foundation that managed the money from gifts and legacies given to the university by graduates. We had the Foundation's investment professionals visit the firms the students discovered to negotiate direct purchases of large blocks of newly issued treasury shares, using cryptos. This returned the firms we invested in to financial viability. The companies used the cryptos to increase their cash positions and catch up on their debts, their payrolls and on purchases that inflation and hoarding had blocked them from.

The influx of cryptos allowed the firms to create more attractive payroll packages to retain their best people and to hire great people from other firms that could not match their offers. With this combination of market investments and direct share purchases, we gained control of the companies we cared about without their management even being aware of it.

Soon the securities markets were quoting prices in both denues and cryptos. With the exchange rates swinging wildly and unpredictably between the two currencies. Then the securities markets started quoting prices only in cryptos. In this way, we became the dominant influence in the Nurena's business sector at no cost to us, just by issuing the cryptos necessary to keep the economy moving.

For all practical purposes the Council's currency, the denue, was dead and we controlled Nurena's economy through our proxies, notably Nurena University.

We started buying supplies from companies we controlled, supplies we would need to realize our long-term goal. These purchases accelerated our efforts to get more cryptos into circulation. In particular we needed copper and molybdenum. Large quantities of these critical items were mined by Excelsior Metals, one of the companies we acquired majority control of. We would need thousands of tons of heavy braided copper cable in the future, and we needed copper and molybdenum in our Tag Blocker manufacturing right then.

We also bought control of two cable manufacturers and increased their output of braided copper cable using our excess copper inventories, but kept these companies also supplying their normal customers so no one would notice the diversion.

The resale crypto price for Tag Blockers dropped far below our target of one hundred cryptos as people used cryptos for many other purposes. Our sales volumes of Tag Blockers dropped too. We set a goal of putting enough cryptos in circulation to inflate the price of Tag Blockers back up to the target – by that time 109 cryptos – and the volume back up to match our production capacity. It took a flood of cryptos to do that. More investment opportunities were found. More strategic materials were stored in more abandoned buildings.

The Supreme Council did not take kindly to losing control of the country's currency. They made trading in cryptos a crime, with the criminals required to forfeit their entire crypto holding. Fortunately, our crypto safeguards made that difficult to enforce. The Council had no other crypto source, so their ability to pay their Council Guards almost vanished. With major defections in their ranks, the Guards and the military found their capacity seriously undermined.

Through the Justice Department, we hired many of the better Council Guards officers, paying them in cryptos. They, in turn, recruited many of the better soldiers, also paying them in cryptos. Soon, we controlled the military and the policing of the country. Most of the remaining soldiers just faded away, since the Council had no way to pay them. Some formed criminal gangs, preying on their fellow citizens. They became our main law enforcement problem.

We wanted a peaceful and orderly country just as much as the Council did, but we didn't use their draconian methods. For all practical purposes the Supreme Council was dead. Now Dargon was our problem, not theirs, as this holograph ranted on communicators and walls. Fortunately, the people behind Dargon still ranted about the Council. Maybe they didn't realize the country's power structure had shifted. If they could be classified as anything, they were anarchists.

We now controlled the military and the police, had a lever on the justice system, and had, for all practical purposes, eliminated the legislative power of the Supreme Council. We were the major force in commerce. Not bad going for a group of less than 500 non-citizens.

Things settled down as the reviving economy brought back some semblance of fairness, even though times were tough, goods were scarce, and the overall economy was slowing down. At least the vast pockets of wealth were eliminated in the changeover to cryptos, so the remaining resources were more evenly shared around. A majority of citizens were actually better off in the short run than they had been before cryptos took over, although elderly pensioners were generally worse off.

Pensions and retirement investments were mostly wiped out. We offset this by starting a universal minimum income plan that at least provided sustenance for everyone. To finance it, we shifted the target inflation rate up to 5% and let the general public know this was a target, not a sign of the previous hyperinflation of denues. This let us release 5% more cryptos into circulation each year to pay everyone an income supplement. We did not have any taxation powers and the Council no longer had enforcement powers.

An era of relative peace settled in that lasted several years, although there were occasional clashes between Dargon's mobs and the police forces. Migrants, particularly from Caprico, were an increasing concern, with the weakened military less able to cope.

Read that as our police forces, our military.

Gangs made up of former Council Guards continued to plague us. What made it all possible was that a majority of citizens came to see our police in a favourable light and started relying on them when help was needed.

CHIEF JUSTICE, THE HON. ANDREW F. ROBERTSON, BA, LLB

The loss of our friends and fellow employees was devastating. We all grieved for the four of them. I was especially desolate over losing Judeth. She was a beautiful, intelligent young woman whom I loved as the daughter I never had. Maybe it was more than that, but I would never admit it. I still love my wife of fourteen years, the mother of our two sons.

Then Jeremy brought the news that Judeth was badly hurt but safe in the migrants' infirmary in the badlands. He even admitted that he was the hovertruck driver who saved her. To tell me that he must really trust me, because my having that knowledge could be dangerous for him. Of course, then I knew where Judeth was. I was inside that mountain once. I asked if I could have Judeth back and Jeremy said why not, as long as I didn't mind that she was a Fractional and as long as I could protect her.

What a shock! No wonder Anthony seemed to know, intuitively, how to deal with me with well-thought-out answers for each of my objections. I thought about it, I really thought about it. I finally saw it as an advantage. Judeth could be my conduit to my new allies, and I loved her. To save my soul, I loved her.

I told Jeremy that I wanted Judeth to come back and work with me for the betterment of the country. Three weeks later, Jeremy rolled a radiant Judeth in a wheelchair into our secret new offices at Nurena U, still wearing a cast on her right arm. Jeremy reminded me that there was still a warrant out for Judeth's arrest and that the Guards weren't too picky about the "dead or alive" part – whichever was easier. We set up a bedsitting room for her right in the athletic complex so she would never be exposed to discovery.

For a while, the justice business was very busy as citizens' trust in the new-style Guards increased and they were willing to testify against the gangs of ex-Guards and other criminals. It helped that we assumed new operating rules that favoured ordinary citizens rather than the rich and powerful that the actual laws favoured. Of course, we could not change the laws, but we could choose which laws to enforce. Creating laws was the province of the vacated Supreme Council, who weren't meeting anymore. It was too dangerous with Dargon's mobs searching for them.

Chapter 16

DR. MARTHA JACKSON, BA, MA, PHD.
(PRESIDENT, NURENA UNIVERSITY)

We started recruiting doctoral students and stealing a few outstanding young professors from other universities. Juanita's list was 80% women. I got the impression that the bar was higher for men than for the women, although everyone on Juanita's list was outstanding.

With our endowment funds bursting with cryptos and corporate investments, our offers were irresistible. In addition, we were offering placement in what was clearly the best-financed and most prestigious university on the planet. To some of our recruits, the second consideration was more important than the first. Not one invited person declined, and our recruiting people had the sad task of turning down unsolicited applications from some very good people who weren't on the list.

Of course, a substantial portion of our endowment fund's investments were actually directed by our benefactors through Juanita's proxy doctoral students, but even those investments were earning good returns. Juanita's doctoral students were holding their own academically too. She had trained them well. These students developed into natural leaders, holding prominent places on the student councils and on several university committees.

Research projects started exploring intergalactic travel and autonomous robotics. Heavy emphasis was placed on mathematics and physics as well as on engineering. Ant's group took over an almost derelict starsled launching facility north of the city and started redeveloping it as a satellite campus of Nurena University. I was directed to put millions of cryptos into this project to create an experimental site. Doctoral students and young professors rotated through it, conducting the practical part of their studies and research.

My job description had really changed. I was no longer on the road begging for money and had time to pay attention to what was happening at the university. I visited the remote campus once as part of my new-found duties and was amazed. Our cryptos had built a large facility with fine buildings, reading and study areas, private ensuite bedrooms, serious recreation facilities, fine dining areas and an enormous empty cavern of a building.

New paved roads were laid out and new power lines disappeared into the distance toward Norland Electric's nuclear generating station. The electricity control room at the remote campus was more complicated than anything I had ever seen. The cables and switch boxes were enormous. I eyeballed the thickness of one copper braided cable and guessed it at thirty centimetres in diameter. Everyone seemed enthusiastic in their work, including the large number of tradespeople working on the continuing development of the site.

I recalled from an investment committee meeting that Nurena University had a significant holding in the shares of Norland Electric. Interesting.

Back at the main campus the next day I was confronted by the issues of protecting Andrew Robertson and the justice system. They had managed to move their operations onto our campus, but at a terrible cost. Also, we no longer had athletic facilities, which really bothered some students and some parents. I couldn't give the real explanation, the move of the justice system to these facilities, so I blamed it on the renovations which were actually happening.

Hearing of the loss of four of Andy's most trusted employees was ter-rible. In a strange turn of human emotions, hearing later that one of the four, Judeth, had been saved somehow turned the tragedy into a muted celebration. It was as if death had been cheated.

Nurena University developed a new faculty called The Nurena Police College. We drew in some of the best members of the Guards as instructors and shifted some faculty over from other social science disciplines. Our students were all young people drawn from the general population. This sat well with the existing Guards as the expansion gave them opportunities for advancement in their new careers. The makeup of the Guards patrolling the streets started looking more like the makeup of the general population as new graduates took over the lower-level policing responsibilities.

We also ran extensive refresher courses for existing Guards—really retraining courses, if truth be told. These courses were well received since the credits helped the participants earn promotion. Although laws could not be changed, enforcement was changing. Among other things, migrants and Fractionals were no longer hunted or detained. This made Andrew's protecting Judeth much easier, although Dargon's mobs were still dangerous.

Chapter 17

ANTHONY CARTER
(BACK TO ME)

We took over a remote starsled launching site by simply walking in and offering to absorb it into Nurena University's payroll and benefit systems, which paid in cryptos. The site was understaffed because of voluntary departures so we could put our own people in some key positions. By agreement, the top administrator there kept up all the reporting protocols and no one at their headquarters ever knew of the change in management.

The plan was coming together, slowly but surely. Two years ago, Juanita moved out of our base and began overseeing the development activities at this rejuvenated launching site, now a satellite campus of Nurena U. Getting her there was a nightmare. Finally, she accepted being drugged and sleeping through the transfer. It was the only way she could tolerate being in the badlands. She started running the technical aspects of our project from there, fully hands-on.

Nita, our oldest daughter and now a nuclear engineer, was studying for an advanced degree in the Nurena U doctoral program. She earned that place on her own, no influence needed. Nita stayed with her mother whenever she was posted to the satellite campus. Our next child, Anton, named after his grandfather, was admitted into the advanced mathematics/physics undergraduate program. Although none of our children could match Juanita's extreme genius, her genetic influence seems to have resulted in five very intelligent human beings. Anton is called Ton by his friends. He is almost as big as I am.

I had to stay at our base in the badlands to juggle the business side of our plan. I sorely missed being with Juanita, but our separation was much harder on her. Without me holding her, her night terrors came back. Her doctor at the remote campus wanted her to take drugs to sleep but she refused, saying she needed all of her brain fully functioning to pull off her part of the project, because it was so complicated.

I had to divert more than our normal allotment of copper, molybdenum and several other metals from regular customers, which was difficult to explain since we weren't advertising what we were doing. The change in law enforcement by the police, treating us like people, made my work easier and safer.

I spent time at the Norland Electric nuclear generating station sorting out who was who. One small step in the plan was having our people take over control. The top supervisor was well past retirement age, so I arranged a generous buyout for him. Now I needed to choose a successor I could control. The plan involved doing something illegal.

I conducted several interviews and identified a middle manager whose integrity was clearly for sale. Next I had to clear the path upward for her by eliminating or arranging lateral transfers for the three remaining managers above her in the management hierarchy. I wanted to make her seem like an appropriate choice to deflect curiosity.

First, I offered retirement buyouts for the older two, citing a need to cut costs (a lie). They accepted as they should have – my offers were stupendous. I arranged a lateral transfer for the third manager to become chair of The Nuclear Safety Board, a global organization. I did this by offering the board very generous funding through him. Deal! Done!

We were now spending so many cryptos on the various payrolls for the Justice Department, the police function, Nurena University, the military and our main project that we had to reverse the trend and have Nurena U start selling assets to take cryptos back out of circulation and hold inflation down to our 5% target. As the project accelerated, we needed to spend more cryptos on it, millions more. Nurena U's asset disposals also accelerated, leaving them holding billions of cryptos. Some of Grant Ames' graduate students, a new generation, were recruited to help with the asset disposals, earning commissions and a course credit.

Originally most of the assets went for more than the university paid for them back in depressed times, but the capital gains gradually got smaller in the rush to maintain balance in the cryptos markets. Then we had to slow down the disposals to prevent prices from descending into fire-sale range. But we needed to keep on issuing and spending larger and larger amounts of new cryptos, putting them into circulation through enormous purchasing transactions for our project. Fortunately, the crypto float was so large by then that the imbalance did not show up immediately as hyperinflation.

With the development and design phase of our never-before-seen transport vehicle largely completed, we needed to complete the construction phase. Juanita named her vehicle Starseeker. This enormous machine was designed to carry its passengers to the nearest stable galaxy, a far more complex challenge than previous migrations to other star systems in our own galaxy. Among other issues, we did not have the luxury of sending advanced preparation proxies ahead.

We started by levelling an area of about two square klicks. By levelling, I mean really levelling. Level to a tolerance of one millimetre, adjusted for the curvature of the planet. Grading required massive tamping down so the entire area was equally stable and could carry heavy loads.

Next, the entire graded area was paved, so heavy equipment could move freely over it.

Two of our manufacturing facilities started building the 3,142 large curved stainless-steel reflector plates that, when assembled, would form a single parabolic reflector over a klick in diameter. The focal point of this reflector would be the place where Starseeker would sit before launch.

Each reflector plate was mounted on a sturdy stalk and equipped with a heavy remote-controlled electric adjusting motor with gyroscopic controls. These stalks were mounted on enormous remote-controlled tractors. The finished parabolic mirror had to adjust itself constantly, so it was re-aimed each night at a dim star that was, in fact, the far distant galaxy.

We never got a hundred percent of them accurately positioned, but Juanita said 98% of them aligned would be enough.

Although each unit did not make much noise, the combination made a shrieking, deafening sound. We needed to use our communicators set to proximity/conference and headphones to talk to each other. The entire system was controlled by a complex computer program Juanita wrote.

There was a window of only six days when a clear path would exist through to the outer edge of our galaxy toward this far-off galaxy. On each night, the effective launch time was only seven milliseconds, so extremely fine calculations were necessary. If we didn't launch during these six days, the next clear path window would not open for thirteen years.

Clouds of dust and pollution often dimmed the night sky, interfering with light transmission. That could make launching dangerous.

Starseeker was designed to travel more than two million lightyears across empty space, carried in a burst of light, then use its autonomous intelligence to unerringly find and descend on a planet that was immediately habitable for its passengers. That was enormously more complicated that just aiming a starsled at a predetermined planet in our galaxy after sending autonomous robots ahead to make preparations.

Specialized contractors were recruited from all over the planet. We continued to stockpile shielded copper cable. The Starseeker construction activities used up most of our molybdenum and other rare metals, so purchasing those materials also accelerated. It was now a race against time to get it done before the markets or Dargon or hordes of migrants caught up with the new dynamic.

Unrest was overwhelming the planet as food scarcity became panic and productivity vanished. Dargon's mobs were increasingly dangerous. Economic and environmental migrants counted in the hundreds of millions around the globe, and regional battles became genocides. News reports showed thousands of corpses piled up against barriers with people scaling over them to get to the top and then falling back to join the piles of corpses below.

Drought was all-pervasive. Climate migrants joined the economic migrants. Mobs from Caprico were overwhelming Nurena's borders and their spread was advancing toward Nurena's heartland, despite the army's best efforts to stop them.

Food was so scarce that entire species of animals and edible plants were wiped out, eaten. Rumours spoke of widespread cannibalism as enemies and recent allies became sought-after food. People were eating anything they could, and many died from ingesting poisonous plants and animals.

Parents were killing their children to save them from suffering and starvation, before killing themselves.

Nuclear weapons were in widespread use around the globe as better situated people tried to kill entire populations of those in uninhabitable zones trying to migrate. In some instances, migrant groups succeeded in wiping out the populations in habitable zones, only to move in and find that the areas they won by genocide were no longer viable because of the radiation poisoning they caused. Nerve gases and biological agents were being used to depopulate potential migration areas on one side and to obliterate potential migrants on the other.

Carbon dioxide reached poisonous levels as enormous fires tipped the atmospheric balance, depleting oxygen levels further. The reduced oxygen contributed to the creation of carbon monoxide, a deadly poisonous gas. Red blood cells, carriers of oxygen to all the cells in our bodies, prefer to absorb carbon monoxide over life-giving oxygen, and our body's cells die without oxygen.

Policing was no longer possible in most parts of the country, although Nurena City remained somewhat stable. Andrew moved what was left of his police forces there. Any semblance of social order was already history everywhere else.

Chapter 18

JEREMY
(ONE LAST TIME)

It was getting more and more dangerous out in the badlands as gangs and individuals moved around, trying to survive. I was doing double duty, still keeping up the Tag Blocker supply and shuttling people and other shit between our base and the new campus. New roads connected the new campus with the city and traffic was moving on it day and night, so I had that to contend with that too.

Ant arranged for powerlines between the remote campus and the Norland Electric nuclear generating station. There were no roads, so Ed and I ended up ferrying engineers over all that territory too. One time a drone actually fired on me but missed because I was making jinxy moves. I was so damn mad I wobbled the hovertruck like I was hit and ran right up the side of a mountain to slow down.

The drone crashed into the mountain just above me. Its wings crumpled and it slid down past me. Those drone pilots need better training.

The Guards were mostly on our side now. I carried ID that said I was a Nurena U employee assigned to a geographic research project. Damned if I knew what a geographic research project was, but the Guards captain who flagged me down didn't know bupkis, so we were even, and at even I'm damn good. I didn't need to pay him off and he escorted me past a bunch of Dargon rowdies, right out there in the boonies.

I got to take Judeth back into the city to keep on working for Dandy Andy, that smooth-talking bastard with his eye on my Judeth. I thought me taking her out after the riot was the end of that, what with there being a warrant out for her arrest. Dargon wanted her too and posted a five thousand crypto reward for her head. Not dead or alive, just her head. Bastard! Everyone was after her.

On the run in, we were chased twice by unidentified hovercraft and buzzed once by a drone. We had to detour around a firefight between who knows who and we were stopped at the city gate. Shit! The sergeant recognized Judeth. I was just about to pull my weapon and fight out of there when she smiled and congratulated me on the run over that bastard Dargon's mob. She approved! Instead of fighting I went back after dropping Judeth off at Nurena U and we got drunk together. Fine woman. Pleasant night.

Getting Juanita from the base to the campus was a strange experience for me. Ant was with us as we crossed at night. Juanita was asleep in Ant's arms in the back row of seats. He made me drive slowly and cautiously, a new experience. We spotted other craft on the move twice and Ant made me pull aside, once into a ravine and once into small side opening, until they moved on. I am not used to hiding.

The launch was spectacular. I was fifty klicks away coming back for the last load of people when a blinding light swept across the entire horizon. A thin, bright flash split the sky a fraction of a second later. It was bright in my eyes for minutes, or that's what it seemed like. The boom was deafening a few seconds later. I barely got to full rev before the ground swell rolled past underneath me. I was almost thrown out of my hovercraft. The kids were on their way.

Seconds later the power station blew, but I was still deaf and didn't hear it. Once I could see again in the early dawn I went into full thrust. We were in the worst scenario we imagined, and I had to get Juanita, Ant and the two supervisors out fast, or they would be radioactive toast.

Chapter 19

(ME AGAIN)
ANTHONY CARTER

I gave up trying to juggle the doomed economy and retreated to the satellite campus to be with Juanita for the grand finale. Construction of Starseeker was complete. The bunker, located two klicks from the campus on the side farthest from the nuclear generating station, was ready. Our last task was laying the shielded copper cables over the ground between the nuclear station and the launch site. The junction boxes were higher than a man. It took two days even with the special cable laying equipment. We were finally ready.

Juanita's and my children boarded Starseeker. All the other children and young adults from our colony boarded with them. Some children of the group that remained with us at the launching station boarded. All but two of the doctoral students and junior professors, among the best minds on the planet, boarded. Those two backed out at the last minute, making room for two standbys. Every one of the passengers was less than thirty years old. In total, Starseeker could hold exactly 1,024 passengers.

Our suborned administrator had already evacuated the staff from the nuclear station by arranging a false meltdown signal. Only our four Fractionals remained to divert the station's entire electric output to our launching site.

We retreated to the bunker. Juanita threw the lever. We had no windows in the bunker, but the glow was so intense some light penetrated the heavy steel and concrete walls. The bunkers were soundproofed, but a heavy rumble rolled through the ground, causing the bunker to shake. Everything jumped around. We were all thrown to the floor. The two supervisors were injured, but not seriously. I caught Juanita and held her.

An hour later, when things settled down, we went out to look at the damage. The satellite campus was in shambles, destroyed. Many of the copper cables laid the previous two days had melted. The copper from the overhead transmission lines was just splashes on the ground. A few of the reflector plates were shattered and those near the centre had morphed from their bright silver finish to a softer copper colour.

The nuclear station was now really in meltdown. The glow over the horizon was bright enough to be seen in the early dawn. Our four volunteers, who knew this might be their fate, had to be dead. The city would be without power forever, with the exception of a few local fusion generators.

Starseeker was gone, our children were on their way to a stable galaxy 2.2 million lightyears away, if Juanita and her team had got it right. There were no test drives on this venture.

We pulled our personal belongings together and boarded Jer's hovercraft for the journey back to our base in the badlands. We needed to move fast, before radiation fallout from the meltdown caught up with us. We heard later that the light from the launch was brighter in the city than our star's light at high noon, blasting across the horizon at ground level. Many people suffered temporary blindness. A brilliant narrow flash of light split the sky reaching into the stratosphere, while actually only milliseconds in duration, it imprinted on peoples' retinas for minutes. The sonic boom shattered thousands of windows and some structures. The earth shook as if in an earthquake and monitors recorded 6.7 on the Richter scale.

The main campus of Nurena U was overwhelmed by Dargon's mobs when the fusion generators overloaded and cut out, shutting down the protective barrier. We didn't anticipate that. Obviously, the backup fusion generators weren't powerful enough to maintain it. Hundreds of students, professors and administrators died in the riot. The Justice computers were destroyed when the buildings were gutted by fire.

We assume that both Judeth and Andrew died there, since we never heard from them again. Jeremy died over and over and over on communicator news broadcasts for the next two days, trying to save his Judeth one last time. The broadcast showed his hovercraft exploding from the force as laser beams struck it, with him tossed through the air to smash headfirst into a wall. It must have happened less than an hour after he dropped us off at our base.

The next week the communicator network blanked out, never to broadcast again. Juanita said it wasn't the satellites so the studios must have fallen to Dargon's mobs.

A few of our spies worked their way back to our base over the next few weeks. The city, the last outpost of sanity, was in its death throes. The planet for all practical purposes was finished.

We paid an enormous price to get our next generation away, in both effort and the lives of some of our best people. Our hosts paid an even greater price, which we exacted from them to make our plan work. I am sure our children's intergalactic migration would not have happened if Nurena had accepted our people, a mere 128 migrants, into their society. We would have just been absorbed and disappeared.

That was fifteen years ago. We all chose sterilization years before that, so no more children would be hostage to our lives. Our base is a hollow, sterile place without children. We have all grown old. Eleven years younger than me, Juanita died last year. We went to bed as usual with her warm body snuggled in the crook of my arm. Toward morning I realized she was cold. She had slipped away in her sleep without so much as a murmur.

I miss her warm body snuggling against me in bed. I miss her head on my shoulder in sleep. I even miss her hair tickling my nose in the middle of the night. Most of all I miss my daytime conversations with my amazing, intelligent, beautiful life-partner.

Radiation has killed all life on the planet, except on our base. Our last fusion engine quit forever two days ago. Our only electricity now comes from depleting batteries. Our masking barrier is gone. There are no more electronic signals on this dead planet for it to block anyway, but radiation is flooding in.

We have formed a suicide pact rather than suffer prolonged and painful deaths from radiation poisoning. I must close this journal now and go to the parade ground for our last gathering. I don't know why I bother with a journal anyway. There will be no one left to read it.

I hope against hope that our children are safe and settled. But wait, they still have over two million years in my time frame left to travel, although it will only be an instant in their time frame, travelling at the speed of light. It is a paradox, and there is no way to know.

Section 3
Growing Up

I am the luckiest of the lucky, born in a stable, prosperous country at the best of all possible times for me: 1933, the depths of the Great Depression. There were not a lot of children born in my decade. My father was a fully employed university professor, so we were relatively affluent. My parents gave the four of us love and guidance, and we had two full sets of grandparents a short walk away who also loved and cherished us.

All my life, an enormous cohort of Baby Boomers trailed a generation behind me. Finding jobs, even careers, was easy since there was not much competition. Hordes of Boomers waited for my left-behinds at every step of the way. Starter jobs as they pushed me up the ladder. Starter homes as we expanded our family and needed more space. Looking for larger homes when we were ready to downsize. All the way through to retirement, I rode the front of that Boomer crest. Even in retirement, masses of working Boomers are financing my fully indexed defined benefit pensions.

My maternal grandparents had a cottage on Sparrow Lake in Muskoka, and I spent my first fifteen summers in that idyllic place, only moving on when I was old enough to have a summer job.

To my credit, I know how fortunate I am, and I will always appreciate it. I was not born with a "silver spoon in my mouth," but with something far more important: love, opportunity, health and a decent brain.

Fingers (50 words)

I had two brothers and a sister. One of my earliest memories is of Dad holding out one hand with the fingers fanned out so each of us could hold onto one of them as we walked across streets. I know that is improbable, but it is what I remember.

DUSTY

We had a grey Persian cat named Dusty when I was a small boy. One week, when I was quarantined in my bedroom with whooping cough, Dusty came to visit and stayed my constant companion, snuggling and purring day and night. Dusty helped me weather that storm of loneliness. He never paid much attention to me before that week. He never paid much attention to me after that week.

How did he know I needed him then? Why did he care?

Kindergarten *(50 words)*

I didn't get to kindergarten until April when I turned five. I was bumped into grade one the following September. All of my life I have felt cheated about that. Kindergarten was the pinnacle of my academic experience. Oh, how I longed to go back and have a make-up year.

GRANDMA'S

Grandma's was a wondrous place, full of fascinating things and interesting activities, only a ten-minute walk from our house. There was a windup gramophone that played *The Whistler and His Dog* from wax records the shape of empty toilet paper rolls. It played faster when I wound it tight. As it ran down, the dog's bark descended into basso profundo.

There was the stereoptic viewer that showed me the burial crypts under Paris in full 3D. There was the button jar, containing thousands of buttons of every shape, size, colour and texture, that needed sorting. Miraculously they needed sorting on every visit.

There was the flower-filled back-yard rock garden that extended down into the valley with switchback paths to the bottom, where lawn clippings and dead vegetation were dumped over the fence. There was the cold-frame greenhouse full of green baby plants in early spring while snow still lingered on the ground around it. There was the back screened porch, perfect for a game of Go Fish with the "best" playing cards, on a warm, rainy day.

And there was Grandma. Always there was Grandma. A tiny lady dressed in loose black, with rings on her fingers, bangles on her wrists and a smile on her face. She would focus her entire attention on me as if I was all that mattered in her world.

Every now and then, Grandma invited one of us over for an afternoon visit and dinner. She greeted us at her front door, which was actually on the side of the house. There was always an afternoon's worth of activities waiting.

Her kitchen was full of wondrous aromas. Grandfather Dixon made the solid oak furniture in her cozy dining room and in her living room. There was a magic player piano in a room between them. Usually we ate in the dining room. On hot summer evenings, we ate in a basement dining area populated with ordinary store-bought furniture, where it was cooler.

Once I got to wish upon a star, and it worked! Soon after, I got the schoolbag I wished for.

After dinner on pleasant evenings, we retreated to the back yard overlooking the valley and waited for the double header to chuff and huff as it pulled out of the valley. The double header was a long, long, freight train pulled by two magnificent steam locomotives, each with four large wheels on our side. The engines announced their passing with long, mournful whistles. They released large puffs of steam into the air to tell us the sound was coming soon. We counted the freight cars, sometimes over a hundred of them.

During our visits, Grandfather Dixon retreated to his woodworking shop, also in the basement. One time he came up carrying a superb, detailed carving of a face he named Socrates. Grandfather Dixon used a billet of firewood as his medium. He gave Socrates to me. It is one of my most cherished possessions. After eighty years, Socrates still holds a place of honour on my bookshelf.

MEMO TO GRANDPARENTS

My grandmother was an amazing teacher. She mastered experiential learning more than eighty years ago. Look at what she was doing for me. And oh, how I loved her. I still love her. She is as clear in my mind today as if it was just last week.

You could do the same for the small children in your lives.

<u>The Button Jar</u>: I was learning to classify, big, medium and small, and to use judgment in creating and filling the categories. I was learning to identify colours and interpret shades of colours. I even cross-classified by colour and size. Shape was a nonstarter because almost all of the buttons were round. Estimating quantities—for example, how many small buttons were in a teacup—and counting to verify the estimates was another button jar game.

<u>Go Fish</u>: Go Fish is a memory game.

<u>Victrola (music machine)</u>: The sound effect of lower and lower pitch as the machine ran down gave us a chance to talk about sound waves and decide that bass waves were longer.

<u>Greenhouse (little glass house)</u>: Combined with the rock gardens, the greenhouse gave us a chance to talk about seeds, plants, sunlight, watering, fertilizer and plant maintenance.

<u>The Trains</u>: Learning to count to one hundred was an accomplishment for a four-year-old. The timing between the sight and the sound of the train whistle revealed the difference between the speed of sound and the speed of light. After a discussion, we agreed that the two must have started out at the same time.

Don't say you have no trains in a valley, no buttons in a jar, no windup Victrola, no garden, no greenhouse. My grandmother just used what was available to her. We talked peer to peer, as equals. There must be many learning opportunities in what is available to you. You just need to find them and use them.

GRANDFATHER DIXON

My biological grandfather died when my mother was a young girl. My grandmother took in boarders to help financially. As mother and her sisters approached puberty, my grandmother decided having male boarders was not appropriate, so she gave notice. One boarder, Leonard Dixon, countered with an offer of marriage. The marriage lasted a lifetime.

We shared a duplex cottage with our grandparents. They had separate quarters on one side while we had a large, two-room space on the other. The long summers gave us plenty of time to get to know them.

Grandfather Dixon was a perverse man. Tall, frail, English accent, rubber-soled canvas shoes, limping with the help of a cane he made from a sapling he had trained to his specification. My older brother, Leon, was named after him. Grandfather Dixon had asked my parents to not do this, but they did anyway. For all of his life, Grandfather Dixon called Leon "Jimmy."

Grandfather Dixon made a cedar-plank punt. Every spring we carried it down to the water, where it leaked prodigiously for several days until the planks swelled to seal the seams. Once, when it was full of water, we released some perch into it. While we were at lunch, the fish mysteriously disappeared. When we questioned him, Grandfather Dixon only said he didn't want perch prints all over the bottom of his boat. We never figured out how he did it.

Grandfather Dixon was an avid fisherman. He went out on the lake almost every evening in that punt, with "Jimmy" rowing. Grandfather Dixon's woven cotton fishing line was wound on a small H-shaped wood plank. He paid the line out by hand and worked the lure constantly. When he hooked a fish, he rewound the line on the plank as he brought the fish in. He was extremely successful.

Grandfather Dixon organized us into a platoon. Attention, at ease, present arms, whole drills. Every morning he rapped his cane on our door and it was flag-raising time. We marched, wood rifle over a shoulder, to the flagpole and unfurled it. Every evening it was the reverse, as we took the flag down. Heaven help us if the flag touched the ground.

We played hide and seek in the woods with Grandfather Dixon. He was a hunter in his youth. When we hid, he spotted us every time. He would pretend to walk past us, then poke us in the ribs with his cane. When it was his turn to hide, we never found him. Once he snaked his cane out from a juniper bush to trip me. He was in plain sight but too motionless to see. Another time he scratched a kitchen match to light his pipe, and there he was, right beside me.

Most nice afternoons our parents took us blueberry picking. We hated it, but we were not allowed to opt out. Years later we discovered that the goal was not the blueberries, but to give Grandfather Dixon a quiet time for his afternoon rest.

SPLIT ROCK

The woods behind our cottage were wondrous, with so many mysterious places and secret opportunities to feed our imaginations. There were juniper bushes, covered with poisonous blue berries, that were so big we could lie in their cores and be out of the world, seeing only treetops and clouds. There were almost impenetrable thickets where we could be Stanley and Livingstone. There were stagnant ponds for frogs and toads.

There was an old pine tree that divided into two trunks about twenty feet up. My brother and I could climb to the top of these trunks and start them swaying in synch. We could touch hands on the inbound phase and be fifteen feet apart on the outbound phase. From up there we could see the entire lake over the cottage roof. One time I fell, bouncing down from branch to branch until my legs hooked over the last one. I was swinging with my face no more than six inches from the ground.

There were wild cherry trees infested with tent caterpillar nests that we could dynamite with the small firecrackers our parents didn't know we had. We had to retreat fast after lighting them or get splattered with tent caterpillar guts.

There were dozens of birds of all sizes and colours, with many more hidden in the trees and undergrowth. Grandfather Dixon could identify every one of them by their song. There were garter snakes sunning themselves on rocks, too stupefied to move. The squirrels and chipmunks would stand still until sure of our direction, then scurry off in the opposite direction. The raccoon would look up and simply ignore us.

There were wildflowers we could pick to bring back in bouquets for Mom and juicy raspberries, well named for their thorny branches that raked our arms. The black crow stood sentinel over all of it, warning every creature in the woods of our arrival.

Those woods were our domain, far removed from the grown-up world around us.

And there was Split Rock, a large boulder about fifteen feet high that was neatly cleft in half, revealing the layers of sediment that went into its formation. The split was touching at the bottom and separated by about two feet at the top, creating a narrow space to climb into. Split Rock was our stagecoach as we pioneered the west, our Conestoga wagon as we fought off Comanches, our ship as we fought off pirates, our fort as we play-ambushed cars passing on the gravel road below.

In later times, Split Rock was a hidden place for courting.

Split Rock was, above all, a private, secret place known only to us. Then one late August morning, as they were preparing to return to the city on what turned out to be Grandfather Dixon's last summer at the cottage, I overheard him say to Dad, "I'm going for a walk to say goodbye to Split Rock."

It was his special place too.

LYDIA

Lydia was a twenty-foot long, vintage, white "touring" boat, with an engine in a covered compartment in the bow, separated by a flat windscreen from the open space behind. A drive shaft under the floorboards went halfway to the stern. There was nothing in the open space except a steering wheel connected by wires to a rudder at the stern.

The large in-line engine had small cups complete with butterfly valves on top of each of its eight cylinders. To prime the engine, Dad or Grandfather Dixon poured small amounts of gasoline into each cup, then opened and closed the valves to charge the cylinders. The engine needed to be hand-cranked into action, sometimes taking several tries. I remember Grandfather Dixon filtering the gasoline through his felt fedora, then putting the fedora back on his head.

Lydia was old and tired when Grandfather Dixon and our Dad bought her. She likely dated back to the days of grand hotels when the only access to the lake was by railroad at Port Stanton. The lack of seating suggested that she was a cargo boat. I remember sitting on a large wicker chair as we thundered along at a sedate pace. One time we were lost in fog. We sidled up to an island looming out of the opaque mist and Grandfather Dixon leaned over, put a hand on the island, and announced, "This is Elephant Rock. The cottage is over that way." He was right.

Lydia was mothballed for the Second World War because of gasoline rationing. Using block and tackle anchored to a boulder, and large logs as rollers, Lydia was pulled up onto the rocky shore and parked for the duration of the war.

Soon after the war ended, Lydia was rolled back into the water and tied up to our dock in front of the cottage. Lydia sank to the gunnels overnight. Dad bailed her out, thinking that she only needed to "soak up" to become "watertight." Lydia sank again overnight, and every night for a week. Finally, Grandfather Dixon used his walking cane to punch down through the punky oak keel and reveal open water. Dry rot had consumed the wood.

Dad and Grandfather Dixon built a sturdy log tripod, secured block and tackle under the apex, and lifted the engine out of Lydia. They dragged Lydia away, and lowered the engine into another boat. In the process, they snapped off one of the priming cups. They sold the engine as a functioning piece of machinery, assuring the buyer that the cup could be welded back on and still work.

That was the end of Lydia's touring days, but not her useful life. Parked on the shore, Lydia became a favourite children's play zone. One year she was carried off by the ice of a spring flood. We assumed she was on the bottom of the lake. Two years later we found her on a far shore, filled with dirt and repurposed as a flower planter.

MOM AND DAD

Mom and Dad were so important to me that I can't reduce them to five hundred words or even five thousand words. Dad came over from England with his family at age ten. They were going to emigrate to Australia, but a ship to Canada was available sooner. Before leaving, Grandad Smith took them on a hired car ride, because he thought they would never get another chance to do that in the backward colonies.

Dad enlisted in the Canadian army at age fourteen and had the good fortune to be wounded a month after he arrived in the trenches. Repatriated, he used his veteran's benefits to take an accelerated high school completion course and complete a university engineering degree program, the first person in his family to pursue higher education. He remained in academia all his life and capped his career as the inaugural dean of the higher mathematics engineering science program.

Mom was the second daughter of a branch of a prominent family. Her immediate family was sidelined by the early death of her natural father. Some years later, she acquired a much-loved replacement father, when her mother married Leonard Dixon. Mom was a natural beauty and, although financially poor, was rich in personality and joy of life.

Mom and Dad met when both sang in the Broadview United Church choir, and Dad won her hand in marriage after a vigorous campaign. Their honeymoon was a trip down the Moon River in a bright red, cedar-strip, canvas-covered canoe, sleeping on rickety camp beds in a heavy white canvas tent.

Mom and Dad had four active children, raised free-range to the dismay of our neighbours and relatives. Mom was the disciplinary member of the team. She could be very stern and firm on occasion, but mostly she trusted us to do what was right, and mostly we did. It must have worked, because all of us went on to productive careers, established families, and paid our taxes regularly.

Dad had amazing concentration skills. Once, at the cottage, we asked him if we could go swimming. He was sitting at a folding bridge table in the same room as us, writing row after row of mathematical hieroglyphics in ruler-straight lines. After about twenty minutes of this amazing focus, he put down his pencil and said, "Sure, let's go," as if no time had passed since we asked the question.

Dad was strong on engineer-type projects. One was building a driveway from the township road to the cottage. This required lifting large boulders out of the way using a four-foot steel pry bar, a log tripod, and block and tackle. One time the pry bar slipped, spun through the air and hit me on the head.

When Dad died, we were all surprised by the flood of condolences that came from all around the world. Apparently, Dad was a world-renowned mathematician. How could we not know that? But we didn't.

Projects *(50 words)*

Dad planned construction projects around the cottage for our weekends there. My two brothers would jump in to save him from arduous tasks. I told them to stop interfering and let Dad do them because we weren't done until Dad was tired. Eventually they saw the error of their ways.

Engineer *(50 words)*

An enthusiastic mother once told my father, an electrical engineer, that her young son, Greg, was good at taking things apart, so perhaps he would become an engineer. My father answered, "The question is not whether he can take things apart but whether he can put them back together again."

Misdirection *(50 words)*

My dad, an electrical engineer, was very excited when I asked him to help me build a crystal radio. Perhaps he thought I was following in his footsteps. Wrong. I just wanted to listen to Foster Hewitt broadcasting Toronto Maple Leaf hockey games in my bed after lights were off.

Sayings *(50 words)*

My mother had a saying for almost every occasion. For example, "If at first you don't succeed, try, try again." My father countered that with, "Repeating the same thing over and over and expecting a different outcome is evidence of insanity." Sometimes their sayings were in conflict with each other.

Hitchhiking *(50 words)*

While hitchhiking to the cottage, dark overtook us. I burrowed into a hay pile and slept. My brothers kept trying, finally huddled over a small fire. "Don, we have a ride." Forty freezing miles in a truck bed. A three-mile hike. Breakfast. My weekend was great. They slept through theirs.

Latin *(50 words)*

We had to study Latin. It befuddled me. I had a zero-term mark before the final exam. My Latin teacher stopped me later and asked, "If you pass, will you take Latin next year?" I answered, "No, sir," and got 50%. He didn't even want me in his class.

Hannibal *(50 words)*

Our Latin teacher wrote a Latin language text based on Hannibal versus Rome. It told of how Hannibal crossed the Alps, how Hannibal drove a Roman army into the sea, how Hannibal tried to defend Carthage. If he had written that story in English, it would have been a bestseller.

Brilliant Teacher *(50 words)*

I once had a teacher who made mistakes deliberately. This was a wonderful learning device that kept all of us on our toes, waiting for a chance to correct him. I don't know about the other students, but I aced the exam in what would normally be a dull subject.

Natural Teacher *(50 words)*

I guided the class discussion by who I called on. Then I called on a student who said, "Sir, you have dyslexia," interrupting the flow. I had transposed two numbers on the whiteboard. I don't need to deliberately make mistakes, it comes naturally. I guess I am a natural teacher.

Best Teacher *(50 words)*

The best teacher I ever had taught physics. In a class dealing with air pressure, he had a gallon can of water boiling over a Bunsen burner. He turned the heat off, capped the can, and proceeded. The can started crumpling as the steam condensed. We needed to know why.

Worst Teacher *(50 words)*

The worst teacher I ever had taught chemistry. He stood at the blackboard writing furiously, his back toward us. We

were expected to copy all of it into our notebooks. I soon
discovered it was already in the text, so I stopped copying
and snoozed. I barely passed the exam.

MY FIRST JOB

In our family, each of us took a summer job as soon as we turned sixteen,
the legal age for working. I don't know why it happened; it wasn't man-
dated. It just happened. The money we made was ours to keep. Having
our own money to spend was exhilarating. Having earned it, we probably
developed good money habits that lasted a lifetime.

My first job was digging rectangular holes about ten feet long by six
feet across and ten feet deep. The holes would later be filled with rebar
and cement to become footings for tall, sturdy, hydroelectric towers that
supported large cables carrying high-voltage current from a lakeside generating station to the city.

The work was hard and, in the heat of summer, sweaty. I developed
muscles I never knew I had. Normally we worked in teams of three. We
carved a step on one wall so the bottom digger could throw dirt partway
up, where a second digger then loaded it on his shovel and threw it over the
top. The third digger moved it away to make room for the next shovelful.

One digger, Socos, chose to work alone. He was remarkably good at
the job. He always finished his hole first, then sat in the cool bottom out of
the sun, waiting for the rest of us to catch up. Once he encountered a large
boulder. He broke it up with a sledgehammer rather than wait for the jack
hammer and dynamite team, and he still finished ahead of the rest of us.
Socos had no English and my friends and I were helping him learn.

We ate breakfast and dinner in a Quonset hut and slept in a large bunk-
filled dormitory. The cooks gave us sandwiches to carry for lunch. There
was always tea stewing in a large porcelain-steel pot sitting in an open fire
fuelled by scraps of construction wood. We just added new tea leaves and
new water from a jerry can, but we never threw out the old tea leaves. It
tasted awful, but the older workers seemed to like it.

One day we got a new foreman, Sam. Sam was illiterate. He couldn't
even write his own name. Sam picked me to write his reports, even sign his

name. He rewarded me by letting me sit under a tree all day long, reading. I would have settled for just getting out of the hole to do the reports, but Sam didn't understand that. His only instruction was "If you hear a helicopter, get in one of the holes." When September came, Sam couldn't understand why I was leaving this cushy job to go back to school.

One night back in the dormitory, a drunk threatened my friend with a knife. Socos was on him immediately, disarming him. Socos threw him onto the floor, breaking his arm and said, "Leave . . . boys . . . alone." No one bothered us for the rest of the summer after that.

MY FRIEND JOHN

John was a friend and an irritant for much of my life. We played badminton together. He was not as athletic as I was, but he was canny, placing shots strategically to pull me off-centre, always planning a couple of moves ahead. Intelligent, really intelligent. He was also wild and undisciplined.

I remember the time, as teenagers, when we were drafted to clean up the badminton courts on New Year's Day after a drunken party the night before. As a reward, after we cleared and stacked the tables and washed the sticky floor, we got full possession of the courts for the rest of the day. Unending badminton. No restrictions.

I saw John mixing the dregs from several glasses on a table and drinking the noxious concoction. Before we were finished cleaning up, he dropped out of sight. We thought he was sleeping it off somewhere, maybe in the furnace room. Then we realized his little MG sports car was missing too. Instead of playing badminton, we went looking for him. We checked his parent's house. No car in the driveway. We checked all the likely spots he might get to. Nothing.

About dawn on January 2, we went by his house again and his car was in the driveway, undamaged. Later we asked him where he had been. He had no idea. He could remember the cleanup. He could remember waking up in his bed. He could not remember anything about the intervening hours.

John's parents despaired of him. He was thrown out of every high school he ever attended, including one for incorrigible kids. As the school refunded his parent's money, they said he was the very first student they had ever been unable to deal with. John never finished high school.

John was forever trying out new business ventures. One was a gas station at a busy corner in a large city. I was a student accountant at the time and kept his books for him. He did not have enough self-discipline for that simple task.

One day I got off the bus to walk to his station and noticed a large crowd around his gas pumps. Suddenly, they burst into shouting and joyous hand waving. As I got closer, I saw canvas flaps being pulled down over the windows displaying the pump metre readings. There was a lineup of cars down the street and around the block, all waiting to buy John's gasoline.

John had invented pump poker. There were five digits displayed on his pump metres, two for gallons and decimals of a gallon, and three for dollars and cents. At forty cents a gallon, the dollars rarely got into double digits.

The deal was to drop the flaps over the display, put the pump's trigger lock on, and let the pump click itself off. In this way, every sale was for a full tank. If all five digits showed the same number, the gas was free. He had odds for full houses, five-digit straights, three of a kind, two pairs, one pair, etc. to qualify for discounts on the price.

John was in his version of heaven. Crowds, action, the centre of attention. "Isn't it great, Smitty?" he said. "I've sold two tanker trucks of gas so far today and the third is on its way."

That night I did some calculating. I had taken a course called Combinations and Permutations, so I knew how to calculate complex odds. The next morning on my way to work, I stopped by John's station to tell him the net result of his pump poker game was that he was selling his gasoline for two cents a gallon less than he was paying for it.

"Show me," John said. To his credit, he understood the logic and could follow my calculations, although he had never seen anything like them before, and he agreed I was right. He didn't thank me. He was mad at me. "God damn it, Smitty, you sure know how to ruin a good thing."

But he stopped playing pump poker.

Another time John went into the vending machine business. He was driving a delivery truck when he came across three vending machines that were out of service, with chains and locks on them. Instead of completing his delivery route, he started investigating and found the leasing company that had repossessed the machines. He made a deal to buy them, no cash down, by just assuming the lease payments.

With that, John was in the vending machine business. A good thing too, since he was fired by the delivery company. He had discovered lease to own with no down payment.

John also discovered cash flows. He could fill a vending machine one day and collect his money the next, and he didn't need to pay for the merchandise for thirty or sixty days. John expanded quickly into every corner of his territory that was unserved, making deals to pay a tiny percentage of the take to "rent" locations in all sorts of buildings.

One time, John showed me a beautiful rendering of a sophisticated layout that included a variety of vending machines, microwaves, and a sink. John befriended or paid the municipal clerks of every community in his territory so they would let him know when a new business or commercial building was coming along.

In the instance related to his drawings, he had spotted a plan that called for a complete cafeteria. John paid for the drawings then telephoned the American president of the incoming company and said, "You don't know me, but I can save you half a million dollars. If I fly down will you give me an hour of your time?" Of course the answer was "yes."

John explained that his installation would save the company two thousand square feet of space and considerable payroll costs over the years. He wanted the space he needed rent-free and would use his own employees at his own cost to run his facility. He got the contract.

John's cash flows were huge, so he bought a service station that had been bypassed by a new highway. It once had a restaurant and still had a fully equipped stainless-steel food-processing-quality kitchen. He stored merchandise in the service bays and had five employees making sandwiches and baked goods for his vending machines. He had five service trucks on the road to load his vending machines. He had two coin-counting and coin-tubing machines in a secret vault in his house that were running almost constantly.

John and his family lived like kings. The only problem? His business was unprofitable. In effect he was riding his own personal Ponzi scheme.

As long as his business was expanding, the expanding cash flows covered up the unprofitability. But like every Ponzi scheme, he ran out of expansion opportunities. John had to start selling slices of his business to pay the bills. The downslide went very fast.

John tried to borrow money from a bank. When his request was declined, he came to me to ask for help getting the loan. After looking over his records I tried to explain that his business was a bad risk and, by the look of it, was going down, so he should salvage what he could from the wreck. John got quite angry and our friendship was never the same after that.

John tried several other businesses, including relaunching a decrepit summer lodge, but was never again involved in anything as spectacular as his vending machine venture. Eventually alcohol caught up with him and he retreated into dementia and died of Alzheimer's before his sixtieth birthday.

MY BEST FRIEND

Moe and I were close buddies for much of my youth. Avid badminton players, we could not team up to play as a doubles team because each of us was a dedicated individualist. For several years, Moe pestered me to meet his cousin. I always declined, saying things like, "I don't want to know your dog of a cousin."

One year he tricked me. We were double dating at a sports centre, and he showed up with his cousin, Jean. She was lovely and a lot of fun. She even cannonballed me in the swimming pool. I don't remember my date's name, but I certainly shifted my interest. I dated Jean for ten of the next eleven evenings.

We were married young, Jean twenty, me twenty-two. My aunt lamented at the wedding that we would starve, but we never did. Jean displaced Moe to be my new best friend.

Goodbye Grade Seven (50 words)

Jean taught in a two-room country school. She had students in every grade but grade five. When her grade seven student stopped coming to school, she reported him to her superintendent. After investigating, he reported, patroniz-ingly, that the student quit legally on his fourteenth birthday to work on the farm.

Subsidy *(50 words)*

After two years of teaching in a one-room country school, Jean had to attend a year at a teacher's college. I gave her $20 a week out of my $100 a month salary at Price Waterhouse to help her make ends meet. It was the best investment I ever made.

Student Accountant *(50 words)*

As a student accountant at Price Waterhouse, I earned $100 a month. My future wife, Jean, landed a job paying triple that as a primary teacher in a school in North Toronto where she had practice-taught, so we got married. It is fair to say I was a kept man.

$500 *(50 words)*

Jean and I were married in a beautiful country church. Jean borrowed $500 from her brother to finance the wedding. They argued happily for years about it. Jean said she paid him back. He said she didn't. Now we will never know. The sands of time have washed it away.

Love, Honour and Obey *(50 words)*

Jean asked her uncle to leave out the part where she prom-ises to obey. In the ceremony, he read out the fateful phrase, "Love, honour and obey." Jean parroted the words automati-cally. Later she complained. He said, "Someone has to be in charge. Did you think it should be you?"

Voyeur *(50 words)*

Moe loaned us a car so we could honeymoon at the Sparrow Lake cottage. One day we drove to Algonquin Park. We skinny-dipped in a remote, tannin-brown lake to cool off. A male canoeist paddled by and wouldn't go away. I think he knew Jean was naked under the water.

Don't Cry over Broken Eggs *(50 words)*

Shortly after we were married, while carrying the groceries to our upstairs apartment on the second floor, Jean tripped on the stairs and broke a dozen eggs. We emptied the egg carton into a big bowl, stirred it up, and had scrambled eggs for dinner three times the next week.

Eyes of God *(50 words)*

Months after Jean's uncle married us, she received a letter from the Department of Records asking her to return the marriage certificate since she hadn't used it. Panicked, Jean telephoned her uncle. His response was, "Don't worry. You are married in the eyes of God and that's all that matters."

Garter Belt Quarter *(50 words)*

A button was missing on Jean's garter belt and she was using a quarter as a substitute. One day we were so broke, we needed the quarter to buy a loaf of bread and a quart of milk. We went behind the store so she could take off her stocking.

DRESSING DOWN

I was summoned to the senior partner's office to be chastised. It was the only time he ever spoke to me. He started by pointing out that I had not received the firm's permission to get married. He told me how fortunate I was to be paid a salary, since students in England paid Price Waterhouse for the privilege of being trained as chartered accountants.

Finally, as I was expecting to be fired, he said, "I have talked you over with the other partners and we have decided to keep you. Since you are now married and have taken on increased responsibilities, we are increasing your salary to $150 a month."

My good buddy, Ralph, was incensed that I was making more than he was because he was a far better accountant than I was, and he knew it. In fact, he ended up staying with Price Waterhouse after he graduated and eventually became a partner.

Accidental Placement *(50 words)*

The "Help Wanted" advertisement was for chartered accountant students. On a lark I went for an interview. At the end, my interviewer asked what it would take to hire me. I said $1,000 a month. After thinking briefly, he said, "Deal." I accidentally went from $150 to $1,000 a month.

Same Tactic *(50 words)*

Many years later, an interviewer used that tactic to skim off our top graduating students right in the middle of Interview Week. He would ask, "What would it take to hire you?" If he liked the answer he would stand up, say, "We have a deal," and shake their hand.

LEAF SATURDAY

For the thirty-two years we lived in our house in the woods, the first Saturday in November was Leaf Saturday. Our smallish lawn in a corner of our twenty-acre prime Carolinian forest was populated with several giant oak trees that shed a deluge of tough, dry, brown leaves. Surrounding maple trees made their contribution. The leaves were so thick on the ground we could shuffle through them, making rattling noises.

Howard was always first on the scene. He got up on the roof and raked it clean, then settled in to drink beer, his contribution finished. Our six kids were there. Other guests arrived throughout the early afternoon and between them they took up most of our twenty rakes. Leaves were gathered into local piles and scooped up by the armload. They were deposited on the sand in a wide clearing at the turn in the driveway. In a few minutes a large leaf bonfire was burning. That was strictly illegal, but no one could see us back in the woods.

Rake, drink beer. Rake, drink beer. The air was cold and fresh. The swirling smoke kept wafting around to chase us. Piling on leaves, we smothered the fire, but it always broke through on one side or the other. Sitting in lawn chairs, we savoured the experience late into the night. I always had two huge eight-rib beef roasts in the oven, one medium rare, one medium well, and about three dozen large baked potatoes. Jean and I spent a lot of time in the kitchen.

One year the transformer outside our house blew up with an enormous bang. The lights went out. The roasts stopped cooking. The water stopped flowing. The furnace stopped heating. We called the Hydro emergency line. Five minutes later a bucket truck showed up. Soon after the rest of the crew were there. The crew chief lived in the adjacent subdivision and was at his house on standby with the bucket truck when my call came through.

Once they got our electricity back, they joined the party. People were getting rides up in the bucket. The Hydro guys got as drunk as everybody else. Fortunately, there were no more emergency calls that night. Later, people were sleeping on every couch, chair and carpet in the house. That was our best-ever Leaf Saturday.

NUNAVUT

Our younger daughter, Martha, is a CPA. She has a successful career performing accounting tasks and auditing the financial statements of businesses, municipalities and other entities in the Territory of Nunavut, which straddles the Arctic Circle. One year we decided to visit her. The airplane was a strange hybrid. The front section held about a dozen seats. Behind a partition, the back section was full of pallets of food, machinery, and other goods.

Iqaluit was a strange city of about five thousand residents. There were no laid-out streets. The few cars would just vector to their destination over the rock and gravel terrain. Houses were numbered by the sequence in which they were built. Number 68 could be right across town from number 69. Taxis did not provide exclusive use but would pick up passengers and drop them off as the cars shuttled around. How the taxi drivers figured it out was a mystery to me.

During the week, Martha had to work. We booked a fishing excursion out of Pangnirtung, a small village situated on a narrow plateau at the base of a mountain range. The air strip paralleled the ocean about twenty feet from it. Our host met us and took us to a smallish plate-aluminium cruiser in the harbour. We had to hurry because the tide was going out and the cruiser would soon be landlocked in mud. The trip was only half full, so the outfitter included some family members, a real bonus for us.

We motored out on the fjord and proceeded to Cumberland Sound. Because of adverse ice conditions, even though it was July, we turned in and camped on a low gravel beach. Camp consisted of large white canvas tents that were set up in advance. Our guide carried a rifle with him at all times, in case of polar bears. Apparently humans are part of a polar bear's food chain. The guide set out a rope on self-propping posts to enclose the camp. On the rope he hung jangly things, like empty food cans with stones in them, to alert him if a bear came into camp overnight.

Jean and I went down to the shore near a small stream and cast out into the ocean. We each caught one arctic char. Jean's was bigger than mine. The cook, a family member who was also a lawyer and justice of the peace, fried the fish for dinner. It never got dark, just descended into twilight. There were huge mosquitoes that flew so languidly I could snatch them out of the air.

There were enormous ice shelfs sitting on the beach, stranded by the receding tide. As the ocean drained from under them, they cracked and fell apart. Each time that happened, a sound like a roll of thunder deafened us. All night long, the thunder and the giant mosquitoes broke into our sleep.

One time, Jean tripped on the rope on her way to the bathroom tent, jangling all the noisemakers. Our guide did not wake up.

Run Up *(50 words)*

I went to audit a Bay Street mining company. Up three floors of narrow stairs I found a door listing twenty companies. I was greeted with the question, "Which one this time?" While working, I overheard one of the men say to another, "Which company should we run up today?"

(Note, that was over sixty years ago. It could not legally happen today.)

Section 4
Caughnawana

I was on a fast-track business career in my early thirties and belonged to the Quebec-based Caughnawana Hunting and Fishing Club. We had a hundred square miles under lease from the Quebec government encompassing the headwaters of three distinct watersheds. The central watershed was filled with lake trout (grey trout) and speckled trout (brook trout). The greys could weigh up to twenty pounds, the speckles up to five pounds, and they often did. Another watershed held pike and pickerel (walleyes) and sauger. We called those coarse fish, not worth going after.

I used my Caughnawana membership to entertain the managers and owners of key client businesses and later built a Pan-Abode summer camp on the largest lake for our family to use.

AJ

AJ was a big man in every sense of the word. Not fat, just big. His nickname was Moose. AJ was a member of Caughnawana. He owned a very large camp built with very large logs. The main room was two storeys high with two floors of bedrooms on each side, the upper ones accessed by internal stairs and balconies. In a past life AJ's camp was a Hudson's Bay trading post. The stone fireplace was big enough to walk into and burned whole logs.

We had a loose arrangement with AJ that he would host us, and we would supply all the beer, booze and gourmet food. He could easily afford his own, but he liked to deal. He also liked our company out there in the wilderness, although he never admitted that. AJ sponsored my membership to the club.

AJ flew a rattly old World War II Seabee that he bought at a government surplus auction. He sometimes flew one of us into his camp if the load limit allowed it. On one flight, I noticed that he was following a zig-zag path and asked him why. He said he wanted a lake ahead on his flight path for when the engine failed. Not if, when. If a lake wasn't available, he would select a big tree to settle down on top of.

One year, AJ's doctor told him his health had deteriorated to a degree where the doctor could no longer certify his flying licence. AJ proposed a deal. If he promised to never take anyone up with him again, would his doctor certify him? His doctor, a true friend, agreed. I never flew with AJ again, but he did often fly in our food and alcohol.

After that, I drove in on forty miles of abandoned logging roads in my four-wheel drive Jeep Wagoneer, equipped with a skid plate that protected the engine and transmission from road damage. I had an aluminium boat stored at the landing. That trip in took up to six slow hours, depending on how many fallen trees I had to chainsaw through to clear my way.

After launching and loading the boat at the end of the road, I had to motor several miles across a lake to a portage that led to the lake AJ's camp was on. The club kept a wheelbarrow at the portage. AJ would leave one of his boats on his side. I would unload my boat, trundle the load across to his lake and load it in his boat for the final run to his camp. It seemed the wheelbarrow was always on the wrong side of the portage, half a mile away.

Going back, I carried all our garbage out on the reverse run.

My favourite memory of AJ is the time we stepped out onto his deck to relieve ourselves after excessive beer consumption. A fellow guest and I, both much younger than AJ, produced high pressure arcs surging into the dark. A moment later AJ said wistfully, "I used to be able to do that," as he splashed his shoes.

Help (50 words)

We held our retreat in AJ's old wooden lodge with a walk-in fireplace that burned whole logs. I woke to a strange sound. Our drunken chef was slumped before the dying embers, a bear-skin rug over his naked shoulders, moaning, "Help." He couldn't find his way back to his bed.

Thunder (50 words)

AJ's camp had a metal roof. In one corner, a nail stood above the metal. A woodpecker was drilling on the nail, making the entire roof vibrate, sounding like rolls of thunder. As we covered our ears, AJ smiled and said, "Boy, that guy's going to have a big territory."

MARTINI ON THE ROCKS

One of our Caughnawana members was an Air Canada pilot. On one May 10, while flying the polar circle route from Montreal to Europe, he passed over our lease and radioed back to let us know the ice was out.

Action stations! The best lake trout fishing is just after ice-out, and the best places are the mouths of small streams carrying slightly warmer water into the lakes. We had an arrangement with a local float-plane service to fly us in as soon as their planes could land on water on our lakes. We were at our camp opening it up the next day but arrived too late to mount a fishing expedition.

That night we lubricated our reels and wound new five-pound mono-filament line onto them. We mixed gasoline and oil for the outboards and made sure they were going to start. We sorted out our tackle boxes and applied silicone to our boots. We boasted about our pending exploits. We made sandwiches in case of fishing failure the next day, and we pan-seared sirloin steaks in frying pans for dinner on the cast-iron wood stove. As part of our preparation, we opened a full bottle of vodka and topped up the air space with white vermouth, then recapped it and put it in the freezer of our propane refrigerator.

Perhaps we also drank too much scotch.

May 11 dawned clear and sunny. The temperature was well above freezing. We ate a hearty breakfast of bacon and eggs, washed our dishes, and set out. Jason and I, with our guide, chose to portage over to Green Lake. We had a preferred fishing spot where a stream flowed in from Grave Lake above it.

It took us about half an hour to get to the portage, half an hour to get everything across and get back on the water, and half an hour to get to our spot. As we drifted on the surface of the still, crystal-clear water, it felt as if the bottom was the ground and we were floating on air twelve feet above it.

I cast my line and slowly retrieved, watching the silver lure sparkle in the sun. On my third try, a grey trout shifted from the shadow of a large boulder and ghosted toward it. BANG, yank and the tussle started. Five minutes later, the trout was in the canoe. We caught three more trout over the next hour, releasing the two smaller ones. We used barbless hooks, so we could shake them off without touching or netting them.

Later, just two days away from the hustle and pressure of our business lives, we watched our guide fillet the trout and prepare our shore lunch in a large black iron skillet, over an open fire. We were sitting higher up on sun-warmed rocks, sipping ice-cold martinis from banged-up aluminium cups.

GEFILTE FISH

Joseph, one of our guests at Caughnawana, wanted to catch a big pike to make gefilte fish, a delicacy he and his family enjoyed eating. Our lake system has lake trout and speckled trout in it, but no walleye or pike. Our guide reluctantly agreed to take Joseph to the adjoining watershed, where walleye and pike were abundant.

They set out on a clear, sunny, early May morning, in a light canoe powered by a small gasoline motor. They crossed over our lake and passed through Scudder's Pond, where we only allowed fly fishing. They portaged up over a mountain ridge and down onto South Garden Lake in the adjacent watershed. The guide completed two trips over the ridge, one with the canoe, the other with the motor, in less time than it took Joseph to get to South Garden Lake carrying only his fishing gear.

They got back in the canoe and motored over the calm water to a sunlit underwater sandbar, known as a place where pike warmed themselves after the rigours of winter. Joseph got out a stubby steel rod loaded with heavy copper line wound on a big drum-like reel. At the end of the line, the guide mounted a large silver Williams Wabler with a big barbed treble hook at its tail. The guide baited the hook with a fish head and guts saved from the night before.

They started trolling and on the third pass, less than ten minutes later, a huge pike swallowed the lure. It wasn't really a fight as Joseph cranked the pike in beside the boat, although it took all of his strength to do it. The guide gaffed the pike under the base of its gills and dragged it over the gunwale and into the canoe. The fish was too big to net. They tried to kill it, but pike are tough. Also, the large teeth in their prehistoric, alligator-like mouths and their razor-sharp gill plates are both dangerous, especially in a small canoe.

Once the pike was in the boat, the disgusted guide said, "Now let's go catch some fish," as they started the trek back. Pike and walleye were thought of as coarse and not worth catching.

Joseph huddled, safe, in the front of the canoe; the guide kept clear in the back while running the motor. That poor pike lay gasping, twitching and bleeding, alone in the middle section all the way back to the portage. Finally dead, it added so much weight the guide needed to take three trips over the pass, one just to carry the pike.

When they finally got back to the camp, we weighed it. That pike came in at over twenty-seven pounds. It must have weighed more before it bled out. That wasn't sport, it was meat hunting. From the moment the pike swallowed the lure, it never had a chance.

It would have been much easier to go to the grocery store.

LINE SQUALL

We were fishing for lake trout in a sixteen-foot V-stern canoe one portage out from our home lake. I was running a small outboard motor and trolling, while Gord was casting the shoreline. His casts were a bit wild and he caught some tag alder bushes. Other than that, neither of us caught anything but bottom. The day felt heavy. The wind was fitful, shifting direction around the compass, not even strong enough to blow away the cloud of black flies around our heads.

Our shore lunch was sandwiches, provided by the cook in case of abject failure. We were surrounded by ever more black flies. A whisky jack swooped down and stole half a sandwich right off my aluminium plate.

By mid-afternoon, discouraged, we headed back to camp. Carrying the canoe, the motor and our fishing gear, we trudged across the half-mile portage to our home lake, with mosquitoes replacing the black flies.

Once organized, we pushed off. I soon realized the wind had picked up a lot, but it was pushing us in the right direction. As we cleared the shoreline, Gord shouted and pointed over my shoulder. I looked back. A heavy black line of ominous clouds surrounded by an orange tinge stretched to the horizon.

By then it was too late to go back. If I turned the canoe broadside, the cresting waves would swamp us. As long as I kept the motor going so we moved faster than the waves, the vacuum behind the boat kept the waves from broaching our stern.

There was a small island ahead, barely above the water. Angling slightly, I was able to hit it dead on. The waves were sweeping right over the island. Reaching agreement by hand signal, Gord jumped out on the left and I jumped out on the right as the canoe was also being swept over. We stood on that island with the waves coming up to our crotches and desperately held on to our canoe. The rain was so intense, we were alone in a grey nothing.

Once the height of the storm passed, we could let go of the canoe, but the lake was still far too rough to get back on. We took the opportunity to put on rain suits. Although we were completely soaked, the suits broke the wind.

To pass the time, we started casting down-wind. Our lures sailed out hundreds of yards. We caught a lake trout on almost every retrieve. Every fish in the lake must have sought refuge from the storm in the lee of that island. We kept four beauties and released the rest. We fished with barbless hooks, so we could wade in and to shake them off without touching or netting them.

Finally back at camp, we found that we were the only members to catch fish that day. While Gord and I stood, mostly naked, thawing out in front of the enormous walk-in fireplace, others cleaned and filleted them.

ROY

We were good stewards of the land, keeping it clean and maintaining good policies of fish and game preservation at Caughnawana. We maintained the dams and we employed our own game warden, Roy. Roy was deputized by the Quebec authorities and had official status.

Roy oversaw our territory from a small yellow Champion float plane. One day he spotted four men using dynamite to fish a remote lake, noted for its large speckled trout. Considering it too dangerous to confront them, Roy landed on another lake, hiked over, and while they were out on the lake, disabled their trucks. They had to walk forty bug-infested miles on a bush road to the highway, where the Sûreté, Quebec's provincial police, waited for them.

Roy did short take-offs in his little Champion by tilting one pontoon up first, then levelling to lift the other. This required very precise control, because he was dead if a wing tip touched the water on the tilt. One club member ran out of gas and emergency-landed on a lake too small to fly out of. Roy agreed to try it for $5,000, set out into the trees carrying a can of gas, and succeeded.

Roy told us we could call him down in an emergency by putting a blanket out on the rocks in front of our camp. Another signal was turning our boat in tight circles on the lake. We needed that once, when some of our party took a wrong turn on a portage and disappeared into the forest. Roy came down, heard my problem, and took off again. Half an hour later he came back to tell me he had found them, had landed on a nearby lake, and had sent them on the path to safety. He told me where on the shore I should go to pick them up.

Then, one year, René Lévesque, Quebec's new separatist premier, cancelled all Quebec fishing leases with no management provision. An American fishing and hunting magazine announced the uncontrolled situation. Fifty yahoos descended on our lake on logging roads and fished it out in a week, leaving garbage floating on the water and on every shore. I saw one of them drag a stringer of at least twenty squirming lake trout out of the water and sling them into the back of his truck before he drove off.

Roy, stripped of his authority, retired. The club, stripped of its purpose, disbanded. We sold out, broken hearted, and re-established ourselves on two remote acres carved out of a vast forest preserve on a large lake in northern Ontario. That was over fifty years ago.

In my head I know Roy must be long dead, but my heart says otherwise. Every time a float plane passes over our Ontario camp, my heart knows that is Roy up there, still looking out for us after all these years.

Pan-Abode (50 words)

Eventually we had our own camp building, reminiscent of Lincoln logs. I contracted to have it trucked in, floated across the lake, and assembled. Construction went well except for a roof over the living room when hunting season started. That was left open to the elements until the following spring.

Shore Fishing (50 words)

Our camp had a rocky shore. One time we saw three enormous lake trout feeding where we had cleaned fish. A guest put a twenty-pound test line on his reel, loaded fish guts on a lure, and hooked one. It zinged his line all the way out before it snapped.

Poaching (50 words)

We had misread the French-language fishing guide and were catching walleyes in another watershed hours before the season opened. Roy landed to challenge us, realized who we were, and flew our catch to our camp so other game wardens would not cite us as we drove back to our lake.

Clash (50 words)

Slowly, slowly, the cat crept forward. The squirrel, oblivious, continued collecting nuts. I could only tell the cat was moving by the closing gap. Zoom! A hawk dropped out of the sky. Cat and hawk confronted, shocked, as the squirrel scolded from a thicket at the base of the tree.

Tingley (50 words)

We closed the camp, crossed the lake and hitched up the boat before our four-year-old daughter said, "Dad, we forgot Tingley." Tingley was her favourite stuffed animal. I told her Tingley was guarding the camp over the winter. She bought it. We drove home with a proud, happy little girl.

A Better Lesson (50 words)

Our cat, Nudge, got stuck up a cedar tree. I rescued him. A second time, the same routine. Third time, a bristly lakeshore spruce. Using my chainsaw, I felled the spruce and Nudge into the lake. Nudge, looking like a drowned rat, streaked past us, and he quit climbing trees.

FOLLOW THE RUGGED ROAD

One of our writing group challenges was to write a poem. This is my effort. It tells of a mosquito-infested night portage through a wilderness in late August, navigating by the light of a full moon. My four-year-old son was riding on my shoulders as we stumbled along, watching and listening to wide V's of Canada geese migrating south.

On the forest trail
As we marched along
From *The Wizard of Oz*
He sang this song
Follow the rugged road
Across the shining moon
In the fading light
Geese forming a V
In their south-bound flight
We followed the rugged road
Over rises and roots
We stumbled our way
Crossing to our lake
At the end of the day
He sang, follow the rugged road
Now high on my shoulders
As we marched along
Mosquitoes buzzing loud
Still he sang his song
Follow the rugged road
Finally safe in the boat
My four-year-old son
In his mother's arms
Was finally done
Following the rugged road

Section 5
Onaping

Some years after the disappointment of losing our place at Caughnawana, Jean and I re-established a family summer escape on Onaping Lake in northern Ontario. By then we were both teachers, her in a primary grade, me in a university. We loved our careers. We enjoyed many happy summers at Onaping as our six children passed through their teen years to grow into fine, tax-paying adults.

THE SEARCH

Jean and I and a canoe investigated several largish lakes in northern Ontario, finally settling on Onaping, a lake made up of smaller lakes and connecting rivers brought together by a series of dams. It was created by the E. B. Eddy Company as a reservoir to maintain water flow down the Spanish River to float its logs on.

We accessed Onaping through Ladisseur's Landing, owned by Lionel Ladisseur, a long-term local resident. E. B. Eddy tried to stop Lionel from putting in docks, because the company did not want its lake taken over by cottagers. Turned out the higher lake levels flooded some of Lionel's land and his docks were on his land. End of argument. The judge even assigned Lionel's costs to E.B. Eddy.

Jean and I puttered around Onaping for three summers, camping at various places along the shore. Onaping is beautiful, stretching forty-eight miles end to end, with bays and hidden sanctuaries to get lost in on the way. By the third summer, we had found most underwater rocks the hard way, by shearing the pin on our tiny propeller with every hit. One summer Jean forgot the oatmeal, so no traditional breakfasts, but fishing was always good, so we ate a lot of fish for both breakfast and dinner.

Onaping is in an enormous forest preserve. There was no chance of buying a piece of land and starting from scratch. Perfect for us, no new neighbours possible. In the upper twenty-five miles there were only fifteen or twenty camps, so our choice was limited. We spotted half a dozen remote camps up the lake that we would like to own.

With so few camps on this magnificent lake, new broker listings never went public. Each broker had a list of locals looking for them. Once we had identified our shortlist of desirable locations, we went to the biggest Sudbury broker to play the game their way. The following winter we got the call. A new listing eighteen miles up the lake. A plywood shack on two acres on a side bay.

The broker was shocked when I said we would take it and arranged to sign the offer by fax that day. He asked, "Don't you want to see it?" I assured him we already had seen it and it really suited us. In fact, we had stopped for lunch on the overgrown area in front of the building one sunny August day the year before.

Later we discovered more of its history. The owner of a bush air service out of Peterborough had spotted it from the air forty years earlier, and he also thought it perfect. In those days a citizen could stake a wilderness lot, build a four-hundred-square-foot building on it, and claim title to it. We found one of his original hand-carved corner stakes. He brought the building materials in by tractor over winter logging roads and across the frozen lake. He landed his float plane periodically each summer to build his "shack."

BULLDOZER

Our son, Victor, paid his way through university framing townhouses. He put a crew together each spring and bid on summer construction contracts. One Christmas he gave us an unusual gift: a weekend of his time. Jean and I picked the August long weekend and planned a project, constructing a building at our campsite on Lake Onaping.

We already had a small, worn-out plywood shack on the best location. We selected a secondary site up the hill, which needed a lot of grading, to erect what would eventually be our secondary building. In May we located a local contractor who took on remote projects and hired him.

One evening at the beginning of July, the contractor's bulldozer came walking across the water toward us. It was on a raft made up of six 200-gallon oil tanks and it had a two-inch clearance. Waves were washing over the tread bottoms. Pushed by a fifteen-horsepower motor, the trip up from the landing took him nine hours.

I asked him how he knew the raft would float the bulldozer. He answered, "My sister is an engineer and she said it would, but I think she forgot about the diesel fuel."

I asked him, "What would you do if your raft sprung a leak or tipped?" He pointed to the small aluminium boat the raft was towing and then to the fishing knife in a sheath on his hip. "I just jump in that boat and cut the rope. Then I look around and hope no one is watching, because if they are, I might have to get the bulldozer back up."

I asked him about the cost of a lost bulldozer. His answer, "I'm a large engine mechanic. I salvaged this machine from an abandoned logging camp. They just drove it into the bush and left it. I fixed it and drove it out. If I lose this one, I know where there are six more."

He went to work, moving large rocks, rolling aside enormous boulders, shifting a lot of sand. He also dug holes for two septic tanks and the trenches for the weeping tile. When it comes to bulldozer drivers, he was a virtuoso. The next day he brought two septic tanks and buried them. Each was made up of two 200-gallon oil tanks joined by high and low pipes, all welded together.

On one pass his machine hit the corner of our existing building, almost knocking it off its pilings. A cloud of bats, thousands of them, flew out screaming. I can tell you with certainty that bats can make sounds humans can hear. After a while, the bats came back in a cloud and disappeared under the overlapping side boards. We looked later and could see their tiny claws clinging to the bottom edges of the boards.

He even carved a gap in a gravel bank so we could insert the world's finest outhouse, then backfilled around it. Our site was ready.

INTO THE DEPTHS

We were organizing to construct a new building at our remote campsite. I once had a magnificent eighteen-foot green freighter canoe powered by a reliable five horsepower Evinrude outboard motor.

I had a truckload of cement blocks delivered to the landing at the end of the road, to be used for the building's foundation piers. Our campsite was eighteen miles up the lake, very remote. Each time I left the landing to head up the lake, I took a load of the cement blocks with me. That canoe could carry quite a few blocks but carrying them really slowed the trip down.

One sunny afternoon, I decided to take an extra-large load because the lake was so calm. When I was partway up the lake, dark clouds moved in and the wind picked up. Soon I had to aim the canoe directly at the wind and the waves to keep wave tops from spilling over the gunnels. I tried to angle toward shore but could not pull it off, missing by, maybe, fifty feet.

Then I was past the promontory and the wind and waves started hammering me from two directions. Wave crests started spilling into the canoe from both sides as I tried to split the difference. I started bailing like mad. Then waves were spilling in, not just their crests.

I shut down the motor so drowning it wouldn't ruin it. By then it was getting dark and I needed a flashlight to see what was happening. I grabbed a flotation cushion just as the canoe submerged with a loud sucking sound. I watched it disappear into the depths with the flashlight still shining on the way down, until it was out of sight.

I tried swimming toward the near shore, but the wind and waves were too strong. I decided instead to just float to the far shore half a mile away. As I started doing this, the outboard motor's gas tank burst out of the lake beside me and jumped clear of the water. The hose must have uncoupled somewhere down there. That tank almost landed on me when it came back down. If it had hit me on the way up it would surely have broken my legs.

I switched from the flotation cushion to the gas tank because the tank had a good handle, making it easier to hang on to. I soon realized I was coated with gasoline and needed to tighten the cap on the tank.

I floated on the lake, clinging to the tank, for most of the night. The clouds cleared and the sky was lit by a million stars, but the wind kept blowing. Then I realized it was going to blow me right past the shore and out into the main lake, so I needed to start swimming again. Finally reaching land, exhausted, I crawled up onto a rough, bushy shoreline, relaxed, and slept.

At dawn the mosquitoes found me. I pushed myself through the bushes and along the shore until I found a small cabin. There was a comfortable chair on the porch and a carpet on the floor. I wrapped the carpet around me and, shivering violently, watched the most beautiful sunrise I have ever seen.

Two hours later, the cabin's occupant came out and did a startled double-take when he saw me on his deck. He took me inside and lit the wood stove to warm me. Seems I was suffering from hypothermia, although I didn't know it.

Later, back out on the deck in the warm sunlight, I saw my son, Colin, motoring down the lake in our aluminium boat, searching the far shore. I waved a towel belonging to my host. He saw it and came over to pick me up.

It took me a couple of weeks to get over the gasoline burns, which hurt like a bad sunburn. We went looking for the canoe without success. Later I saw a Ministry of Natural Resources depth chart that told me I managed to sink that canoe in the deepest part of the lake. It is about a hundred and forty feet down, still full of cement blocks no doubt.

BUILDING

With the ground prepared, Jean and I took the next steps. I had designed a 448-square-foot cabin, had the material requirements worked out by a local building store and placed the order. Delivery was scheduled for just days before the target construction weekend.

Our son Victor and his siblings invited a bunch of their friends up for that long weekend.

Jean and I collected rocks from nearby beaches and transported them to our waterfront. We built wood frames for twelve support pillars on round patio stones sitting on the gravel. We carried the stones up the hill. We mixed cement in a wheelbarrow. We put the rocks and cement in the frames and tamped them down to make sure there were no cavities. It took over two exhausting weeks, eighteen days gone.

We borrowed the bulldozer barge, received the building materials at the landing, loaded, ran up the lake and unloaded on our shore. It took two round trips of nine hours each way, four days gone. We worked out a food plan and shopped. We bought a BBQ to help feed the crowd. There was already a propane stove in the original building. We bought a ridiculous amount of beer.

Finally, the day came. Twenty crew members arrived, some after dark. Shuttling them up the lake took several trips. Tents to set up. Sleeping bags to set out. Tent mates to establish. A large bonfire. Dogs and burgers and beer, beer, beer.

The next morning, it started raining. Some were hungover, but task-master Victor still got enough of them going. Breakfast, then carrying materials up the hill to the building site. It was a people-train marching by. Victor was at the shore sorting the materials in the order they would be needed. Then the rain stopped, and the sun came out.

Victor sat on a rock above the action, directing. When necessary, he moved down to explain or help. First the pillar tops needed to be levelled using a clear hose full of water as the tool. Then the beams had to be placed and secured. Next the sixteen-foot joists had to be laid and secured. Then the plywood floor had to be laid and nailed down. We ran into our first glitch there. We had two kegs of three-and-a-half-inch spikes, good for framing. We did not get the two-inch nails needed for the floor and roof plywood.

There were people pounding those spikes with hammers, sledge-hammers and the backs of axes and hatchets. One person used a stone. Everyone was pounding. Then the framing started. Each side was laid out on the floor, assembled and then raised. The trusses and plywood roof led to more pounding of spikes. It was a whirlwind of activity. By the end of the weekend, we had a building.

I never cooked so much food in my life.

LOST AND FOUND

Four teenagers—two of our children and two of their friends—set out for an afternoon fishing excursion on our large lake full of narrows and passages, separated by spaces of open water. As dark approached, they had not returned. Searching was not an option with so many paths they might have taken. I paddled out on the bay and placed a lit lantern on a rocky point beside the entrance, to tell them where to turn in.

Jean and I slept fitfully, hearing false sounds of their motor throughout the night. In the morning, with no sign of them, I went out to retrieve the lantern, then we ate a silent breakfast, fearing the worst.

Those kids finally motored around the point and into our bay near noon, none the worse for their night out on the lake. They told us they had a grand time. They caught several decent lake trout before realizing they were lost. They stopped to ask directions from a couple cooking their dinner at a shore-side campsite. Giving bad directions, the campers did tell our guys to be careful leaving from there, because there was a rocky reef about fifty feet straight out. Our son revved the motor, got up to speed, and absent-minded, ran right over it.

The motor popped up on tilt, breaking the tilt lock. With its skeg gone, its cowling rocketed into the front of the boat but missed everyone. The bottom of the boat was chewed up and leaking seriously. Thrown to the floor, the occupants were bruised but otherwise unhurt. Ever resourceful, they paddled to shore and set out replacing the shear pin to revive the beat-up motor. As the guys focused on this task, difficult in the dark, the girls got a fire going and started cooking dinner.

Their dinner consisted of lake trout fillets cooked in empty beer cans with the lids pried off, tucked into corners of an open fire. Their utensils were long-nosed pliers and sharp-edged fishing knives. After dinner, they closed out the evening singing campfire songs and moving to the smoky side of the fire to fend off mosquitoes. I don't think they slept at all.

In the morning, daylight showed them the way. With a limping motor and a leaky boat, they worked themselves back to camp, bailing all the way. When they arrived, all they wanted was a full breakfast, then off to bed.

Those kids had a great night of fun and adventure. They were full of it. Although I tried to patch the boat with tar and fabric, it still leaks. The motor needed an overhaul at the marina. Jean and I lost a lot of sleep in our anxiety.

Is this picture fair?

Why is it that, as kids, we can be so carefree, so sure of our immortality, yet in the passage of time we morph into adults and turn into concerned worrywarts? We should have more faith.

SORRY, I DIDN'T GET THAT EMAIL

Several of us share a wilderness fishing camp on Lake Onaping in northern Ontario. Lake Onaping stretches forty-eight miles end to end, made up of a series of smaller lakes and joining rivers flooded together by seventeen dams. It parallels Highway 144 about seven miles east of it.

Three years ago, the series of cell towers on Highway 144 added a tower at Halfway Lake to fill a dead zone. One of our members received a text while listening to music in the outhouse. We have a hotspot, the only one on the lake. The outhouse is now called the Communication Centre.

Cell reception is a carefully guarded secret. We don't tell our wives. We don't tell our employers. In this way we don't need to lie, saying "Sorry, I didn't get that email." We still just say, "Sorry, I was at the fishing camp."

THE WONDER OF A CHILD

Maddy rushed up from the dock on her first-ever day at our fishing camp, dashing up the thirty-two stairs in record time to boast about the dock-bass she had just caught. She held her hands wide apart to indicate the size. She must be a fast fisherperson learner, since our dock bass rarely exceed six inches.

Indeed, this was one of the smaller ones, as I discovered when I went down with her to take it out of a bucket of water, remove the hook, and release it.

Of course, I had to bait the hook again.

I think I was up and down those stairs twenty times releasing fish and baiting hooks. I have always suspected it was the same fish over and over, but that doesn't matter.

A few years later, Maddy was the first of my grandchildren to learn to run an outboard motor, sooner than all of my grandsons. If she couldn't find a companion, she would go out onto the bay by herself, trolling along the shore while managing both her rod and the motor effectively.

Maddy grew up on a hobby farm, is an accomplished horseback rider, and learned to manage large animals including a goat, a donkey, a llama and of course many horses. She is now a beautiful twenty-some-year-old young woman running a farm-sitting business with her significant other, and still the most successful fisherperson the camp has ever seen.

TWO IN ONE

My teenage grandson, Cameron, insisted he was old enough to drive the cargo boat down the lake to the landing, to pick up arriving people and their stuff. We reluctantly let him try it.

Partway down the eighteen miles, while running at full throttle, Cam's hat flew off. He swerved hard right to go back for it, still at full throttle. The boat skidded into the shoreline, smashing the lower foot of the motor. Stranded with no idea what to do next, Cam curled up and went to sleep. The waves rocked the boat against the shore until the small auxiliary motor dropped into running position and its foot was destroyed by the pounding.

That evening Cam was rescued by locals, who took him to their cabin for the night. Our camp was equipped with a radio phone system on a party line. His rescuers were on the same party line. They could not call us directly, so they called Cam's mother back in the city and asked her to relay the good news that Cam was safe. Cam's mother called Cam's dad at our camp and asked, "Do you know where your son is?" A trick question. Dad lied. Mom blew a gasket. Frosty, very frosty.

The next morning, Cam's dad went down the lake to retrieve Cam and the boat. He was told to sit on the porch and wait by Cam's rescuers until "young Cam finishes his bacon and eggs breakfast."

DISASTER AVERTED

My wife Jean and I owned a very nice fishing camp on a large lake north of Sudbury, Ontario. We sold it to one of our sons and three of his friends, who timeshare it. Most of the same people still go there as guests of one or other of the new owners. Our grandson, Cameron, decided to hold his stag there during our son's time slot.

One of the other owners, Martin Neary, left a bottle of whisky behind for Cameron and his guests to enjoy at the stag. The label was signed by Martin and his entire family, with best wishes expressed.

At the last minute, Cameron's stag was cancelled when he couldn't get time off from work, so Jean and I, a couple of our adult children including the part-owner, and several friends used the camp instead.

On our last night there, after hectic preparations to leave the camp pristine for the incoming group, we ran out of alcoholic beverages. Thinking nothing of it we opened and consumed the bottle Martin left for Cameron, intending to replace it when we got back to civilization.

Much to our surprise, both Martin and Cameron were very angry about it.

I sent an email to all those involved with the attached document. It worked. A crisis that threatened good relationships between two of the camp's owners morphed into a joke. Martin even added to the joke with his own proclamation.

SUPERIOR COURT OF THE DISTRICT OF PARRY SOUND

In the matter of the diverted whisky in the Unincorporated Township of Fairbairn,

We the Jury find as follows:

The entire blame rests with Cameron Malcolm Smith, who failed to make a scheduled appearance at The Camp on Eighteen Mile Bay, Lake Onaping, Fairbairn Township, District of Parry Sound, Ontario, Canada (The Camp), where he would certainly have shared it with the occupants then in residence.

This failure left the occupants of The Camp in a difficult ethical quandary. Clearly carrying the whisky out was not an option. That would be the equivalent of carrying out a full jerrycan of gasoline or a full cylinder of propane. It just is not done.

The option of leaving said whisky in the camp over the winter was also dismissed as unacceptable. If someone broke into said camp over the winter and found it, the camp would be broken into every winter for the next dozen years on spec. This option would also have unfairly passed the ethical dilemma on to the close-up crew, since it was already established that Cameron Malcolm Smith would not be in attendance then either.

A third option was finally chosen, broaching the bottle and sharing in around, as Cameron Malcolm Smith would have done had he been there, honouring his good intentions in absentia. Of course the occupants toasted Cameron Malcolm Smith and his intended bride in doing so. The plan was, and is, to replace the said bottle of whisky to Cameron Malcolm Smith in a timely fashion and in a more civilized setting.

In keeping with the ancient saying "a bottle in the bush is worth two in the town", Cameron Malcolm Smith will receive two (2) un-broached and pristine bottles of Jameson's Select Reserve Black Barrel Irish Whisky on the evening before his wedding, with compliments from the entire Neary Family, although unfortunately not signed ones.

Cameron Malcolm Smith should have many opportunities to share said Irish whisky with friends and acquaintances at this timely time in the traditional manner. It should also provide Cameron Malcolm Smith with sufficient Irish courage to face the festivities of the following day.

In closing, Jean Isobel Smith denies being the sponsor of this decision, although freely admitting that she was an enthusiastic participant.

Finally, kudos to Martin Neary's taste. That was damn fine whisky.

MINORITY OPINION

The issue was a management problem. The person put in charge of the bottle could not be trusted.

CONCLUSION

Two bottles of Irish whisky were delivered to the groom's party the night before the wedding and contributed to its success. A copy of my notice is stapled to the camp's living room wall and we all still get a chuckle over it.

Out of the Ashes *(50 words)*

I heard a strange metallic scraping sound. Two days later, I found a small red squirrel covered with grey ash huddling in our wood stove. I lifted it out with the ash shovel and gently placed it on the deck. It shook itself, looked around, perked up, and scrambled away.

A Different Perspective *(50 words)*

Morning coffee on the deck. Sun up and sparrows singing. Trails of mist on the mirror-calm lake. Nine loons drifting in the bay. As they came closer in an arc, a small bass surged onto the rocky shore, flip, flipped along and splashed back in, outside the circle of death.

The Raid *(50 words)*

Our camp is in the wilderness. One day, Colin left the back door open. A mother and four baby racoons marched in single file and cleaned out the cat-food dish. They tore open the kibble bag and ate a lot of that too. Satisfied, they marched back out, single file.

Running Up the Lake *(50 words)*

Running up the lake in the dark, we got lost. Eventually we pulled in to shore, set up a campsite, and made our dinner. In the morning we looked out of our tent and saw our camp across the bay, only about a hundred metres of open water away.

Pushing the Limit *(50 words)*

We heard silver bells tinkling on our aluminium boat. Gunning, Jake drove it up over slush and close to shore. We jumped out and pulled it the rest of the way. Jake pitched the tent while I started a fire. Five days later we walked out on the solid ice.

Get Off Our Property *(50 words)*

Our remote camp is the only one on a side-bay eighteen miles up a lake. One day we spotted a fisherman a quarter of a mile away on "our" bay. An indignant guest marched down to the shore and yelled at the top of her lungs, "GET OFF OUR PROPERTY!"

Failed Experiment *(50 words)*

Our camp runs on a twelve-volt system. One time the batteries were so low only one fluorescent light worked. Steve came in and decided to check the situation out. As we shouted, "Don't touch that!" he switched off the last light. It wouldn't come back on. We ate by candlelight.

Sold *(50 words)*

When we told the owner of the landing where we access the lake that we had sold our camp to two of our sons and two of their friends, he said, "Fantastic. Now you are the guests and they do all the work." That is how it has turned out.

20/20 *(50 words)*

There is a saying that hindsight is twenty-twenty. I think that means we can see and understand our mistakes after the fact. This seems to imply that we can learn from our mistakes. If that was true, why do people keep making the same mistakes over and over again?

Oh Well *(50 words)*

The young boy was riding on the bow of the fishing boat when his shoe fell off. He looked around to see if his mother was watching, then shrugging his small shoulders he said, "Oh, well" and kicked off the other shoe to join its mate on the lake bottom.

Section 6
Academic Career

I was on a fast-track management career at age thirty as general manager of a small Canadian subsidiary of a larger US firm. It was tough sledding because the main product was obsolete and there was no money for diversification. I was not comfortable in that role. I felt the responsibility heavily of holding the economic fates of over a hundred relatively low-skilled employees.

Looking for an alternative where I could make a good living without this weight of responsibility, I decided to take a run at academia. Although my education did not go past high school plus a professional accounting designation, I did have a business track record. In addition, I had recently published an article in a respected journal and scored a very high number on a graduate business (GMAT) test.

HARVARD

I was accepted at the MBA level everywhere I applied. The Harvard Business School also bumped my application over to their doctoral program since I had listed an academic career as my goal. That program was admitting a small group of child geniuses and scheduled a mini MBA-type program over the summer. With this bonus program available, they also offered me admission.

Naturally, I took the shortcut. I found myself learning alongside seventeen- and eighteen-year-old geniuses. Most were hand-picked from disadvantaged areas of the United States. One already had a PhD in some esoteric branch of mathematics. I asked him, "Why math, since you are clearly interested in business?" His answer was that at age fifteen he lacked credibility, but math was objective so the professors could not deny him.

Harvard uses cases to teach and examine. I was very good at cases, probably because of my business consulting experience. A case describes a business situation that needs resolution. Usually the facts focus on symptoms of a problem and the students must delve behind these symptoms to find the underlying problems, then offer a solution.

Here is an example. A large company had a policy of managing their divisions as independent firms competing in their separate markets. These divisions sometimes bought from each other, but only if the deal beat outside competitors. A vice president received emails from two division managers concerning a price argument between them. The emails contained a lot of cost and price information.

Normal students focus on the cost and price information. Brilliant students see that the emails should not even exist. Their existence indicated that the vice president was subverting the system. His actions were the real problem.

I found studying with these kids amazing. They had enormous academic smarts, but I knew the world better, so we could trade.

One of these geniuses was coaching me in finance. The night before the final exam, he gave up on me, saying, "Don, you just don't understand finance." When the exam results came out, I scored an A and he scored a B. In frustration he exclaimed, "Damn it, Smith, you are the only person I know who gets A grades on C knowledge."

STREET SMARTS

A colleague of mine has a saying: "There are two kinds of smarts in the world: academic smarts and street smarts. If you can't have both, take the street smarts every time."

Here is an example. Andy got into the business school's MBA program on the strength of family tradition; his father was a graduate. It probably helped that his family gave a lot of money to the school. Andy's older brother had failed out two years earlier, and Andy was not about to let that happen to him.

At the start of his first term, Andy approached the doctoral program's administrator and got the names of doctoral students specializing in the five subjects he would study that term. He interviewed his candidates until he found the ones he wanted as tutors. I was one of his choices, to help him with accounting. Andy offered an outrageous sum and I needed the money.

When my turn to coach him came, Andy had me prepare a detailed and comprehensive analysis of that case. Next, I drilled him on my solution in depth, over and over, testing him as we went, until he could deliver it by rote. Andy had three classes each day. This detailed preparation took so long that Andy only had time to prepare for one class each day.

Andy worked out a timetable that had him preparing for one out of three classes each day, but he alternated between the courses, so he prepared for nine classes in each course over the term. In the one class each day for which Andy was "prepared," he volunteered actively and delivered a dominant performance. In the other two classes each day he stayed silent and practically hid. Because of his strong performance when he did participate, his professors left him alone in his quiet classes.

When exam time came, Andy went to each of his professors and told them he panicked on exams and that his exam performance would disappoint them, but his classroom performance demonstrated that he knew the material. Andy must have been very persuasive, because he passed every course and he certainly did not have much of a grasp of the subjects, at least not for the accounting course.

Andy achieved the same outcome in his second term.

I left Harvard to take up my own academic career in a different city. In his second year, Andy faxed me the cases he chose to prepare for. I faxed back my analysis and recommendations. He then called me long-distance and we went through the drill. Obviously it worked, because Andy got his MBA.

I feel no guilt about helping Andy game the system. He will go into the family business and some day he will run it. He will do very well because he knows how to surround himself with talented people, how to motivate them, and how to use their judgment and advice.

Andy will also do his school proud, and his family will continue to support the school generously. Everybody won.

Helping *(50 words)*

One of my university service assignments was staffing twelve sections of our Introduction to Accounting course. The candidates came from our very intelligent MBA graduating class. A characteristic I considered essential was being able to take satisfaction from helping others succeed. That was always easy to spot in an interview.

MICHAEL

I admire people who do the most with what they have. Michael ranks up there with the best.

Michael was a student in my first-year Introduction to Financial Accounting class. He was proud of being at a university. His high school guidance counsellor recommended a vocational stream, but he persisted in following the academic stream. He completed grade twelve, although it took him a couple of extra years to do it. He was admitted to our university as a mature student.

In 1972 I was developing and testing an audiovisual programmed learning system for the mechanical aspects of my accounting course. Many of my students covered that material in high school and were bored by this early part of my course. Students who did not cover the material in high school were at a serious disadvantage. I wanted to eliminate the boredom and level the playing field. Besides, teaching mechanical content was boring for me and a poor use of precious classroom time.

Michael was my best tester, working through new material diligently and talking to me about parts he did not understand. Together we created very effective modules that had remedial branches for almost every imaginable error a student could make, and some unimaginable ones.

In this process, Michael spent far too much time on accounting and far too little time on his other four courses. As a result, he scored a strong B on my course, scraped through two of his other courses and failed two. Probably he should not have tackled a full course load anyway.

I learned much from Michael. One thing I learned is that "slow learner" is an accurate and meaningful term. Michael was a slow learner. It took him longer to get there, but he persisted, and he did get there in the end.

I realized that our entire education system was upside down. We usher students through in lockstep, grade after grade, and judge them by how well they master the material—A, B, C, D, and F. We need to make time the variable instead, moving students forward as they master the material, and always demand that they do master the material before moving them on—A, A, A, A, and A.

Of course, we all reach our limit, but this approach should help each of us get closer to that limit. I can't fathom relativity, although I do accept that time flows differently under different circumstances. Relativity is one of my limits.

Michael dropped out of university and my life, but I heard that he landed a useful job as a bookkeeper, so he did benefit from our collaboration as I did. All the students in later sections of the course also benefited from a more effective learning experience, thanks in large part to Michael.

Michael is one of my life heroes.

I had an opportunity years later to test this theory and it worked. I put a writeup on that in the last section of this book under Serious Writing if you are interested.

WANNABE ENTREPRENEURS

I ran the accounting and finance segment of a program for wannabe entrepreneurs. We provided the support of four coaches, covering the areas of accounting and finance, marketing, personnel and strategy. We ran classes and also provided a lot of individual help related to their specific business goals.

Participants were expected to prepare a comprehensive, detailed business plan, including assumptions about the amounts and timing of investments, sales volumes, prices, costs and revenues. I put their numbers into a computer model that forecast monthly profits and cash flows. I often questioned their assumptions to keep the models realistic.

Here are three participants' stories.

Karen was a single mom with two daughters in ballet classes. She designed and sewed their recital costumes because she could not afford to buy them. Soon, she was making costumes for their classmates. Then for groups from other ballet studios. She thought it might be a business. Karen's financial model came up WOW!! I told her to start looking for other people to sew costumes. My six-month follow-up found five busy, grey-haired workers, coordinated by Karen's mother. Karen was out talking to an opposite-season figure skating club. Her cash flow was so strong she was buying the building.

Mike, a retired middle manager, wanted to start a commercial internet portal. His cousin already owned one in a different city. Mike's financial model came up UGH! I sent him back to refine his assumptions. No, he had it right, based on information from his cousin. I told Mike to look for something else, but he went ahead anyway. His business did not survive long enough for a six-month follow-up visit. His cousin's business fared no better.

Jason was a cheerful, gregarious man. He wanted to start a coffee pub. His investment assumptions included spending about $70,000 on fixtures and furniture. I thought his operating assumptions were optimistic, but still his financial model said OK. Jason mortgaged his house to finance his business. My six-month follow-up found him in serious trouble. His cash flow barely covered the wages of two employees, with little left over for rent, supplies or Jason himself. Jason was playing Mein Host, mingling with his "guests." I advised him to get rid of the employees and get behind the counter himself. Not long after, I walked past his location and saw that a new business was occupying the premises.

The message? Preparing a good, comprehensive business plan is an essential first step to starting a business. If the plan says GO, the plan can help you succeed. Testing and refining the plan can improve your odds. If the plan says NO, you can save heartache and financial ruin by accepting that message, making modifications, or moving on. Some business concepts just aren't viable. It is best to find that out ahead of time.

VALUE OF AN IDEA

A friend of mine had a saying for wannabe entrepreneurs: "A great idea and $2 will buy you a cup of coffee, but don't try to get the coffee without the $2."

JONESY

Jonesy is a bartender at The Legion. He's good at it. He knows all his customers by name and by what they drink. He can cut off a customer who has had too much so nicely they aren't insulted. I got to know him at the hockey arena Saturday mornings. He knows everyone and he was always ready to pitch in and help. He could not take on fuller commitments because of his job.

If a midget game needed a timekeeper, Jonesy volunteered. If a bantam game needed a scorekeeper, Jonesy volunteered. When the Powder Puffs coach didn't show, Jonesy got behind the bench and ran the team. He knew every girl by name and position. He was the volunteer equipment manager for the Junior D team, which got him a seat on the team bus for away games.

I hired Jonesy to bartend at my daughter's wedding. He asked me how many were invited. I told him about 120. He said OK, get a licence for 240, the liquor board always underestimates. Helpful thing to know.

The day came, I bought and brought the booze to match the licence, which he posted on the wall. Everything was going nicely: sit-down dinner, toasts to the bride and groom, speeches, and onto the dance floor. Then a swarm of party crashers showed up. The groom, Greg, has eight aunts and uncles and they have a lot of children, his cousins. Maybe some friends were there too.

Now I know how the Egyptians felt when they were swarmed by those locusts. It wasn't Greg's fault. He was as upset as I was. But what could we do? Spoil the party?

About 10:30 pm, Jonesy took me aside and told me we were about to run out of booze. He offered to borrow some from The Legion if I got replacements back to him before it opened the next day. I agreed. Jonesy took away a bunch of empties to keep the bottle count right and came back a few minutes later with two mixed cases of liquor.

A bestseller was a Dutch gin called De Kuyper. It tasted like turpentine, but Greg's family emigrated from Holland a generation ago and they liked it. At about 1:00 am, the bar ran dry again and we shut it down. The beer supply was still good, so the locusts carted it off to party somewhere else. Jonesy gave me a list of what to buy.

The next day I hit the liquor store as soon as it opened. The staff didn't even blink at the order and helped me pick the bottles off the shelves. It almost maxed out my Mastercard. I met Jonesy at the back door of The Legion ten minutes before it opened, and all was well. That was typical Jonesy. He risked his job, maybe jail, to help out a casual friend from the arena.

I got to know him a lot better after that, and eventually he told me his story. Here it is.

***

I'd been long-haul trucking for more years than I can remember, driving for AGI Transport. Eighteen months ago, I got a chance to own my own rig when Secord's Hardware offered me a contract as an independent. The deal looked good on paper. The mileage rates were what they were paying AGI, so Secord's wasn't lowballing.

I checked the dealerships and found Jenny waiting for me on a lot. She was $249,900, including a full set of both summer and winter tires. The financing was fair: 6% with the payments spread over seven years. Jenny's a beaut, named after my niece, and should last more than seven years. Jenny's a silver-grey eighteen-wheeler with lots of chrome. I took her through the wash at the truck stop at least twice a week to keep her bright and clean. I polished her chrome wheels whenever I was on standby. I loved Jenny.

The payments were $3,637.53 a month. Somewhat scary, but a lot less than what I would bring in. I was able to get that down a bit by paying $20,000 up front, borrowed from Dad. That brought the monthly payments down to $3,345.36. I jumped at it, signed on the dotted line with the finance company. Dad had to sign too, as a guarantor.

Dad is not exactly wealthy, but he owned his house and has a couple of pensions. He had a reverse mortgage on his house to give him some extra spending money and has helped us a couple of times in the past. He's been on his own for six years since Mom died.

Jeff, my contact at the bank, set up a high-interest savings account for me as well as a business account. He told me to put twenty cents of every dollar I earned into that savings account, because I would need it when an engine blows, Jenny needs new tires, or whatever.

At first I did that, and it got to be a lot of money. Then some things went bad. Rob, my oldest son, needed braces on his teeth. The furnace quit in January. The roof started leaking. Ordinary stuff, but a lot of ordinary stuff. I started paying some expenses out of the high interest savings account. Then I took a shortcut by not putting money in.

Six months ago, I pulled into one of the truck-inspection stations and they took me off the road. No tread on the tires. I knew I needed eighteen new tires, but where was I going to get $24,000? So, I just crossed my fingers and ignored it. Secord's sent a big truck carrying a forklift and a team of four men to take their load off Jenny. They billed me over a thousand bucks for that and took it out of what they owed me.

The finance company repossessed Jenny five days later and towed her away, after being notified that they owed storage of almost $1,000 at the roadside inspection station. Jenny sold at auction for $130,000, hardly more than half her original price. I still owed $211,828 on the financing, so I was short about $81,000. The finance company didn't bother coming after me. I had nothing. They went straight after Dad.

Dad had to sell his house. Of course, we took him in. After all, I did cost Dad his house. He has our master bedroom with the ensuite, furnished with his bed, his favourite chair and his TV, so he has a place to crawl into and escape the turmoil. Our three boys share the second bedroom on a bunk bed and a single. Rob grabbed the top bunk as the oldest. That room is a chaos of scattered clothes, sports gear and school stuff.

My wife Gloria and I share the small bedroom. It's too small for a decent size bed so we have bunk beds too. I have the upper, I guess because I am older than Gloria. We share the smaller bathroom with our three boys. Dad's leftover couch and chairs are in the basement, the rest of his furniture and stuff fills the garage. I gave up my car to make room in the driveway for Dad's car, so with Gloria's car we are still a two-car family.

Secord's cancelled my contract, not that it was any use to me. AGI wouldn't hire me back because I went into competition with them. A question of loyalty, they said.

The lifesaver was a government program that paid me to go to college for three months and earn my bartending licence. I have a four-night gig at The Legion now and freelance at parties most weekends. The pay is OK and the tips are appreciated. Gloria drives me to work most afternoons after getting home from her job and I Uber back home at night.

At least I don't owe income tax. Turned out I lost money after all the dust settled. I worked my ass off for over a year and earned nothing.

Oddly, Dad is the real winner out of this fiasco. He loves my boys and they love him. He drove them to hockey practices and games last winter and now he's driving them to soccer. He stays and cheers them on. He discusses pro players and argues with them about who's best. Turns out he was lonely in our old house. Not anymore.

It's not working out so well for Gloria and me. She works days, I work evenings, so we don't see much of each other. She hasn't invited me down from the upper bunk yet. When I told Jeff, my banker, my sad story, he told me his family's rule, "Never co-sign for more than you can afford to lose. Hope for the best but plan for the worst."

JAMES

James commuted sixty miles to our MBA program every day. In addition to class time, study groups and assignments, it was just too much for him. One day as he slept in my class, I threw a stick of chalk at him to wake him up. To my horror it hit the desk in front of him and exploded across his face. He stayed awake for the rest of the class and I never threw chalk again.

Eventually our faculty gave James an ultimatum. Find accommodation nearby or drop out of the program. He chose the former and turned out to be a fine student.

NUMBERLESS

We had a student in our MBA program who had absolutely no number sense. He did not understand that four was bigger than two, much less that it was twice as big. He attended Jesuit schools right through university and he never took one course containing numbers. In his first year with us, he topped his class in the three "soft" courses and failed the three number-oriented courses, including my accounting course.

In a faculty meeting we voted to pass him into the second year of the program "by faculty action," because he was a very intelligent and impressive person and a fine student leader. Our argument was that he would be a credit to our school after graduating and would always find ways around his deficiency.

He won the gold medal in his second year by avoiding all courses that had numbers. This is an almost impossible feat, since number-based courses are normally easier to score nearly perfect on.

Motivation *(50 words)*

Our dean was a great motivator. When the university got its first server, he emailed all of us, offering prizes to the first twenty respondents. I won and picked my prize from a huge box full of toys. I think there were enough toys in there for every faculty member.

Dawn of the Computer Age *(50 words)*

We had a very smart dean, Alex. At the start of the computer age, many students were computer whizzes while we, the faculty, were clueless. Alex established computer labs and our students developed computer courses, both student-run. No student could graduate from our business school without a student-trained Microsoft certification.

Shared Ignorance *(50 words)*

Our MBA students were writing an exam in a large gymnasium alongside many students from other faculties. A proctor from another discipline reported to our dean that two of our MBA students were discussing their exam in the washroom. Our dean shrugged and said, "Shared ignorance never leads to wisdom."

Shouting *(50 words)*

We were advising a group of middle managers planning to be entrepreneurs. One rough and rugged participant wanted to start his own debt collection agency. He submitted every assignment IN CAPITAL LETTERS. I complained that it felt as though he was shouting at me. His answer was, "I AM SHOUTING."

Publish *(50 words)*

As part of their jobs, university faculty members are expected to complete research and publish it. This was so important we had a saying, "Publish or Perish." A colleague of mine, a Jesuit priest and full professor, once told me that the saying at Loyola University was "Publish or Parish."

Diseconomic *(50 words)*

I taught a seminar to government economists explaining where financial reports deviated from sound economic principles, and why. The goal was to prevent them from taking accounting reports at face value. One indignant participant asked, "When will accountants do it right?" When I answered, "They won't change," she stomped out.

New Family Base *(50 words)*

My bright young student from Hong Kong spoke excellent English, participated actively and scored high grades. Seems her family sent her to Canada and her brother to Australia, competing to determine where to establish a new family base. Her brother would need to be very good to win that contest.

She also drove a neat BMW two-seat convertible.

Exam Cheats *(50 words)*

The exam was over. I was shutting down late writers. With one, another student was dictating an answer. I confiscated the paper and said both were disqualified. The helping student asked, "Do you know my name, sir?" I conceded, "No." As he walked away, he said, "Then fuck off, SIR."

Self Taught *(50 words)*

The professor sat silent at the back of the room while his students ran the class. I replaced him. The students rebelled. We compromised. I sat at the back and had ten minutes at the end of each session to comment on anything they had missed. I rarely needed it.

From this experience I learned that classes went best when the students did most of the work. I used this insight throughout my teaching career.

The professor, sadly, suffered from a fatal brain tumour.

Two Reports *(50 words)*

On my first written assignment students wrote poorly organized reports. Maryanne's was the exception. I attached Maryanne's report to all of them for hand back as an example. Maryanne came up to me later, saying there was a mistake because she only got two copies of her own report.

Intermittent Reinforcement *(50 words)*

His mother asked the small boy if he brushed his teeth before getting into bed. He answered "No," so she got him up to do it, saying "Why do you try this on me? You know I will send you back to brush them." His answer, "Mother, once you forgot."

Bastard *(50 words)*

The butterfly bounced across a field of daisies, touching down from time to time. The flowers yellow heads and white petals swayed in tune with the gentle wind, in dancing waves. I thought to myself, "butterfly?" That makes no sense. Perhaps their original name was "flutterby" and someone bastardized it.

Fog Flight *(50 words)*

David was flying his Cessna on visual reference. Fog. Easing off altitude, David tried to get under, to land. A cliff face loomed. Banking right, he missed. "Phew, close call." David finally got down. A ground crew member asked, "What happened to your wing?" David looked. The wing tip was gone.

Section 7
Serious Writing

I have a few areas where I disagree with the way my world works. Maybe I am right, maybe I am wrong, but here are a some of them, anyway.

PERSONAL CAPITAL

We are all capitalists. Some of us have money capital invested to earn a money return. Almost all of us have skills capital, which can also bring in a money return. Our skills capital is usually developed through time and effort – commitments to education, training, and experience.

Most of us have personal capital in physical skills as well. Exceptional people can hone these skills to a high level through rigorous practice, to bring in a lot of money. Professional athletes are examples. By developing and applying our personal capital, we can earn income in any country where residents are free to exploit their personal capital for their personal benefit, always within the limits of reasonable laws.

In Canada, our governments commit a large portion of our economic resources to helping young people, and some not so young, develop skills capital, by providing free education through at least twelve years and subsidized education after that. We try to make this personal capital development available equally to every Canadian resident and encourage each to pursue this development to the limit of their ability.

Anyone who does not take advantage of this free or subsidized opportunity to develop their personal skills capital is a fool.

Of course, having fully developed skills capital for all its residents also advantages a country and all of its residents. Increasing the sum of the personal capital of all of us makes all of us better off. In Canada, personal capital is by far our largest money-earning capital resource.

But capital, both personal and financial, can be undermined or extinguished by changing times. More recently, our governments have developed skills retraining for people whose skills capital has been compromised in this way. Anyone who does not take advantage of the opportunity to develop replacement personal skills capital is also a fool.

In recent years, the value of physical skills has diminished for all but the most talented, as machines and automation have displaced much manual work. By the most talented, I give as examples the one-in-ten-thousand who achieve professional careers in sports or entertainment. There is little room for second-tier skills in these fields.

In contrast, the value of skills capital and especially intellectual skills capital has increased significantly and is in broad demand. Although there are still the most talented one-in-ten-thousand superstars, there is plenty of room for people with average talents to succeed. An example is software development, where most people can learn to program, but only superstars can imagine what is possible and get it done. The superstars may become billionaires, but ordinary people can still earn decent livings.

It will be interesting to see how artificial intelligence changes the value of skills capital. Possibly a balance of intellectual and physical skills, like those employed as tradespeople such as mechanics, electricians and plumbers, will land near top of the value charts in the near future.

GOVERNMENTS ARE MY PURCHASING AGENTS

Governments are my purchasing agents. They purchase services for me and my fellow citizens and residents that I could never hope to buy on my own.

Municipal governments purchase personal and property protection, courts and law enforcement, fire protection, garbage collection, local road maintenance, winter snow clearing and much more. A long, long list of services I badly need, but could never buy on my own.

Provincial governments purchase a higher level of personal and property protection: higher courts and law enforcement, highway maintenance, health care and hospitals, education. An even longer list of services I badly need but could never buy on my own.

The federal government provides overarching services at the national level and feeds money downward from its superior money collecting systems.

I fund these services through fees for service, property tax, sales taxes, income tax and more, as we all do. I read that in total we pay about half of our personal incomes in one sort of tax or other. A bargain at the price. Doing without these services is unthinkable.

In Canada, we buy a safe, stable, comfortable environment. We have a well-educated population to move us forward generation by generation.

Those of us with higher incomes obviously pay more, but we also benefit more. We get to keep much of what we earn with legal protections and social enforcement. We are surrounded by a large population that can work for us and buy from us. That safe, stable, comfortable, mostly forward-looking environment and well-educated population are the basis of our success.

We may object to some of our government's spending priorities. We may think our purchasing agents could be more efficient. That is where politics comes in. We can switch out the teams. But stop complaining about paying your taxes. However you cut it, you are getting the bargain of a lifetime just living in this safe, stable country.

THE CASE FOR VALUE-ADDED TAX (VAT)

Income tax on corporations is stupid. It subsidizes weak producers and the arithmetic just doesn't make sense. It is an expense of doing business and will be passed on to the customers, with a markup for profit. The tables below demonstrate the costs.

Cost and Profit Margin Structure		Without Tax	With Tax
Cost of Materials		100	100
Cost of Direct Labour (people running machines, etc.)		50	50
Cost of Indirect Labour (sweepers, maintenance, utilities, etc.)		150	150
Cost of Management and other overhead		75	75
Income and other taxes (part of other overhead)		nil	50
Subtotal		375	425
Markup 20%		75	85
Price of product	Could be	450	510

Income tax caused the product to be priced $60 more (13%) than it would have been without the tax. Because business is competitive, that would be a real price difference in the marketplace. Ultimately customers

213

pay the tax. In the long run, in a competitive market economy, it could never be any other way. Only subsidies or foolish investors can create the conditions to allow a producer to sell below cost + markup.

SUBSIDIZING INEFFICIENT PRODUCERS

The problem is even worse when you consider less efficient producers. Assume a competitor who is less efficient has no taxable profit.

Cost and Profit Margin Structure	Without Tax	With Tax
Cost of Materials	110	110
Cost of Direct Labour (people running machines, etc.)	75	75
Cost of Indirect Labour (sweepers, maintenance, utilities, etc.)	170	170
Cost of Management and other overhead	90	90
Income and other taxes (part of other overhead)	nil	Nil*
Subtotal	425	425
Markup 20%	85	85
Price of product	510	510

* The inefficient producer does not pay income tax because he has no profit.

CONCLUSION

Corporate income tax is a hidden tax on consumers and provides a subsidy for inefficient producers. Governments miss a lot of the tax benefit. Inefficient producers get competitive protection. This inefficient tax, which promotes economic inefficiency, also disadvantages exports and may give imports a competitive edge.

Value added sales tax (VAT) provides a level domestic playing field, with the same amount of tax paid across the supply chain for the same end-priced product or service. VAT also provides a level playing field between domestic products and imports selling at the same end-price. It is an efficient tax policy that does not disadvantage exports.

Since VAT is not a cost to the company, it would not be marked up as internal costs are.

REPLACING THE LOST GOVERNMENT REVENUES

Without corporate income tax, there would be no logic for special tax treatment of dividends. Dividends and other corporate payouts could then be taxed at full rates.

Implement or expand the use of VAT. Tax wealth consumption, not wealth creation.

If every country followed this logical tax policy, there would be no "tax rate shopping" through manoeuvres such as manipulated transfer prices.

Some argue corporations should keep the money because they are better at using it.

VAT AND THE HIDDEN ECONOMY

VAT would also partially tax some businesses in the hidden economy. If a business is not registered, it cannot claim back the VAT on its inputs. If it is registered, it is no longer hidden.

NON-PRODUCTIVE CORPORATIONS

A zero-income tax rate would be a mistake for non-productive corporations, set up for example to manage financial assets, property assets or other non-productive assets, allowing indefinite tax deferral. Logically these corporations should be taxed on a flow-through basis. The business owners should pay personal income tax on their share of the corporation's income in the personal tax year that the corporation's fiscal year ends in, as part of their personal tax obligation.

The after-tax profit left in these companies would be added to the owner's investment base. Money taken out would be subtracted from the owner's investment base and treated as a return of capital, tax free.

If taking out money reduced an owner's investment base to zero, money taken out beyond that point should be taxed as a capital gain.

YOU CAN'T STORE RABBITS

I have an adopted son whose heritage is Indigenous Canadian. He was born with fetal alcohol syndrome. Somewhere in this combination, his mind works so differently from mine that we frustrate each other every day. He has absolutely no money sense. Zero. If he has it, he spends it. If he doesn't have it, he still gets along somehow, until he doesn't. He lives in the day. The past is gone. The future is not now so it doesn't count. Maybe there will be rabbits tomorrow, maybe not. No sense trying to predict the future.

In other areas, he excels. We had a camp on a complex lake system. He always knew where we were on that lake and how to get back home. Without him along, we sometimes got lost. He reads text at about a grade four level, but he can read a blueprint accurately and spot errors professionals miss. He can make fine things with his hands and has an eye for beauty. He can make an outboard motor run when the rest of us have given up.

I got to thinking about this. He descends from thousands of years of hunting, fishing and gathering for a living. In that society if a hunter caught a surplus of rabbits, say ten where four would do, he had to spend them. Thus, he and his dependents chose to either pig out or share with neighbours or maybe both, because you can't store rabbits.

I come from a heritage where labour is rewarded with money. Money can be stored. Two thirds of Canadian families own their own homes. That is a money storing system as we pay down our mortgages. From the day we start work we pay into the Canada Pension Plan. That is a money storing system. Some of us are fortunate enough to have employee pension plans. That is a money storing system.

From about age forty-five, with the kids grown, many of us start thinking about retirement. Twenty years more working followed by Twenty years not working. At that age, many of us accelerate our money storing. Unlike rabbits, money deteriorates only slowly through moderate inflation, except in places like Venezuela. There are foolproof ways to offset inflation and long-term ways to beat it. Over the long term, stock markets have always gone up.

My heritage is to plan for the future and store up for it. His heritage is use it or lose it. I wonder how much heritage memory is in his makeup, or is it all the syndrome?

SELF-LEARNING

Our business school had a serious inequality problem. About half the undergraduates entering a pre-business accounting course studied accounting in high school; the other half did not. In the business school we taught using the case method. This has students reading to learn concepts and subject content outside the classroom, then applying that learning in the classroom to analyse real business situations. Understanding financial information and being able to analyse it was an important skill.

We ran an Introduction to Financial Accounting class in our university's second year to prepare them. Competition to gain admission into our business program in their third year was fierce, with grade point averages the main determinant. Some emphasis was also placed on how well students did in the second-year accounting course. In that course we believed students who studied accounting in high school had an edge. Many who did not never caught up. In effect, a high school choice was a significant determinant of who got into our business school.

To help level the playing field, I developed an accounting learning system that included three-panel easels with flip charts, large paper data-entry forms, and cassette tapes with recorded instructions, challenges and feedback on them. The cassette players had a stop switch. I recorded information on the tapes and included a beep to tell the user when to stop the tape to deal with a challenge. The earliest year printed on a flip chart was 1972.

The demand was overwhelming. The business school librarian set up six large tables, each with four electric outlets for the cassette players at four workstations, to be used exclusively with these self-learning modules. We rationed the modules' availability over time to spread the demand and the librarians started booking appointments. The problem was compounded when MBA students suffering from the same inequality discovered the system.

I got to know one of my students in the undergraduate accounting course very well. He confided to me proudly that his high school advisor told him university was beyond his capability, but he applied and got in anyway. He seemed to be using my system every time I went past the library. He was an effective participant in the class discussions and passed the final exam with a solid B+.

Unfortunately, he failed two of his other four courses. He must have spent too much of his learning time on my course.

This gave me an idea that I got to test when I came back to academia years later. Some people master content faster than others, but given enough time, almost everyone can eventually master it.

In our schools, we march all our students onward at the same pace and differentiate them by how well they master course content within that set amount of time. That's plain stupid. The goal is for them to learn the material. We need to unlock the time dimension to allow students as much time as they need and demand mastery of the course content from every one of them.

This implies a pass/fail evaluation. They either demonstrate mastery or they don't.

I was recruited back into academia years later and took another run at my concept using a new tool: microcomputers. In coordination with a programmer, we developed a far more powerful learning system paralleling the original one's content. We were able to track user errors, and by analysing those errors, we created remedial loops to set the users straight. Our system collected enormous amounts of data for us to analyse, to help us improve its effectiveness.

It worked.

I was able to collect a lot of data in one term where the students agreed to help by completing information questionnaires. With this, we were able to analyse their exam results for both the midterm exam, which examined technical aspects of accounting, and the final exam, which tested how well they could interpret and use financial information in business settings.

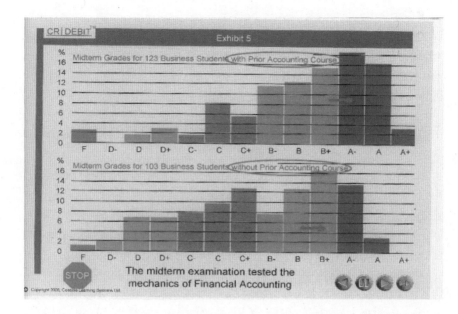

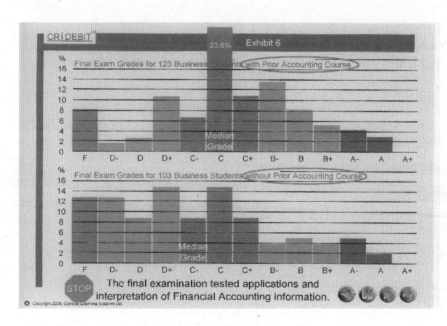

Past distributions of grades on both the midterm and final exams were bimodal, with the nodes centred around D+/C- and B+/A-. We did not actually know why, but we assumed whether students took a high school accounting course contributed to it. The most interesting finding coming out of our data up to the midterm this time was that the bimodal distribution almost disappeared. Another difference was that midterm exam grades for all students were much higher than previously recorded, although the exam was at a normal level of difficulty.

In the second term, where we followed traditional teaching practices, the bimodal distribution resurfaced, although it was weaker than in prior years. In the second term having taken a high school accounting course was a major success factor. It is likely that many students who studied accounting in high school were already headed for accounting careers.

Another interesting observation was that of the 680 students that registered in the course, 661 students completed the course and received a grade – a 97% completion rate. A typical completion rate after dropouts and did-not-writes was about 70 to 75%. Of those receiving grades this time, only ten failed. This is important to the university, with more students going on to higher-level courses. Universities are paid on a per capita basis by tuition and government grants and cannot afford empty seats in classrooms.

There were seven modules available. Students could try a module as often as they wanted, with their best result counting towards their grade. One mark was allotted for a score between 80% and 89% and two marks for a score between 90% and 100% on each module. Thus 14 marks were available, but the number entered into their grade calculation maxed out at ten marks, giving them some flexibility.

Ninety-five percent of students **with** high school accounting got all 10 marks and 35% went over the 10-mark maximum. Eighty-three percent of students **without** high school accounting got all 10 marks and 49% went over the 10-mark maximum. Apparently, many students valued the learning even after no marks remained available.

Students **without** high school accounting took longer to complete modules successfully than students **with** high school accounting. The median time students **with** accounting spent on the first module was 79.8

minutes. The median time students **without** accounting spent on the first module was 110.7 minutes – 39% longer. Some students took over three times as long. Over the seven modules, students **with** high school accounting took a median 6.9 hours, and students **without** high school accounting took a median 9.3 hours – 35% longer.

It was fairly clear that making a student's time commitment a variable vastly reduced the overall grades spread when compared to outcomes from traditional approaches, as I expected it would, and the overall grades for all students moved up dramatically.

Twenty-five years later, self-learning has made enormous strides forward. It is most effective when the material to be learned is information oriented. It allows teachers to act as learning facilitators, helping their students develop the skills they need to succeed, rather than wasting precious classroom time helping them learn the information underlying those skills.

AGE PROFILING

If it is illegal for our governments to profile by ethnic group or race, why is it acceptable for the Ontario Ministry of Transportation to profile by age? The Ministry is profiling me by age. Some years ago, I, along with every other eighty-year-old Ontario driver, was required to take a driver test in order to keep my licence. The test was ridiculously easy for anyone who could read and had English as a principal language, but that is not the point. I was profiled because of my age is the point, and it should be illegal. This test has been subsequently replaced with another one that tests for dementia, but the unacceptable age profiling still goes on.

It is a myth that older drivers are more dangerous than younger drivers. The 2009 US Census data, published in 2012, shows that drivers seventy-five years and older were tied as the least frequent drivers having accidents among all age brackets, at four accidents per 100 drivers (**4%**). The table below shows the accident frequencies for all age brackets:

Age Group	Accident frequency per 100 drivers	Fatal Accidents per 100,000 drivers
19 years old & under	20	38
20 to 24 years old	14	36
25 to 34 years old	9	24
35 to 44 years old	8	20
45 to 54 years old	7	20
55 to 64 years old	5	18
65 to 74 years old	4	18
75 years old & over	4	28

Source: www.census.gov › *The 2012 Statistical Abstract* › *Transportation*

Conclusion: As drivers age, their accident rates decline *at all ages*. The more important statistic is the reciprocal. *Ninety-six out of every 100 drivers seventy-five years old and over did not have an accident in the census year*. It has been suggested that the uptick in fatal accidents for drivers seventy-five years old and up comes about because elderly people tend to be more fragile than younger people. It is still an insignificant number. The important fact is that *99,972 out of 100,000 drivers seventy-five years old and over were <u>not</u> involved in a fatal accident in the census year*.

Canada and Ontario do not publish statistics dealing with accidents per driver in driver age brackets on their webpages, but Alberta does, and its statistics support the US information.

Age of Alberta Drivers Involved in Casualty Collisions Per 1,000 Licenced Drivers in 2012

Age of Driver	Male N	Male %	Male Rate / 1,000	Female N	Female %	Female Rate / 1,000	Total N	Total %	Total Rate / 1,000
Under 16	115	0.5	7.6	51	0.2	3.8	166	0.7	5.8
16 - 17	489	2.0	15.0	372	1.5	13.0	861	3.5	14.1
18 - 19	762	3.1	18.4	515	2.1	14.1	1,277	5.1	16.4
20 - 24	1,895	7.6	14.5	1,340	5.4	11.4	3,236	13.0	13.0
25 - 34	3,421	13.8	10.7	2,312	9.3	8.0	5,734	23.1	9.4
35 - 44	2,694	10.9	9.4	1,853	7.5	7.2	4,547	18.3	8.4
45 - 54	2,462	9.9	8.6	1,549	6.2	5.9	4,011	16.2	7.3
55 - 64	1,744	7.0	7.7	956	3.9	4.7	2,700	10.9	6.3
65 & over	1,165	4.7	6.5	601	2.4	3.8	1,766	7.1	5.2
Unspecified	89	0.4		47	0.2		526	2.1	
Total Drivers	14,836	59.8		9,596	38.7		24,824	100.0	

Source: Licenced Drivers – Service Alberta – Registries Services, as of December 31, 2012.

Thus, both the US Census data and the Service Alberta data show that drivers in the "over 65" age bracket are safer than drivers in any younger age bracket. The US statistics show that this advantage persists with drivers over seventy-five years of age. These statistics clearly show that older drivers are safer drivers, so why are we being targeted by government profilers?

Reliable internet sources suggest one in three people seventy-five years old and older suffer from some level of cognitive impairment. Presumably most still drive because this category remains very large, yet the inclusion of the large number of people with this disability in the US accident statistics for drivers over seventy-five years old showed no impact on the accident frequency per 100 drivers. Apparently, older drivers suffering from some level of cognitive impairment are still very safe drivers.

There are reasons why older drivers are safer drivers, in addition to having more experience. Drivers over seventy years old are usually retired. They do not need to drive in the chaos of rush-hour traffic to get to work. They can run errands in daylight hours and avoid busier, more dangerous night and weekend driving. They have plenty of time available and can leave early, so they do not need to hurry to their destinations. They sometimes move out of cities to less stressful small towns or rural environments. They may reduce the range of their driving and stick to familiar places. They drive a lot fewer hours and kilometres than younger drivers who work and/or have young families.

Our insurance company knows the truth of the matter. My wife and I were both in the "over 75," category and we were also both in the lowest rate category our insurance company offered. So why were we being targeted by government profilers?

Another problem is Ontario legislation that requires doctors to turn in their patients, if the doctors think these patients might have reduced driving skills due to cognitive impairment or dementia. This is clearly a conflict of interest for the doctors, whose imperative must be to act in their patients' best interests. Their patients' best interests on driving rarely intersect with society's perceived interests. Hundreds of Ontario doctors harm thousands of their patients every year by turning them in to the Ministry, even though statistics show these patients are most likely very safe drivers.

It is important to recognize that reduced driving skills are not the same as reduced safe driving. Many older drivers modify their driving choices and ranges to compensate for reduced driving skills that they recognize in themselves, and thus remain very safe drivers.

I do not understand why the medical profession has allowed the Ministry to compromise their professional integrity by requiring them to report their patients. It clearly creates a conflict of interest. Doctors acting to deprive their patients' driving privilege are rarely acting in their patients' best interest, and they do their patients great harm.

I know of two drivers who descended into dementia and still drove. In both instances, they eventually had a series of minor fender benders in the early stages of their disability. One died without ever being involved in a serious accident. The other did finally cause a serious accident. For drivers descending into dementia, this pattern of repetitive minor accidents might be very common and could be a signal that they should lose their driving privileges.

Getting all ages of dangerous drivers off the road does have merit. A better approach might be to base the removal of all drivers on individual driver performance rather than profiling tens of thousands of safe older drivers. How about an approach where every driver involved in an accident resulting in an insurance claim more than once in a twelve-month period, regardless of fault, is required to take a medical exam? This would be followed by a driver training course and an on-road driving test administered by the Ministry. Failure at any of these three steps would cost the driver their driving privileges. A secondary backstop could be three insurance-reported accidents in a sixty-month period.

This approach would include all drivers regardless of age, so it is age-impartial. Remember, with drivers over seventy-five years old, 96% will not be involved in an accident in a twelve-month period, and this statistic includes drivers suffering from some form of cognitive disability. The odds are strongly in favour of these older drivers with this system and it will remove some younger dangerous drivers who aren't currently even on the Ministry's radar. It should also be much cheaper than spending resources on thousands of safe drivers to find the few dangerous ones.

One possible reason for the objectionable government profiling of older drivers may be the enormous news coverage of the rare event where a driver with severe dementia kills a bystander in some horrendous way. Obviously these drivers slipped through the Ministry's far-flung net. I wonder how many of them had earlier, smaller accidents that would have grounded them using the individual driver performance model suggested above. This approach might catch a large majority of dangerous drivers suffering from dementia before their serious accident. Delving into the insurance records for their accident history could tell us if that would be so.

This approach would also resolve the doctors' ethical conflict issues. Doctors would not have any legislated involvement with the Ministry under this plan, as they should not. It is bad law. Risking a few extra fender benders is better than taking thousands of safe drivers off the road.

Ontario Road Safety Annual Report (ORSAR) 2009 – Table 2.20:

Driver Age Groups – Number Licensed, Collision Involvement and Per Cent Involved in Collisions, 2009

Age of Driver	Drivers Licensed			Drivers Involved in collisions			% of Drivers of Each Age Involved in Collisions		
	Male	Female	Total	Male	Female	Total	Male	Female	Total
Under 16	0	0	0	84	26	110	N/A	N/A	N/A
16	42,425	36,927	79,352	677	424	1,101	1.60	1.15	1.39
17	60,091	53,296	113,387	3,740	2,438	6,178	6.22	4.57	5.45
18	67,852	60,372	128,224	4,802	2,892	7,694	7.08	4.79	6.00
19	75,135	66,620	141,755	5,098	3,066	8,164	6.79	4.60	5.76
20	76,910	69,273	146,183	5,045	3,164	8,209	6.56	4.57	5.62
21 - 24	311,724	288,579	600,303	19,566	13,106	32,672	6.28	4.54	5.44
25 - 34	782,542	771,724	1,554,266	44,099	28,054	72,153	5.64	3.64	4.64
35 - 44	898,838	864,866	1,763,704	45,688	29,296	74,984	5.08	3.39	4.25
45 - 54	987,443	919,089	1,906,532	45,521	26,698	72,219	4.61	2.90	3.79
55 - 64	724,165	663,929	1,388,094	28,176	14,956	43,132	3.89	2.25	3.11
65 - 74	421,668	363,714	785,382	12,728	6,768	19,496	3.02	1.86	2.48
75 & over	269,615	225,141	494,756	7,712	4,332	12,044	2.86	1.92	2.43
Unknown	0	0	0	38,446	0	38,446	N/A	N/A	N/A
Total	4,718,408	4,383,530	9,101,938	222,936	135,220	358,156	4.72	3.08	3.93

This table includes people in the driver's position of parked vehicles and excludes drivers of some vehicles such as bicycles, snow and off-road vehicles, etc.

The Extra Mile *(50 words)*

If you want a great reputation, deliver more than you promise. If you contract for a second level analysis, also deliver the third level. If you promise a hundred-thousand-dollar profit, deliver a hundred and twenty thousand. I know people who promise the stars and disappoint by only delivering the moon.

Section 8
The Survivors

I lost my beautiful wife, Jean, to leukemia after sixty-three years of happy marriage. Then I spent many evenings in front of my fireplace, stunned. Our children went out of their ways to include me in their family's activities and I appreciated it mightily, but it was their lives, not mine. I came out of my shell months later and realized I was lonely. Very lonely.

I am by nature a problem solver. It just took a while for me to identify the problem. Jean and I were good friends with another couple, Carol and Steve. Carol lost Steve to cancer a few years earlier, after fifty years of happy marriage. I lost track of Carol over the intervening years, but we had a mutual friend, Maureen. I decided to go through Maureen, track Carol down, and find out how she was doing.

It took a while, but I finally got Maureen to call Carol and set up a three-way lunch date. It took a while longer for Carol to respond, but eventually we had lunch in her apartment. Carol was exactly as I remembered her, pleasant, attractive, fun, and still on her own after five years. We all enjoyed a great afternoon that stretched on and on. I decided there and then to pursue Carol.

Six months after our original lunch with Maureen, Carol gave notice on her rental apartment. At the end of the following month, January, we moved Carol to my apartment. Combining two households of furniture, smaller items and kitchen stuff into one shared home was no small challenge. We have a happy blend of our possessions here with the spillover either given away, sold, or temporarily housed in a rental storage unit while we decide what to do with it. We have what amounts to an open-air terrarium because our combined plant holding is so large.

My brother, my children, their partners and my grandchildren are all happy for us and all of them like Carol immensely. Carol's siblings profess to liking me and are clearly happy for us. Carol has no children.

In her past, Carol painted beautiful pictures, but she quit about the time Steve was diagnosed with terminal cancer. Many of her paintings are now hanging on our walls. Last week, she picked up a paintbrush for the first time in seven years and started painting again. I think Carol's soul has finally come back home.

For us this is not a new story, it is another chapter added to our existing stories. We put Steve's photograph on the table in front of us on his birthday and shared memories about him. We sat in quiet contemplation in front of the columbarium where Jean's ashes rest and reminisced about her on her birthday. They are still a part of our now-shared lives.

As we sit together in front of our fireplace, we are both so thankful that we are sharing our lives instead of each of us sitting out the pandemic alone.

Section 9
Lucky Linda Loon

I hatched in my nest on the shore of Lost Lake in early June. Life was dangerous at first.

One time, a motorboat passed too close and the waves washed over my nest and nearly drowned me.

My mother let me ride on her back when we went out on the lake for the night to escape the fox and the racoons.

If I went swimming on my own, a large pike might just swallow me up.

Soon I could swim and catch small fish, but try as hard as I could, I could not fly. My wings were not strong enough.

The summer came and I got to be as big as mother, but not as big as father.

I still could not fly, but I could catch fish as well as anyone.

I was very fast under water and could chase a fish down.

I liked my name, Linda Loon.

Then fall came. The days were sunny, but the nights were cold. The birch trees all turned yellow, then their leaves fell off.

One day, there was frost on the ground and ice on the edge of the lake.

We went to a loon convention/ Mom and Dad flew off, leaving me behind, because I still could not fly.

Soon the ice stayed on the lake even in the daytime.

I had to move to a small rapids where the water flowed fast.

As ice covered the lake, I had a hard time finding enough fish to eat.

I had to dive far under the ice then come back to the rapids to breathe.

A loon needs a long runway to take off.

My wings got stronger, but now I did not have enough clear water to take off and fly.

I was almost ready to give up when a big storm came along.

There was thunder and lightning and a strong wind.

At first the waves were only near the rapids, but then the waves got under the ice and the ice started breaking up.

Then the wind pushed the ice off the lake and onto the far shore.

I took a run on the top of the water and flapped my wings as hard as I could. I was flying for the first time!

On my way south to North Carolina's ocean coast, I stopped off on Lake Ontario for two days to eat and rest.

Then I flew on to North Carolina and found my mother and father.

Everyone in the bay calls me Lucky Linda Loon.

When I told my story, everyone was impressed.
I like my new name even better than my old name.